Partner Track deals with topics some readers may find difficult, including the death of an elderly and much beloved pet.

PARTNER TRACK

CAT WYNN

carina
press

carina
press®

Recycling programs
for this product may
not exist in your area.

ISBN-13: 978-0-335-55588-5

Partner Track

Copyright © 2022 by Cat Wynn

For questions and comments about the quality of this book, please contact us at CustomerService@Harlequin.com.

Carina Press
22 Adelaide St. West, 40th Floor
Toronto, Ontario M5H 4E3, Canada
www.CarinaPress.com

Printed in U.S.A.

To my Big Love, Ozzie Bear,
Who lived in such a way
That he used up
His whole entire
Great big
Perfect and good
Heart.

PARTNER
TRACK

Chapter One

A bead of sweat slipped into the dip of Perdie Stone's cleavage. The thermostat was cranked to hell in the deposition room in the small North Dakota town. But she strove to remain cool, calm, and collected like an attorney who had her shit together, and not hot, stressed, and messy like an attorney whose twisted underwire happened to be digging into her rib cage.

The defendant, an oil executive, sat flanked by his army of lawyers neatly lined up in charcoal suits across the table. Their shapes reflected like cubist art against the high-gloss polyurethane finish.

Ordered from greatest to least, the defendant took the helm, followed by big-time defense attorney Carter Leplan in the second chair. With broad shoulders encased in a bespoke jacket, Carter was a full-blown hotshot compared to Perdie, and a newly minted partner at his defense firm.

Perdie fingered through a messy stack, locating a document. "On June seventeenth you planned to drill fifteen hundred feet on my client's cattle ranch—"

"Two thousand feet, my dear," the defendant, Thomas Brown, interjected. His eyes, while crinkled due to late middle age, were relaxed, and he stroked the white stubble on his chin. "Fifteen hundred is too shallow. But not surprised you don't know. Doesn't look like your firm's put in much in the way of resources." A few interns towards the end of the lineup tittered, and the corner of the defendant's mouth curled.

Perdie forced a smile. The jab hit a little too close to home. She sat all by her lonesome on her side of the table, save for a disinterested videographer. But it was only because Frank Stetsel, the managing partner at Joy and Schulz, had dumped the case on her. He deemed the potential payout either too unlikely or too small for his hourly billing rate.

As a result, Perdie had undertaken the whole shebang alone from the document review to the brief writing to the depositions. This was her work, small payout or not, and she'd better not fuck it up. Her eyes shuttered briefly. "My client reported suspicious activity on his property. Were your men conducting tests not disclosed in the agreement?"

"Objection, Ms. Stone, asked and answered." Carter shook his head with an eye roll, signaling to his client how silly Perdie's questions were. He spoke with the confidence of a person who'd never given a wrong answer in class. "You've produced no convincing evidence that Mr. Brown is attempting to shortchange the deal. If anything, Mr. Brown is renowned for his generosity. A pillar of his community. Our motion to dismiss documents the process in plain English, assuming you got around to reading it. But if you're struggling to keep up, I can write it out in smaller words."

Perdie blushed, shuffling the papers in front of her. "Allow me to get to the point, then."

"Would love to finally hear one." That earned a

chuckle from his client. Carter smiled, flashing straight white teeth.

Oh, it would feel good to take this guy down. With haste, Perdie leaned in to— *Shit.* A miscalculated swipe of her backhand sent her stack flying.

An intern at the end of the line moved to help, but Carter held up a hand, prompting the intern to plop down. Appearing to take his time, he pushed out his chair and then sauntered over to Perdie's side of the table. After brief eye contact, he knelt to the mess of papers, and collected each piece by piece. Then he straightened and harshly tapped the edge of the papers to the hard surface until they aligned in a uniform rectangle. With what she could've sworn was a sympathetic smile, he handed the stack of neatly straightened papers to Perdie.

"Thanks," she gritted. Whatever strategy Carter Leplan was employing to throw her off her game, it was working. Perdie was thrown off her game. Big-time.

"A little old for a new hire…" The defendant mumbled, elbowing a straight-faced Carter when he returned to his seat, straightening his suit jacket.

Perdie's hand froze while flicking through the papers. *You know what? Fuck it.* She dropped the stack on the table. "Mr. Brown, who's Lana?"

The question wiped the smirk off the defendant's face. He cleared his throat, almost too quietly to hear. "You'll have to be more specific. When you run a company with three thousand employees you know a lot of names."

Perdie didn't have to flip to the document with the emails discussing Lana, she simply pushed them towards the defendant. "That surprises me as you and your lead scientist have an awful lot to say about Lana. Let's refresh your memory, shall we? Be *my dear* and read those emails loud enough for the court reporter. Start with June fourteenth."

She leaned back and crossed her arms over her white button-up. White had been a poor choice. Next time she'd wear black when she sent a man to his funeral.

The defendant shifted in his chair. "It says: 'Banging Lana on the down-low. She's a juicy one but can't let her husband know.'"

Uncomfortable snickers scattered across the table. A serious look from Carter rendered everyone silent.

"And the next three," Perdie prompted.

The defendant pursed his lips but then lowered his gaze to the paper. "'Lana looks shallow on the outside, but when you dig, she runs deeper than expected.'" He glanced up, but Perdie nodded for him to continue. "'Visiting Lana Friday night. Think I'm starting to enjoy sneaking around. High predictions Lana is a…gusher.'"

This time actual laughter spouted from the other attorneys. Perdie merely lifted a brow, suppressing a smile.

"Objection." Carter's voice was tinged with exasperation. "The defendant isn't being deposed for what he does after hours."

Perdie steepled her fingers, resting her elbows on the table. "Mr. Brown, is it your assertion that Lana is just someone you *do* after hours?"

The defendant turned pale, eyes shifting to Carter. Carter shook his head in response. "Objection, again, irrelevant. And…" while his tone was flippant, casual almost, he caught Perdie's eye "…*indecent.*"

Don't let him distract you. Carter Leplan was a known superstar at his firm, but he wouldn't get the best of her, not today.

"Counsel, as you well know your client has no implication of privilege and is therefore compelled to answer. Lana's name appears over seventy-five times in the emails."

A beat passed, and then the defendant shrugged. "Lana's a gal I used to see, nothing more, nothing less. I might be crass, but far as I can tell crassness isn't illegal. I thought lawyers like you were supposed to be elite. Maybe they don't vet 'em like they did in my day."

A smile. "Maybe they don't. What's Lana's last name?"

"What?" The defendant's jaw ticked, but Carter rested a hand on his client's forearm.

"Surely Lana has a last name? She's a person, yes? A person with a last name?"

"Ms. Stone, you're grossly overstepping." Carter gave her that distracting look again.

But she was ready this time, steeled against his tricks. "Stop interrupting my deposition, Leplan. Or should I use smaller words to help you understand?" She over-enunciated her next line. "You don't know Lana's last name, Mr. Brown?"

The defendant glanced over at Carter but this time kept his mouth shut.

"Perhaps..." Perdie spoke smoothly. "Lana's not a person at all. Could it be Lana's the code word for undisclosed oil reserves you located on my client's land before he signed a contract? And if so, isn't it true you withheld information to undercut his payout by several million?"

"That's preposterous." Carter leaned back in his chair.

Perdie tilted her head. "There is a very strange set of numbers at the bottom of each email involving Lana. What are those numbers, Mr. Brown?"

The defendant huffed. "Phone numbers?"

Perdie scratched the tip of her nose with her pen cap. "Probably, right? But I called and wouldn't you believe it? Didn't work."

The defendant crossed his arms. "So?"

"They appear on *your* emails. What else could they be? Oh, I know…" She tapped her fingers against the surface of the table. "Coordinates perhaps?"

Silence permeated the room. The defendant might stonewall, but Perdie knew how to wait it out. A lawyer trick. Seconds ticked.

Finally he scowled. "Perhaps."

Perdie reached into her briefcase, retrieving her phone. "Ah, your memory *returns*. If I input these coordinates on a map, would you know where they'd lead?"

"How the hell would I?"

Perdie punched them in and turned the screen to the defendant. "You recognize this location?"

The defendant closed his eyes, then sighed. "I might."

"It's my client's cattle ranch, isn't it?"

Again silence.

"Interesting. Now, why would every email referencing Lana, *the gusher*, also contain the coordinates to my client's cattle ranch?"

"Objection!" Carter called out.

"For what?" Perdie snapped.

"The connection you're implying is specious at best and fantasy at worst."

"Well then, perhaps the defendant would rather explain this *fantasy* in front of a jury of his peers. We still have seventy-one more emails about Lana to get through."

Carter rubbed his forehead. "Now just wait. I think we all need to calm down." Was it possible Carter was flustered?

"Interesting, you seem to be the only one who needs to calm down." *That's* what he'd get for giving her a sympathetic smile.

"I merely meant that my client needs a minute to process the information."

But Perdie was already certain the case wouldn't see the light of the courtroom. Carter's client wouldn't want the emails to get out in front of a jury. No other ranchers would do business after hearing about Thomas Brown's penchant for scamming the good people of North Dakota over a little hydraulic fracking.

The row of attorneys frantically flipped through papers, whispering to one another. They'd missed this Lana business in their document review.

And now Carter's client was outed as a guilty fraudster, and Perdie would be hailed the unlikely heroine of the case.

This settlement could be, would be, huge. *Millions.*

She smiled. "He can have all the minutes he needs because we're done here. No further questions."

The defendant sat shocked, and Carter patted his client's shoulder with a grimace. As a defense attorney, Carter would get all his billed hours paid out anyway.

Still, the lawyers and interns down the line would get hell for what had occurred in this room today.

As for Perdie, this was all playing out perfectly well. Before she'd left for the deposition, Frank hinted at a partnership opening. Doubtful he had her in mind at the time, but now she'd really polished a shit-box case into a gleaming Hope Diamond.

As Carter spoke hushed words to his client, he ran his hands through the waves of his thick toffee-brown hair, tempting her eyes with the movement. He caught her gaze for a second with a knowing look, a smirk played on his lips.

Oops. She snapped away and jumped into action, collecting her papers and briefcase.

The rest of the men surrounding the table were gathering their briefcases, hissing accusatory words at each other, and loosening ties.

Perdie's cue. If she wanted to catch her plane in this snowstorm, she'd have to fucking move it. Congratulations could come later. She got to her feet, offering curt nods as she wielded around the table.

"Ms. Stone, a word?"

"Send it in an email, Leplan. I've got a plane to catch." At the door, she snatched her coat and the suitcase awaiting her and pushed her way to freedom.

She welcomed the fresh air of the hallway. She couldn't wait to get to her condo in Charleston, South Carolina. It was fifty-eight degrees and sunny there. The first thing she'd do was fling her bra across her bedroom and free herself from tit jail.

When she reached the elevator, she exhaled in relief and pushed the down arrow multiple times, tapping the pointed toe of her four-inch Louboutin against the wheel of her suitcase.

Work would be good when she got back to her office in Charleston. A shot at partnership at Joy and Schulz would have to be in the cards. She'd had to sneak and fight and claw her way into the associate position at the prestigious firm. A miracle she snagged the job in the first place with the weird way her brain worked.

But now she wanted—no, she deserved—more. Why couldn't anyone else see that?

Ding.

She clicked her way inside the mirrored chamber. She'd change into her flats once she was safely in a car zipping towards the airport. That would feel almost as good as taking off her bra.

She unbuttoned the top of her shirt, waving the flap of material to fan her skin and pulled her long mahogany ponytail loose. As the doors slid, she hesitantly lifted her arm and inhaled an investigatory whiff—

"Hold it." A large hand forced the doors to part.

Startled, Perdie dropped her arm. *Shit.*

Carter Leplan shouldered his tall frame inside, taking up too much space next to her. With him trailed a scent of chilled peppermint. How could he smell so fresh after hours crammed in that sweaty depo room?

She willed away the creeping flush on her cheeks. There was no way he'd caught her checking her own armpit stank, right?

Right?

Carter stared ahead, seemingly unaware of her, but when he cleared his throat and tugged at the cuff of his sleeve, she could see in her periphery the smirk across his features.

She rolled her eyes as the doors closed.

Oh, what the fuck ever. It didn't really matter what he thought of her because after her certifiable win today she'd never see his Harlequin-book-cover-looking ass ever again. At least not in person. He worked for a swanky firm in San Francisco, far across the country. Basically, as far away as he could get without ending up on another continent.

Also, they couldn't be further apart in life experience either. While Perdie had come to the law in her late twenties after a series of poorly paying, demeaning jobs,

Carter Leplan had graduated top of his class at Harvard Law at the ripe old age of twenty-four. And at thirty-two, he'd made partner at his firm. His firm's talented little golden boy. Actually not so little. In reality, he stood well over six feet, dwarfing Perdie even in four-inch heels, but she endeavored to ignore that fact.

Everyone at Joy and Schulz knew about Carter Leplan. Especially those attracted to men.

It was standard practice to look up fellow attorneys, but Carter's bio picture presented like a Vogue ad for Armani suits. Maybe in her twenties she would've longed for a man like Carter. But now, at her age? Pass. Carter Leplan's money was too deep, his skill too slick, and his bespoke suits too…well, *spoken. And screw that, thank you very much.*

"You're good." His voice surprised her, and unwelcome goose bumps rippled up her arms. "I'll begrudgingly grant you that the optics don't look great on Lana. Ever consider switching sides? We could always use someone with your talent."

He was playing games. Still, she arched an eyebrow, taken aback by the comment. "Complimenting the enemy is a bold strategy."

"Enemy, huh? Well, if you're my enemy, then maybe *I* should switch to *your* side."

Her jaw dropped, barely concealing a scoff. But there was something familiar in his tone. "Wait. Are you flirting with me? In the elevator?"

He tilted his head, gaze flitting over. "Very easy to blackmail someone in an elevator for a slip of the tongue. They warned us about that in law school, but clearly I didn't take the lesson to heart."

Was it getting hot again? Suddenly, it was like she was in a sauna.

She undid the buttons at the cuffs of her sleeves. "Blackmail would certainly go against my code of ethics, and as such, I wouldn't be so inclined." She rolled the material up her arms, securing either side with a hard yank, airing out her hot skin. When she was finished, she leveled a look at him. "But kinda sounds like you fucking want me to."

The corner of his lips curled. "Depending on your demands, I might insist on it."

"Ha." A snort escaped from her, but she covered her mouth with her palm, eyes going wide.

Bad Perdie, bad.

This kind of interaction was a road to professional nowheresville, and she should cut it out posthaste. It certainly wouldn't help the precarious position she was in career-wise. If she needed to flirt with someone, she had plenty of nonlawyer dudes in her phone for that.

Besides, hadn't she just smoked this guy in a boardroom? What was he so chipper for anyway?

The floor jolted and the elevator doors glided open, signaling the end of their conversation. *Phew.* She was out of there like the last day of school. With a nod, she turned to leave.

See you never, Carter Leplan.

But as the wheels of her suitcase bumped over the ridged, metallic threshold, his hand touched her bare elbow.

Chapter Two

"Hey, where you headed?" Carter asked, his touch fleeting. "The exit is this way."

Whoops. She glanced down the dead-end hallway.

"Need to order a car," she mumbled.

Carter held his phone between his thumb and index finger. "You're in luck. Got one coming. Airport, right? We can share a ride. Give us time to further discuss blackmail demands."

She hesitated, and a glimmer of *something* passed over his face. Nervousness?

His eyes were hazel with a greenish glint, and her proximity allowed even closer inspection. She discovered on the bottom quarter of his left iris a patch of muted cerulean, swirled with white speckles. Her gaze zeroed in on that patch of color like she was searching the glitter in a chunk of pyrite.

"It's okay, everyone stares at it."

Perdie's eyes snapped into focus. Caught staring? *Embarrassing*.

Time to adopt a new course of action. Maybe leaning *into* the flirting was a more winning strategy. Call his bluff, as it were.

"Like you needed something to make you look even

more like an international pop star." She patted him on the arm, his biceps rock-hard against her hand. *Of course it would feel like that.* "Don't worry about the ride, Leplan, blackmail's off the table anyway. I could never stand to see any harm done to a pretty face like yours."

She'd meant it in good fun—after all, he'd started the alleged flirting. So why did the crests of his cheekbones flush at her words?

Carter's phone lit up in his hand. "Come now. No sense in two cars going to the same place." He reached for her, gently removing the folded coat from her grasp and holding it up behind her, prompting her to push her arms through the sleeves. "Wouldn't be very environmentally prudent, would it? We care about that kind of thing where I'm from."

Rude. Her eyes narrowed. "That's rich considering your fracking-happy client. And if you're implying Charlestonians don't care about the environment, that's good old-fashioned slander. You shouldn't prejudge because we're Southern."

They walked to the glass doors to leave the building, and Perdie's muscles vibrated at the feel of Carter's hand hovering around her lower black.

He spoke distractedly as he ushered her out. "Well, you know how it goes. Everyone's entitled to fair representation under the law."

The car rolled close to the curb, and Carter hastily stowed their luggage in the trunk. *Welp*, there went her chance at changing shoes. Her toes ground against the trap of the ungiving leather triangle. With gritted teeth, she ducked into the compact backseat. She'd persevere through the pain. She'd made it all day, she could take a few more minutes.

Carter nestled in, his long legs surpassing the cushion edge, the side of his hip and shoulder pressed against hers. Suddenly, Perdie grew hyperaware of every inch of her skin. She was worried that her cobalt pencil skirt was riding up on her thighs and grateful for the cover of her long winter coat. She also welcomed the blast of cold when they'd stepped outside, otherwise she'd be sweating again.

The driver's eyes appeared in the rearview mirror. "Airport?"

When they confirmed, he shook his head. "If you say so…this is my last lift for the night."

Perdie didn't like the sound of that. The weather was bad, yes, but this was North Dakota. Weren't they used to this kind of thing?

She grabbed her phone from her purse and checked her flight status. Delayed but only by thirty minutes.

To avoid further conversation, she flicked through her messages. She took the time to answer a few from one of her dating apps. Hookups were fun—feelings left at the door, underwear in a handbag.

She bit back a laugh at a message from her best friend and roommate, Lucille.

Ruth Bananas Ginsberg read the caption of a picture of their black pug, Bananas, of whom Lucille and Perdie shared joint custody. Bananas was dressed in a makeshift judge's robe and necklace posed next to Perdie's copy of *Black's Law Dictionary*. A small snort escaped Perdie's lips.

"Can I ask you a personal question?"

Perdie's head snapped up to find Carter watching her intently. Hastily, she locked her phone screen. "You can try."

"How old are you?"

If she were in a sitcom, this is when she would've done a spit take. "Seventy-eight. But I have an excellent skin-care routine." Not true, in reality she had a mediocre skin care routine. One she often neglected.

"You're thirty-nine."

"Okay?"

"I googled you and did the math."

She tilted her head. "Then why ask the question?"

His brows drew together. "This might be out of line, but I'm surprised given your time at the firm that you aren't a partner. Especially since I've seen your work. Competent to say the least."

If he'd googled her then he also knew about her shitty local law school and pathetic career history, and the implications *still* embarrassed her. She was more than her mediocre credentials, but it often didn't feel that way.

"We can't all make it big in record time. Some of us come from more humble beginnings." She hoped to sound lighthearted, but inside she bristled.

"Ah. So, you googled me too."

She blushed. "Please, you know we all do that shit. Lawyers are a nosy bunch. We'll take any ammunition we can dig up on one another."

"Find anything good?" He leaned back against his seat and stretched out his arms on either side. Then he propped up on one elbow, tugging at his hair, his head angled towards hers.

A thrill ran up Perdie's spine at the somehow intimate gesture, but she tamped it down. Still, perhaps she could push professional boundaries *a touch* in the name of a little fun. "Yeah, search results were enlightening but strange because every link with your name led to the same page with only one single line of text."

He gave an expectant smile. "And what did that single line of text say?"

She leaned in. "It said you're a giant fucking douchebag."

He let out a crack of laughter. Perdie smothered a smile. At least he had a sense of humor about himself, even if the whole thing was wildly unprofessional.

"Google said that?"

"Yep." She nodded. "Page one and everything. Super weird. A sponsored ad even." She held her hands up, expanding like a marquee. "*Carter Leplan is a giant fucking douchebag.* You should hire a professional to purge those results."

His eyes danced with mirth. "Wow, someone must have it out for me. Think I could sue the search engine?"

"I know a good lawyer if you do." Before she could stop it, she found herself sharing a smile with him.

Was the air cooking from the car's heater or had the mood abruptly warmed?

Then Perdie froze still as ice when the whisper of his breath caressed the shell of her ear. "You have a little something—"

The shadow of his hand swooped in her periphery. Her skin prickled at the barely there glide of fingertips, brushing away a tendril at her temple.

"Hmm. Fleck of paper." He held his index finger to her eye level, then circled his lips, and with a short huff, the speck fluttered away.

In response, Perdie squeezed her thighs tight as if she could lay-away the tingling sensation for when she got back home. Her vibrator was a-calling.

"Which terminal?" asked the driver.

Her eyes shot open—Jesus, when had she closed them?

"Right here." Carter folded forward, cool as a cucumber. The shared moment vanished.

They exited the car, Perdie's feet smarting with every step on the pavement. A painful reminder: she needed to shake this Carter guy off her back so she could dig through her hot mess of a suitcase, switch her shoes, and maybe run to the bathroom to change clothes.

Unfortunately, he was dragging her luggage with his own. *Fucking polite bastard.* She should tell him that she needed *out* of her business attire, but she couldn't bring herself to do it. A part of her wanted to maintain the illusion that she was a put-together professional woman. One who could wear heels all day without having to make a spiritual bargain with the Patron Saint of Stilettos.

Although she'd do well not to care so much.

She shouldn't forget that Carter wasn't just a pretty face, wasn't merely an exceptional lawyer, but was likely a fuckboy extraordinaire, playing with her for a wee bit o' fun. As she was older than him and less powerful, she was low-hanging fruit, waiting to be plucked. And lord knew she'd never been opposed to plucking.

Upon entrance to the terminals, Perdie mentally prepared to part ways. She didn't want to get attached lest she become overly comfortable with the attention of such a beautiful person. Better to cut ties now. She made her way to the Arrivals and Departures monitor, intending to double-check her gate number.

Carter rolled up, wheeling both his own and her luggage. "Damn. Looks like we're not going anywhere soon."

Every flight out of North Dakota had been canceled.

Perdie consulted her phone: 7:37 p.m. Central Time, 8:37 p.m. on the coast. Too late to get her company's travel agent on the line to reroute her destination. Was there any other way to flee North Dakota? Planes, trains, or automobiles? A ridiculous notion. Travel was out of the question tonight. She'd have to find a hotel somewhere and hunker down.

And her fucking shoes still hurt like hell.

"Gimme that." She grabbed her suitcase handle. Carter's hands shot up, clearly sensing she was at the end of her rope.

She dragged her suitcase to the hard plastic waiting chairs behind them and plunked down. With deliberation, she toed off her heels, letting them clatter to the floor one by one.

Groaning, she dropped her head back and wiggled her liberated toes in ecstasy. "That's the ticket."

"Ahem."

Carter. Of course, he was still there, waiting for her. He rolled his suitcase to the chairs, then seated himself, spread out like he owned the place, hand thrown across the backrest beside her.

Her spine straightened at his nearness, but then she leaned over to gingerly unzip the front pocket of her carry-on. She reached inside for the flats but they were smushed beneath her toiletry bag. Hmm, this was going to be tricky without opening the entire pouch, revealing the mess inside—she'd packed in haste that morning. And okay, fine, she was messy.

She gripped the heels of the shoes, a little finesse would jiggle them out and—

The shoes emerged from the bag, flinging a small silver object along with them. The object hit the tile with a hollow clink and as if magnetized to expensive Prada, rolled directly to the tip of Carter Leplan's loafers.

Her vibrator.

"Oh no!" She clambered onto her sore feet, pulling down her hiked-up skirt and coat, before slipping two wobbly steps—nylon and tile were not a great mix—and floundering like a baby lamb squarely onto Carter's lap.

She landed with an *ummph*.

As if reflexively, Carter caught her waist, holding her steady. "Jesus, you okay?"

She stilled in shock but her heart raced, chest rising and falling. And yet his body beneath her was…very comfortable. Warm, hard…*big*. Heat remained high on her cheeks. "No, I've passed away. From humiliation."

Carter's grip softened.

She twisted to see his face. "You saw, didn't you?"

He smiled softly. "No idea what you're talking about. I don't see a vibrator anywhere."

Despite the moment, she let out a miserable chuckle. "Don't judge me."

"Light blackmail, perhaps?"

"It's just a vibra— You know what? Doesn't matter. We're adults. I'm a grown woman."

"That—" he shifted weight uncomfortably, his voice strained "—you are."

"Oh, ah. Right." It dawned on her that she should really *move*. In fact, she really should've done so minutes ago. *What's the holdup, P?*

She struggled momentarily to lift herself, her bottom wiggling against his lap as she had to grip one of his shoulders and one thigh for leverage, and then she felt it, protruding hard against her backside. "Oh!"

Well, well, well. Her jaw almost dropped but she snapped it shut.

His hands fell from her waist entirely. At first he grimaced. But then he lowered his gaze with a wistful, embarrassed smile, scratching at his forehead to avoid eye contact.

"Maybe call it even on the blackmail?" he asked, voice thick.

Although still gripping his shoulder and thigh, Perdie slowly extricated herself from his lap, balancing herself carefully onto the floor. "Deal." She dusted at her clothes with her back to him for a few moments.

She also discreetly swooped up the vibrator, tucked it into the pocket of her suitcase, and with little hops, slid the flats onto her feet, marveling at the relief. Now she had a reasonable center of gravity. Falling on Carter's lap a second time would bear much more serious consequences.

Carter adjusted his coat, then rose from the chair. "I was wondering when you were going to do that."

"Huh?"

"Change out of those heels. Looks like hell to walk in." He nodded absently, having apparently recovered from their encounter, now scrolling on his phone. "There's a hotel connected to the airport. According to my weather app, the snow is expected to worsen every hour for the next four hours. That rules out another Uber. Staying here is our best bet."

Our best bet. They were in this together now by virtue of a lawsuit and a shared ride. She had only herself to blame for that second part. A shared intimacy burgeoned between them, the kind of intimacy that developed when people faced emergencies together.

But Perdie had to admit it was more than that. Nestling into his lap was too intimate. And he…he was too good-looking, eyes darkened and hair tousled like he'd been up to something illicit. Which, well, they almost kinda had, hadn't they?

Easy plucking, indeed.

She didn't need reminding of any potential career ramifications of her flirting. Not that it was against any rules, technically speaking. Rumors permeated around more than one senior partner. But these were all men in positions of power screwing around with subordinates. Everyone tended to look the other way.

If her managing partner caught wind of these antics... something told her she wouldn't receive the same benefit of their feigned ignorance.

Carter gestured towards the walkway. "Shall we find the hotel?"

Perdie extended the handle of her suitcase. The least she could do was get a good night's sleep. "We sure should."

But oh lord. Would she?

Chapter Three

"Sorry, we only have one available room."

Carter's large frame leaned against the edge of the reception counter, while Perdie stood, arms crossed. Perdie couldn't believe the way the front desk clerk said the words *one available room* as if they were completely normal words to say.

Frustrated, she rubbed at her face. It was going to be a long night, and she was currently living out the life of some kind of warped romance novel heroine, except she wasn't lithe, gracile, and blonde, and her bra hurt like all fuck.

"You take the room," she said to Carter. "I'll find a hotel nearby." At this point she ached for nothing more than to wallow in aloneness. Having Carter around made her clothes feel too tight. It was time to be rid of them and him once and for all.

"Oh no, sweetie. The other nearby hotels are booked," said the desk clerk. "We've been conferring since the storm started more than two hours ago."

Perdie shook her head slowly, weighing her lack of options. "I'll wait in the terminal. No biggie."

In her youth, she'd spent a night or two in an airport terminal, using her suitcase as a pillow and a bra as an eye mask. Usually with Lucille though, after canceled spring break plans. Never as a full-grown adult with a respectable checking account.

"Nope, not happening. My mothers would slaughter me alive for letting you sleep in an airport terminal." Carter canted his head towards the reception desk. "You take the room. I'll figure something out."

Perdie rolled her eyes. "Don't put me in this weird position where I have to accept the room because of your misguided sense of chivalry. It makes me feel like I owe you."

"I'll take the room." The voice chimed in behind them. A line had formed, and they were both in danger of losing the only hotel room available. She had to act fast.

"No, it's ours," she spit out.

The desk clerk's eyebrows shot up.

Perdie, panicked, glanced to Carter. "I was thinking maybe we'd…share?"

An arch look crossed his face, and then he slowly dug into his pocket, retrieving his wallet. "Two keys please."

Perdie beseeched the woman behind her desk. "Tell me there are two beds in this room."

The woman's smile tightened as she typed at her keyboard. "There are two beds in this room…"

Perdie let out an exhale of relief. Finally, one thing going right.

"Except there's only one." The desk clerk gave a rueful smile. "I'm so sorry, ma'am."

Perdie's body slumped at the words. She mumbled to herself, "That checks out."

The woman slid two plastic key cards across the counter. "You're welcome to a complimentary chocolate chip cookie."

* * *

The green light flashed as Carter shouldered his way through the door to their room. Behind him, Perdie clutched three plastic-wrapped cookies to her chest like they were stolen Fabergé eggs.

It was fair to say she was freaking the fuck out.

She set the cookies on the counter directly next to the door and then stood in the doorway, fidgeting. Carter neatly settled their suitcases into a corner. He shrugged off his winter coat and suit jacket and hung them in the closet right in front of the entryway.

She watched him with fascination. She never bothered to do such things in hotel rooms, instead letting her clothes hit the ground like slop.

Carter padded into the room while loosening his tie, then turned suddenly to face her. "Coming in or are you just gonna gawk at me?"

She stiffened. "I'm working out logistics."

He whipped his tie off with a whoosh. Perdie winced inwardly at the intimacy of it all. A little jump in her belly told her that her body wasn't going to behave.

"What logistics?" He tossed the tie onto the pristine white down comforter.

She gestured broadly at the room, as if it were obvious. "There's one bed."

"Previously established. And?"

"Don't act like I'm weird. One of us'll have to sleep on the floor. Or in the tub. Or, I don't know…on this chair right here." She kicked the flimsy rolling office chair to the wall with a sad thud.

For the first time since they'd begun their journey, Carter showed a glimmer of frustration. He stabbed his hand through his hair and reclined at the edge of the bed, his long legs spread wide. Manspreader, of course. Ugh, but it was kinda sexy. How confusing. "Can't we both sleep on the bed, like adults? It's big enough for a nice divide down the middle."

Perdie crossed her arms then quickly dropped them when she got a glance at her resulting cleavage. Carter got a glance of it too judging by the way his gaze went heavy then quickly shifted.

Trying to find something to do with her hands, she scrunched her hair to the side. "Adults don't just sleep on beds together. They…"

He perked a brow. "They what? What do adults do in bed together?" The corner of his mouth twitched.

She glared at him because there were winners and losers in this conversation, and so far she wasn't earning any prizes. She was a thirty-nine-year-old woman and this baby Ken doll was getting the best of her, riling her up both above and below the belt. Men almost never affected her as such, and she didn't like it one bit.

"You're right." She threw her arms up. "We've made it this far, what's sharing a bed with a stranger for a night?" Her hands came to her hips, a defiant pose. "You want dibs on the first shower? Or should we share that too?"

If he walked out in nothing but a low-slung towel across his hips, so help her god she might turn into a pillar of salt.

But she could survive this one night.

Tomorrow she'd be back on the beach and he'd be… doing whatever it is San Francisco lawyers did—drinking ginger shots at farmers markets? Going to a dog wedding?

Who was she kidding? She'd done those things. She couldn't even mock this man properly in her head. Hell, she'd officiated at a dog wedding. It wasn't her fault that

Bananas was in love with Pudding, the dog in the condo across the street, and that their love was too pure and too true to not invite all their friends and family with gold-threaded hand-calligraphed invitations to *watch the union between this dog and this other dog joined in holy wedded dogtrimony, for better and for worse, through sickness and through health, for as long as they both shall live (in dog years) at their Sullivan's Island beachfront ceremony—*

"Perdie." His voice cut through her thoughts. "I think you're inadvertently sending some mixed messages. But look, if you're worried about me trying to take advantage of this close-quarters situation, you can rest assured that I won't. My moms raised me right. I don't hold on to outdated notions about opposite-gendered people sharing spaces together."

"That's a mouthful."

He dug his hand into his pocket to retrieve his phone. "This isn't the eighties. You're welcome to call them up to verify. Of course they'd also be more than willing to spill all the blackmail material you could ever want. They'd love the chance to tell all the most embarrassing stories to a willing listener." And with a smile, he held out his phone.

Perdie didn't call his moms plural. Instead, she stalked off to the bathroom and showered first, carefully planning out the activity to reduce the sexual tension surrounding them.

She wouldn't step out until she was fully dressed, and she would avoid allowing her clothes to stick to her damp body. Unfortunately, since she wasn't planning on spending the night with anyone, let alone a beautiful man who was also her competition, she had little in the way of sleep clothes packed.

She gingerly toweled her hair and body, careful not to leave a huge puddle of water on the floor like she might normally do. Lucille was a saint for living with her for all these years with habits like those.

An unprecedented level of self-consciousness overcame her, and every single sound even from her smallest movement was unbearably loud. She hoped Carter couldn't hear. She was out of clean underwear, so she had no choice but to go commando under her cotton sleep shorts, prompting her to shave everything in case said shorts were on the see-through side. *Better safe than prickly* was her motto.

With a heavy heart she snapped on her abused nude bra beneath the camisole she'd pulled from her suitcase.

There was no way in hell she was going bra free in front of Carter. *Back in jail, girls.*

When she burst through the door, her hair, now wet and curling at the ends, shed errant droplets, painting unanticipated, see-through spots down her camisole. Tiny, indecent windows to her soul. *Oops.* She held a towel over her chest.

"Have at it." She indicated her thumb to the bathroom door. The sight of Carter sprawled out on the bed, though, stopped her in her tracks.

His large body was stretched out with one sockless foot resting over the other, iPad on his lap, brow furrowed. His immaculately fitted white dress shirt was unbuttoned at the top, revealing a light sprinkling of chest hair that made Perdie press her tongue to the roof of her mouth, and his sleeves were rolled up on his forearms so several inches of tattoos peeked out from the cuffs.

Carter had tattoos? It shouldn't really surprise her since plenty of people did. Hell, Perdie had a regretful purple-and-yellow flower back-tatt done in someone's basement when she was nineteen. Everyone had been doing it at the time, and she'd so desperately wanted to be like everyone.

He lifted his head from his work, his hand rubbing the back of his neck, up and down and up and down. "Thanks." His voice was hoarse. He made his way from the bed, barely brushing against her as he passed by. She'd been holding her breath and realized she should've moved out of the way. She'd accidentally forced their touching. *Oops again.*

Soon enough the familiar drone of running water soothed her. She buried herself under the white down comforter, paddling her sore feet against the coolness of the sheets. A long exhale left her body, and she deflated. Two truths existed in that bed. The first: she was exhausted. And the second: she was horny as all get-out. The faint scent of chilled peppermint wafted from Carter's side of the bed.

Her brain began etching naked images of him in the shower. *Stop it, stop it, stop it.*

God, she wished she could take care of her own business. Her head lolled on the pillow, staring longingly at the suitcase holding her vibrator, barely out of reach. She was like Jack stretching across the water to Rose on that piece of spare driftwood Rose definitely could've shared...

It was too risky to vibe one out while Carter was in the shower anyway, and she was too tired to get out of the bed now. Although, after its little tumble on the airport floor, she'd been sure to wash her vibrator thoroughly while in the shower. A girl had her priorities.

She settled for scrolling through her phone, vision blurred with fatigue.

She texted Lucille: Luce, you won't believe where I am right now.

No answer. Probably because it was a Friday night and Lucille was busy chasing after a man who would never love her back. That guy was the actual worst. Perdie didn't want to think about that now.

She scheduled a semi-promising date on one of her dating apps. He was cute at least, an ER doctor who worked for the medical university in downtown Charleston. And that was the last thing she did before dozing off into an unknowable dreamscape.

Perdie vacillated somewhere between awake and asleep when her dream began to unfold. First, the heat in between her legs had grown to a full fire now licking at her belly and breasts, her breathing heavy, her limbs tingling. Then she perceived a body, heavy and hot, strong and hard pressing against her, searing skin sealed to her own. She wanted it. Or wanted something. She babbled incoherently, asking for what she needed, and her hand snaked between them and traveled down her stomach, into the waistband of her shorts and—

"Perdie." A strained voice nudged her awake. "Perdie."

Her eyes snapped open, focusing in the pitch black of the room.

"Perdie."

Awareness of her body washed over her. Her leg tossed over Carter's hip, her arm thrown across his chest. She held him tightly, like a muscled body pillow.

Worst of all, her free hand had breached the elastic waistband of her shorts.

She scrambled, pushing her back against the headboard, drawing her knees in close. "Fuck." She rubbed her face, her voice still drunk from sleep. "Shit…fuck…shit."

He drew himself up on his elbows, the white of his T-shirt stark against the darkness of night. Now wasn't the time to notice, but his hair was tousled in perfect, backlit waves. Like a tatted-up Disney prince. Ugh, great, now she had a fetish. Ridiculously, she ran her palm over the top of her head, finding her hair still damp from her shower.

"How you feeling?" The question was warranted but there was a teasing quality to his voice.

Her breathing slowed, and her speech regained balance. "Think I was having a nightmare."

"I don't think *nightmare* is the word you're looking for."

She frowned. "It was a nightmare. I was having a bad dream."

Even in the dark she could make out the mischief on his face. "Yeah? About what?"

She hugged her knees tighter to her chest. "Shut up, Carter."

Carter leaned back and brought his hands behind his head, biceps bulging. "You're all out of breath, shaking, sweaty, clutching your knees. Must've been a doozy. I read the best way to get past a bad dream is to talk about it. So, tell me every single sordid little detail. I'm here to help." He paused as she glared at him, and then cupped a hand to his ear. "Well, I'm waiting."

"Stop it."

"You were practically whimpering."

She pressed her lips together in shame. "Was not."

"Grinding against my hip too."

"Oh no," she groaned, then pushed the bottoms of her palms into her eye sockets. Maybe if she couldn't see him, he couldn't see her. Peeking from behind her mask of hands, she squeezed out more words. "It was a very... specifically...weird...nightmare."

He chuckled softly. "You mean the kind of specifically weird where you try to come against my hip?" The smile on his face faded.

Her gaze crept over to him, his athletic body, his laser-cut jaw, his Disney prince hair. "Don't say it."

He leaned forward. "I can assist with that, you know. Hip and otherwise. I have the tools."

She released her grip and leaned forward to match him. "So do I."

"Not like this you don't."

Heat flushed her chest, neck, and cheeks. Cocky bastard. Had she ever been with a man this sexy in her entire life? She flipped through an internal Rolodex: *only in my fucking dreams.*

"No touching," she whispered but her words held no bite. "No touching opposing counsel."

"If no touching is the rule, then you should've taken your own advice. You were wrapped around me like a boa constrictor."

With a glance down the comforter, she could see the tented shape below the waistband of Carter's flannel pants. *Yowza.* She almost choked, but a scoff escaped instead. "I can't help what I do in my sleep. It doesn't mean that I want *you* to touch *me*." She ran her thumb across her lower lip, peering up at him.

His gaze grew hot. "Go ahead, tell me no. Tell me to take my pillow and sleep in the bathtub. Tell me to go. I will." He leaned back, crossing his arms in front of him as if to say she wasn't the only one who could withhold. "But I don't think you want me to go."

She nodded slowly, her voice a whisper. "I don't know what you're talking about..."

He shrugged. "I could do it without ever even laying a finger on that flushed pink skin of yours."

Pain surprised her when nails dug into her palms. "How can you tell that it's pink in the dark?"

"It is, then?"

Her cheeks burned, and her voice came out small, breathy. "H-how would you do it?"

Stark silence fell between them. Her tongue skated across her lips, her chest rising and falling in anticipation. His voice sliced the silence like a knife.

"Get the vibrator."

Chapter Four

Perdie rose from the bed, knees shaking. Perhaps she suffered from narcolepsy and was dreaming again. Or maybe, this was simply an everyday sexual hallucination. She *had* done a lot of MDMA in college. Whatever the case, she found herself peering over her shoulder at Carter while she dug through her bag to retrieve her best silver friend. Even in the dark, she could feel his eyes on her.

She clutched the vibrator to her chest, steadied her uneven breath, and teetered to the extremely hot, *extremely* forbidden man in the bed. "This is a *terrible* idea…"

With a click, the lamp on the nightstand flipped on. "Stop."

Perdie froze.

Carter was poised upright at the end of the bed, the light from above illuminating him like a sexy vampire. "What'd you just say?"

"I said this is a terrible idea," she stuttered. "But… but I was joking."

Carter regarded her skeptically. "We don't have to do anything. I thought I was picking up on a vibe."

"You were. It's just…well, I'm a little nervous given our professional situation."

"We could talk instead."

"No!" she exclaimed a touch too fast. "I mean… I'm not opposed to…your *original* suggestion."

He tilted his head with a shrug. "Or we could sleep. You look a little tired."

"Carter! Wait, are you teasing me?"

A glint flashed in his eye. "Halfway. I think you really are uncomfortable about something."

"I would die if anyone at the office found out."

"Oh, I see. I don't think either of us would have anything to gain by that happening."

"It's nothing, forget it. A reputation thing. But on the other hand…" Perdie gazed wistfully at the vibrator at her chest. "Carter, you were right. It wasn't a bad dream…"

Carter muffled a surprised cough in his fist. "Well, then." He cleared his throat. "We're two smart people. Maybe we can figure ourselves around any *unprofessionalism*."

Game the system. Loopholes. She was intrigued. "What'd you have in mind?"

"Letter of the law, not the spirit."

"Go on."

"I won't lay a finger on you."

Her eyes narrowed.

"But we can still…" He raised his brows with a suggestive shrug. "I'm a rule follower by nature, but I've always been sympathetic to those in need."

"Hold on, am *I* the one in need in this scenario?" Perdie tilted her head. He stood abruptly and walked to the little rolling chair by the entrance of the room. "Where're you going?"

He dragged it back, nudging it behind her knees, prompting her to sit. She hesitated then plopped down.

Curious but compliant. Then he settled at the end of the bed across from her and reached for the lip of her seat. Perdie swallowed a yelp when he jerked the chair between his legs so that they were face-to-face, mere inches apart.

"Yes," he said. "You are."

Holy shit.

As if in cinematic slo-mo, his hands traveled towards her breast. Her heart rudely pounded in anticipation. Would he grab her? Kiss her? Throw her on the bed? But he said they wouldn't even touch. *Holy shit times two.*

Instead, without so much as dusting her skin, he delicately pinched the head of the vibrator peeking from her clenched hands. He gave her an expectant look. "May I?" And she loosened her grip, allowing him to slip the toy from her hold. Her hands fell to either side of the chair.

He held out the vibrator and flicked it on and off as if conducting an experiment. Like a mad scientist who'd walked out of a *GQ* photo shoot.

"What's happening?" Perdie whispered, mesmerized.

His focus returned, and he leaned in so close, breath tickled the shell of her ear. *Click.* Buzzing permeated the room. "Don't move," he murmured.

Never in her life had Perdie been so aware of every inch of skin on her own body. Her spine tensed against the back of the chair, eyes squeezed shut, tongue pushed against the roof of her mouth. Like a jolt of electricity, the vibrator made contact with her sternum.

She let out a surprised huff, eyes popping open. But the sensation normalized quickly, as Carter shushed her, smoothing the metal tip gently, almost lazily down the valley of her cleavage and along the bottom, half-moon swell of her breasts. Her nipples pebbled through her threadbare camisole.

"Ah-ha. Suspicions confirmed," he said, the vibration now trailing upwards over the round slope, closer...closer to her aching nipple.

"What suspicions?" Her words were breathless.

"That you're a very bad girl." Carter's voice was soft and teasing but belied the hint of threat. He let the vibrator slide to just outside her areolas, then circled them slowly. "And I like that. Lift up your shirt. Bra off."

"Bossy," she muttered. She awkwardly leaned forward to unsnap her bra, pulled the straps through her shirt, and then hastily tossed the garment to the ground. *Ahhh.* Removing her bra made her already sensitized skin feel like it was ready to burst into flames.

"Shirt. Now."

She pulled the hem of her camisole from her belly all the way to her chest, letting the material fold over, cutting off the top half of her boobs.

He groaned at the sight of her, but even as her back arched he mercilessly avoided her naked nipple, instead repeating his actions with the vibrator on the other breast. Already, she was desperate. If only he'd move to where she really wanted him, or better yet...

"Use your mouth." The words were out before she could stop them. "Put your mouth on me."

His face was tight with concentration at the task at hand. "Can't touch. Would be *unprofessional*."

"Do *something*," she whined.

The hum of the vibrator fell silent and she almost cried out in despair. Her poor throbbing nipples.

"Lift your leg onto my thigh," Carter directed.

She blanched. If she did that...she'd be...*exposed*. To *him*.

But maybe she wanted that. And she still had her clothes on. Well, kinda.

Slowly, she raised her foot, but not to his thigh; she lifted it until it rested on the muscled slope of his shoulder, a bend in her knee. His eyes drooped at the contact, and his head tilted towards her foot as if he might nuzzle her there, as if the technically illegal touch mattered to him. Then he leaned forward to get a better view.

"Are you wet, Bad Girl? Tell me you are so I can imagine what you'd feel like all over my hands, my tongue, my cock."

Oh my.

"I'm—" Perdie inhaled sharply at the buzzing contact suddenly pressed against the fabric covering her pussy. Given that they were in the light, he could probably see that she'd soaked the meager sleep shorts. Her hips undulated of their own accord, the precipice of an orgasm already stirring.

"How's it feel?" he whispered. He was a shadow above her. A handsome, filthy, surprising shadow.

"Unexpected," she bit out. Her head fell back when he exerted more pressure, then began moving with the motion of her hips.

"I wanna come," she murmured. She was quickly losing her grip on any good sense.

"Fine." Carter dipped the rounded tip of the toy to her entrance, barely breaching the barrier through her shorts, until returning back to her covered clit, the vibrator slick with her fluids. A shiver racked her body. "But only because I like to make a woman come fast." He rolled the toy flatly against her. "The first time."

"I'm close already." It seemed every muscle in her body was contracting.

"Push this aside." Carter lifted the vibrator and indicated her shorts. "If my hands touch your pussy, I'll be buried inside you faster than you can say *thank you, Counselor.*"

She almost giggled at the corny expression. Though in a haze, Perdie wrapped her fingers around the fabric, and with a harsh pull, she was completely open to him.

Momentarily, Carter stilled. Eyes darkened. He licked his lips and took a breath as if in prayer before gently circling the tip of the vibrator around her clit. He was coming off the edge of the bed now, an obscene view of the action.

She whimpered unabashedly, toes curling. "Please. Please…"

"Are you going to come without me ever laying a finger on you, Bad Girl? I shouldn't let you."

"Nooo…" she moaned.

"But like I said, I'm the giving type."

"Yesyesyesyesyes," she hissed as he replaced the toy against her primed skin, this time no barriers beneath the vibrations and her clit. Her hips rolled. The pleasure was metallic, like a shock wave, ten times stronger. *"Mmmmph, that's so good…"*

She needed something to anchor her. Something to hold on to. She desperately grasped at anything, the side of the chair, her own breasts, and everything around her until finally, she found Carter's shirt, fisting the material, her leg fell but her knees spread wide. She winced. "Almost…there…" She yanked his body to hers, mouths centimeters from touching.

Carter stilled. At first, he seemed shocked, but then he groaned when her hand traveled to the nape of his neck and she pressed her lips to his. She worked a tongue over him, his mouth finally opening to it, then going wild, tongues thrusting in and out. The kiss growing deeper, harder, messier. He broke away when tight moans began to escape her. "That's right… I want you to come hard… come so hard you see god…"

With her orgasm spilling over, he kissed her again, this time to muffle her cries.

A sharp sensation swallowed her whole, her back bowed until finally the waterfall within her subsided into a still pond. A pond where she could see herself clearly.

She broke away, collapsing into the chair, rolling back so that both her feet landed on the ground, gulping for air, rolling her head and shoulders to stare at the ceiling. Carter leaned back against his hands, his eyes wide, breath heavy.

"Sorry for breaking the rules," she said.

"Worth it, worth every second."

Carter and Perdie lay together on the bed, both of them wide-eyed and out of breath. A quiet awkwardness lingered.

Carter reached for Perdie, his hand coming to caress a lock of hair fallen over her eye.

But she craned away. Fun times were over now. "What are you doing? No, don't do that."

His hand stilled in midair. "You can't be serious?"

Perdie's eyes shifted to him, then back towards the ceiling. "It's unprofessional."

He laughed in disbelief. "Are we still on that? I made you scream like a banshee not five minutes ago."

She snorted. "Yeah, and you know the rules."

"I thought we were having fun."

She let out a heavy sigh, pulling her shirt down,

He raised an eyebrow. "I didn't say you could do that yet."

She leaned over the side of the bed, fishing for her discarded bra. "Game's over, Pretty Boy. New rules effective now. Office rules."

His eyes narrowed. "Oh, I see."

Perdie's own weight shifted as Carter rolled from the bed. She pretended not to watch, when he adjusted his erection as he walked to the bathroom. The tap turned on from the bathroom and then he returned, tossing the tiny vibrator back in her bag.

Even though, in her mind, she'd shut down any chance of future encounters, even though she'd already experienced a mind-blowing orgasm, desire coaxed back into her body. She should probably feel guilty for being the only one who'd had an orgasm. She could extend their game for a teeny bit longer to offer him a little, tiny quid pro quo.

"Carter."

He turned at the sound of her voice. His muscular torso, hard and taut as his hand messily rubbed the hair at his nape.

"Do you expect me to return the favor now?"

His face softened once he processed the question. "I'd commit a series of unforgivable crimes for it, don't get me wrong...but I just wanted to watch you come. Been thinking about making you come since you opened your mouth in that deposition room."

She choked on her words. *Well, fuck.* "Carter..." She cleared her throat, and his eyebrows perked. "Will you bring me a cookie? I'm starving."

Perdie sat crossed-legged at the end of the bed. The fun was over but at least she could fantasize about it in bed for a few weeks until some other hookup came along to whisk away the memories.

She peeled the plastic wrap off the greasy cookie and took a bite. A friendly distance stretched between them now, the sexual tension blown off like so much dust in the wind. Now, they could be cool with each other. They could forget anything weird had even happened between them and act like mature, professional adults.

"So what's going on with you at your firm?"

His question made her stop midchew. "Why do you keep asking all these questions?" She dusted crumbs from her lap.

"You seem...paranoid?"

She whacked his biceps, and his hands went up like he was under arrest.

"Okay, okay. Like I said. Someone with your talent should have made partner by now. Or is that not how it works over on your side of the coast?"

"It might usually work that way. I came to my position through a different path than most."

"So no summer clerk program?"

Perdie laughed. "Oh sweetie, not even close."

He inclined his chin. "Go on, what's the story then." Reaching over, he broke off a chunk of cookie and popped it in his mouth. "This is terrible." When he went for seconds, she slapped his hand.

"Get your own."

"I like yours better. Tell me the story."

"Okay, fine." She took a beat to swallow. "After I graduated, the economy went straight into the trash, and I was saddled with a mortgage-sized student loan from a shitty law school with no prospects to speak of and no clue what to do...so I got one of those recruiters who hooks you up with contract gigs. You know the ones, where they pay you nothing and you work in the basement?"

Carter shrugged. "Sure."

Not a chance he'd ever had to consider that kind of work.

"Anyway, that got my foot in the door at Joy and Schulz."

"And you wowed them so much with your work that they hired you as an associate on the spot?" He winked.

She nudged his foot with her toe. "Not exactly. I was assigned to a case under one of the managing partners. Lots of rushed deadlines and things like that. Well, I had nothing better going on, so I pulled all-nighters to get work done. The work was monotonous, but it was easy to bill hour after hour. Because I would always hang around upstairs late into the evening with the attorney leading the case, one day I decided to…move into an empty office."

She paused, laughing at herself. "Smallest office on the floor too. Look, that might not seem like a big deal to you, but before all that I had only ever worked jobs that required me to stand behind a counter all day. So an office was a big deal to me. Nobody said a word, maybe because we Southerners are too polite. And, well, I kept on. Until one day I walked in, and an IT guy was setting up my new firm computer and work-issued cell phone and there was an official printed offer sitting on my desk."

"So, you moved your way into a job."

She gave a rueful smile. "Sometimes you have to take things that aren't even there."

"Sounds pretty impressive to me?"

"Maybe, but I don't know that I've ever been able to shake the stigma of not going through the formal interview process. They didn't *choose* me. Even after so many years, I still feel like everybody's assistant sometimes.

Not worthy. I've watched three other attorneys who came in after me make partner."

"That's not right. You should demand they consider you."

Perdie laughed. "Oh, you sweet summer child. Tell me something, Carter. What do your parents do for a living?"

Carter scratched the top of his head. "Why do you ask?"

"Because I already know. Your mother's a federal judge."

"My other mother is an artist."

"Did you know that my mother is a bartender at a biker bar called Shooters? Such a cliché, right? You and I? We don't come from the same kinda place."

"And yet we both ended up in the same place."

"Right. On different sides of the table." She offered him the last of the cookie.

"But your bra is from La Perla." There was a glint of mischief in his eyes.

"Well, you know what they say about lipstick on a pig…"

He frowned. "You can't possibly think that about yourself."

She rolled her eyes. "Relax, a little self-deprecating humor is all. But what you have to understand is, I can't stomp through the office swinging my big metaphorical dick around demanding promotions. It's more complicated than that for me."

"They wouldn't fire you."

The concern on his face amused her. He really had no idea.

She sighed. "Maybe nothing so obvious, but they'd ostracize me. Conveniently forget to include me on emails.

Ice me out of their good old boys' jokes. Keep me off the hot cases. There are only two other women in my practice group, and they look like beauty pageant queens. It's a whole different ball game for us."

"A friend of mine from Harvard works at your firm. Ferris Joy? We used to party together back in the day. You should talk to him. Or, hell, I can talk to him for you."

She tilted her head, surrendering to a yawn. Ferris Joy was the son of the named partner of Joy and Schulz, and there wasn't a chance in hell she'd talk to him. "You trying to help a girl out? You're kinda sweet, you know that? For a lawyer." She stretched her arms over her head and fell back onto her pillow. He followed after, both of them, on their backs, respectably distanced. "But don't worry that pretty face over me."

He rustled in the sheets next to her. "Maybe I want to."

She laughed softly. "Trust me, it's not worth the wrinkles. Besides, you'll forget all about me when you fly back to California. I'm sure you have a glamorous life like a TV star. You look like one at least."

"Yeah, you keep saying that."

"And what about you? You like it over there at that fancy West Coast firm representing those rich cartoon villains?"

The bed vibrated a bit with his chuckle. "You know, I never really considered working anywhere else. Just followed the yellow brick road. University to law school to big law. Not much room for questions in between."

"Sounds like you need to change things up. Ask yourself the big stuff. What if you got it all wrong? Wrong firm? Wrong state? Wrong life? Ever wonder if you'd done it differently where you'd be now? Sometimes I do. You ever have dreams too big to chase?"

"I've always wanted to climb Denali. That's a big dream."

"I could never climb a mountain." Perdie's eyes were heavy, but she opened them to see he was looking at her. She couldn't figure out his expression, but whatever it was, it pinged something deep inside somewhere. A little too intense for her liking. "I'm afraid of heights."

He looked back to the ceiling. "Are you afraid of heights, or are you afraid of falling? Because when faced with a cliff, everyone's afraid to fall. But there's a difference."

Chapter Five

"Carter Leplan has ruined my pussy, and I'll never forgive him for it." Perdie shoved a tortilla chip with guac into her mouth, salted flecks sprinkling down her soft cotton V-neck. The happy crowd and upbeat music at her favorite taco joint weren't doing her mood any favors, but at least there was guac. She always had guac.

"I know, baby girl, but it's only been two weeks. Less time than the kale's been in the fridge." Lucille sucked down a frozen pineapple margarita and signaled a server for two more. "Some people go *years* without having orgasms. Some people go entire lifetimes." The *some people* Lucille was referring to was herself.

"I'm sorry. That was insensitive of me." Perdie pinched the bridge of her nose. "So why did you spend the last two weeks with Hampton?"

"Because he's the love of my life, Perdie. He wants four kids, and you know how much I've always wanted four kids, I already have their gender-neutral names picked out: Winter, Avery, Quinn, and Devon. Hampton's over six feet tall. He uses designer beard oil, which is self-care. *And* he told me we could be monogamous once he gets the funding for his microbrew-at-home start-up." Lucille stroked a shiny strand of black hair, then flicked it over her shoulder. "That could be any day now."

"Luce. I'm trying to understand, I really am. But he's never even given you an orgasm."

Lucille rolled her eyes, her margarita sloshing onto her hand. "He's come closer than anyone else." She gazed solemnly into the wide-rimmed glass. "I believe he's the chosen one. I mean, someone's gotta be."

Perdie shook her head then leaned forward to look her best friend in the eye. "Lemme let you in on a little secret. There are no chosen ones. There are only the ones that you have chosen. Make better choices."

"*Psh*, you don't get it. You never grow attached to men even when they fall all over you." Lucille tipped back her glass to finish the dregs, wiped her mouth with the back of her hand, and then twisted on her stool to face the curly-haired man who had just approached their table. "Except for you, Noah. I'm sure she will grow very attached to you. You seem very attachable and whatnot."

Noah's eyes grew wide at the acknowledgment of his presence as he rejoined them after taking a work call. "Oh, well, thank you, I think?"

Noah was Perdie's date for the night, and she had an embarrassed notion he might've heard everything she and Lucille were talking about. She hadn't planned on making the date a threesome with Lucille, but since Perdie's return to Charleston two weeks ago, Lucille had holed away with good-for-nothing Hampton the *entire* time. So when Lucille arrived home earlier that evening, dark circles under her eyes, her crop top and skirt wrinkled, they needed a major best-friend catchup and she'd brought Lucille along on her date with Noah.

Perdie crossed her arms, eyes on Lucille. "Noah, you're an ER doctor, right?"

"No, I have a fellowship for developmental neurogenetics at the medical university."

Perdie did a double take. "Damn. Okay. Well, fuck. The point is, you're a smart guy. Tell my friend Lucille that she needs to choose better."

Before Noah could speak, Lucille cut in.

"No, you tell Perdie that sometimes things are meant to be and you have to stick with them to find out. Like… like…" She circled her wrist, snapping her fingers. "Like you and Perdie could be destined for marriage. You gotta have faith. You can't cut and run because things aren't perfect."

"Things can't be perfect if you keep picking douchebags named Hampton."

"He's not a douchebag, he avoids auxiliary social interactions to preserve his dopamine."

"That's not how dopamine works."

Noah's head vacillated between the two. They stared at him for a response. He stabbed a thumb to his chest. "Oh, my turn now?" For a moment it seemed like he might not say anything, but then he shrugged. "Have you ever considered talking to the guy?"

Both of them narrowed their eyes at him.

"What do you mean?" Perdie asked.

"Talking about what?" Lucille asked.

Noah's eyebrows knitted together as if he were trying to explain quantum physics to toddlers. "Like…regular talking. Asking, answering. Exchanging information to make educated hypotheses about the other person and your potential compatibility?"

Silence.

Lucille tilted her head. "Why do I need to talk to some guy when I have Perdie to talk to? That's not what I need a man for. I need a man to have four kids with."

"Well technically you don't need a man for that, just the relevant genetic material." Noah rubbed his chin, regarding Lucille thoughtfully.

Perdie threw her hands up. "Right? Lucille, I told you I'd happily raise four children with you."

"Perdie, it's nice that you say that, but you don't mean it. You don't want kids. If you did, we'd already have two by now."

Perdie conceded with a nod. "Fine. It's true. I'll make an amazing earth-goddess mother though."

Lucille patted her hands. "Not if you keep shit-talking Hampton, you won't."

Perdie snatched her hands away, eyes wide. "Cunt," she whispered. Then the two broke out into laughter. "Noah, give us more words of wisdom please."

"Oh, I wouldn't say I have words of wis—"

"Just do it, Noah. Don't be a little bitch." Lucille collected three tequila shots from a server, and placed one in front of each of them. "Bottoms up, y'all."

The shot glasses hit the table with a collective thud. Perdie tensed her face to stop from gagging, but Noah had almost no reaction.

He cleared his throat. "Uh, fine. Perdie, I think sometimes emotional things manifest themselves in physical ways which is why you might be having some…you know, problems right now."

Perdie shoulders tensed. "Oh, so you heard all that before?"

"I may have. But the sentiment stands."

She tapped the tip of her nose. "What are you, some kind of guru?"

He shrugged. "I've done a lot of therapy. My upbringing was *unusual*. I could refer you to someone?"

Lucille pointed her finger to Perdie. "Burn."

"I could refer you to someone as well." Noah gave her a deliberate look.

"Oh, we got a live one." Perdie chuckled.

A small smile played on Noah's serious face. "I understand there is still a stigma against therapy. Especially in the South, but I have found it has profoundly improved my life."

"I don't need therapy." Lucille's voice slurred slightly. "I'm doing great. I'm doing fine. I'm doing—oh." Her phone lit up on the table, and she snatched it.

Perdie rolled her eyes, taking a sip of her margarita. "Hampton?"

Lucille looked up through dark lashes. "Hate to bail on our first date."

Perdie nodded. "But you love to fuck a douchebag."

"My destiny calls." Lucille popped out of her seat, collecting her bag. "Sorry, Noah. I had fun. Love the curls."

She leaned over and kissed Perdie on the cheek and sauntered away. "I'm taking Bananas with me, byeee," she called back before Perdie could protest.

To Noah's credit, he smiled and waved. "Well, she's nice."

Perdie sighed as Lucille's petite form disappeared through the exit. "She's perfect, and I love the little weirdo."

For a moment, Perdie fixed her gaze on Noah. She was a little tipsy, enough to feel the warm hug of tequila wrap around her insides, and she was feeling generous.

Noah was actually quite handsome. His eyes were dark brown and framed with enviable thick black lashes. His jaw was strong and dusted with a hint of stubble. And his soft, deep brown ringlets somehow perfectly framed his face. Lucille wasn't telling stories out of school. Perdie almost never grew attached to men. And if she did, she often forgot them when the next guy came rolling around. Maybe a little romp with Noah was exactly the kind of palate cleanser she needed.

She crossed her legs, leaning back in the chair. "So, you wanna go back to your place?"

Perhaps it seemed abrupt after the whirlwind three-person date, and it would be unbelievable to think he'd accept after what she'd said about Carter, but if Perdie knew anything about men…

Surprise only flickered in his eyes for a moment before he tossed his napkin on the table and slapped his hands on his thighs. "Yep."

A famous Swedish designer had decorated Noah's home, and the pristine, nearly mansion-sized house didn't quite fit in with the sprawling magnolias dripping in Spanish moss that lined the streets. But Noah didn't quite fit in with Southerners either.

Inside the minimalist abode, Noah consulted his extensive collection of organized wine.

"Don't care. Any red'll do," Perdie prodded, peering over his shoulder.

Noah nodded and chose a bottle, then poured them each a glass. Without meaning to, Perdie clenched the stem of the expensive glassware. She forced a sip, anything to calm the tense feeling in her shoulders, which she shouldn't be feeling in the first place. She should be looking forward to a little easy fun. Therefore, she was determined to follow through on this hookup.

But when Noah approached, her body stiffened.

"Yes?" he asked, bending at the waist. He was asking to kiss her.

Well, here fucking goes. She nodded tightly. "Mmm-hmm."

His hand came to cup her jaw. She should be excited. Noah was hot. And nice.

But then his mouth descended on hers. Perdie miscalculated his aim and their first contact landed his lips on her nose.

"Oh shit, sorry." Perdie's wineglass still dangled from her fingers, but she grabbed onto the nape of his neck with her free hand. "Let's try that again."

Finally, teeth clattering, hands groping, their bodies connected.

But when they knocked into the counter, Noah bumped Perdie and red wine spilled down her shirt. "Oops!" She set both their glasses on the counter.

Not ideal so far.

It didn't help that when she closed her eyes she was seeing…hearing…smelling the chilled minty waves of Carter Leplan.

Noah must've sensed something because he pulled away. "Are you sure you want to do this?"

"Don't worry about it…" she murmured, clutching Noah's T-shirt, drawing him back in.

But Noah broke the kiss between them and placed both hands on her shoulders. "You know, maybe your friend's right. Some people are destined to be together. I don't think we are two such people."

"Wow, you're not going to even try to hook up with

me." Perdie was so used to using men only for this purpose that she grappled with what to do. And she hadn't even really considered whether she truly wanted to hook up with Noah. Old habits.

"It's not really my style. More importantly, I'm not sure you're into it."

Perdie walked towards the living room and collapsed onto his slate couch. "Maybe we could be friends?" That was something people said to each other, right?

Noah smiled, joining her and sitting across from her on a matching couch. "I think we'd make good friends. You and Lucille were the most fun I've had out in a long time."

Perdie chuckled. "Not so sure what that says about you, buddy."

A weird thing happened after that: they got to talking like friends might. And Perdie learned about Noah's job and his part in developing a medication for seizures that was stolen by a large pharmaceutical company.

She gave him her card. "I think you have a patent case on your hands." Perhaps a long shot but still potential millions on the line. She could make Noah a rich man, and her firm would take a nice hefty slice of that payout.

Knowing there was no one to come home to at her condo, Perdie crashed on Noah's couch. He graciously brought her blankets and pillows and some water.

When she got up in the morning, she clutched the doorframe to steady herself, her other hand grasping the top of her head. She wasn't the drinker she'd once been, but she always seemed to be testing fate.

Silly of her to sneak out. She shot off a text, thanking Noah for being so cool about her meltdown and suggesting they keep in touch.

It was too bad she was already so preoccupied with someone else because Noah was going to make some lucky girl very happy someday.

And as she was not that girl, escape was imminent. Outside, the bite of fluorescent sunlight ate away at her corneas. She shielded her eyes as she half stumbled onto the sidewalk. She looked down at the light pink splotch marring the front of her gray T-shirt, and her stretched and worn jeans. Rubbing a fingertip under her eyelids, she erased the inky remainder of her mascara. She no doubt looked a hot fucking mess. At least she wasn't in heels and work clothes stranded at the airport during a blizzard. Or lying on a bed in a hotel with a stranger. She mentally slapped herself for thinking about Carter.

A botched hookup was no big deal but fixating on one night with one man was simply unacceptable. Why was it he'd gotten under her skin so much? Good looks, money, skill, power? Too obvious. His interest in her? It was no small blessing she didn't have Carter's personal number, or she'd probably give in to the overwhelming urge to text him a time or a thousand. His firm's website listed his work number under his site bio, but even she wasn't desperate enough to contact him that way. Or worse, his work email. They'd briefly exchanged emails to settle the case, but she'd be in trouble if she started composing love letters. HR would get a kick out of it too.

Perdie chewed on her lips. She was lost in the middle of a neighborhood she'd never been in before. She would need a car to get her. She consulted her phone to order one when the screen blacked out. A glitch in the matrix? Nope, a dead battery.

"Dammit." How had people gotten places before the invention of smartphones? Her car was parked at the taco joint, and she had not one iota of a clue how to get out of this Stepford-style residential neighborhood. The houses were also growing theatrically larger and larger the farther she traveled.

Panicking, she hurried, looking both directions for a sign of anything familiar. All that surrounded her were swaying palmetto trees and grandfather live oaks gilding the fancy brick.

She'd have to head back to Noah's and borrow a charger. While they'd established a new friendship, she inwardly cringed at the idea of turning up on his doorstep with a dead phone. She was doing some kind of subverted walk of shame and as such she'd like to finish out the task. He would probably offer to give her a ride home, of course, but...

As Perdie spun on her heel the other way, she ran smack into the middle of a hard figure.

"Fuck me." Her headache slapped inside her skull on impact, and she blinked up at the person in front of her, the face and body backlit like a mirage in the sun.

"Well, that's an enthusiastic greeting."

A prickle of familiarity ran up her spine at the deep voice. *Carter motherfucking Leplan?*

"Oh my god. What are you doing here?" She glanced around to spot the teleportation machine from where he must've emerged.

Before Carter answered, a woman appeared at the entrance of the house they stood in front of. Not just any woman, but a blonde, perfectly coiffed Southern belle wearing a royal blue Lilly Pulitzer jumpsuit. The kind of jumpsuit that required supreme confidence in one's body to pull off. And she was pulling it off.

"Carter, darling, come on in." The woman smiled, not giving Perdie so much as a second look.

He smiled back. "One minute, Aubrey."

A hot surge of jealousy shot through the bottom of her belly. Had Carter Leplan come all the way to Charleston to see a woman? A woman who wasn't even her? She pinched the sensitive skin inside her forearm. *You have no right to be jealous. No right.*

Carter ran his hand through his hair, stepping under the shade of a tree. Her rogue brain took over then, the vision of him almost too much to handle when combined with a hangover. She had thought about him a lot these last few weeks. *A. Lot.* Her eyes swept down his body. His hair was shorter than when she'd last seen him, the sides shaved closer but still that beautiful toffee-brown wavy hair. And he was wearing a gray T-shirt, displaying muscled biceps with a half sleeve of tattoos on his left arm. Expensive-looking raw denim hanging on his hips, all the way down to...

A pair of black-and-white Chuck Taylors.

She looked down at her own outfit. Gray T-shirt, worn jeans, black-and-white Chuck Taylors. Of course she had the added element of a big old red wine stain. *Cute.* Still, the sight of their matching outfits made her slap her hand to her mouth, an unfortunate giggle escaping.

She dropped her hand at his surprised look, straightening up. "Is that your sister?" she asked before she could stop herself. Years of diligent rom-com watching had taught her that men were often out meeting their sisters early on Saturday mornings and *not* their lovers.

The corner of his mouth lifted. "Don't have a sister. But I'm pretty close to my sister-in-law."

She looked down, shuffling her feet. "Oh, so like a cousin or a really young aunt or something then?"

Amusement played across his features, but he stood stock-still, challenging her. "Nope and nope."

She fidgeted. "Okay, then. I gotta—"

"It's something personal," he said, scratching the top of his head. "Can't really...talk about it yet."

She pressed her lips into a facsimile of a smile. "Well, whoever, I mean, *whatever* it is you're doing here, I hope it all goes fucking amazing. Great seeing you." She pulled a big step to the right of him, but he moved with her. She pivoted to the other side, but he moved with her again. And again once more.

"You mind?" She stopped, hands on her hips, exasperation dotting her voice. The sun broke through the leaves, and in the dappled light his eyes looked especially green.

"You live around here?" he asked.

She paused, unsure how to respond, but then held up her dead phone. "No, actually. I might be stranded. Kind of a wild night..." Her voice trailed off. "Hey. Do you mind if I order a car from your phone? Promise I'll pay you back." She wouldn't but it was nice to say.

He crossed his arms. "I'll give you a ride."

She shook her head. "Oh no, really. I don't want you to keep Amanda waiting."

"Aubrey."

"Whatever."

He held up his index finger. "Just wait. Just give me one moment. Don't—don't go anywhere. I'll be right back."

She held her hands up to decline but then let them drop. What exactly were her choices right now anyway? Still, she was suspicious. "Okay, I'll wait right here."

He jogged into the house, closing the door behind him. Instead of giving in to the urge to eavesdrop through a window, she picked away at her manicure—black gels, but she would maybe change it up tomorrow. She was thinking red. Red like—

"Okay." Carter reemerged and waved her over to a large SUV parked out front. The car beeped when he clicked the key fob. "Let's go."

Chapter Six

Perdie breathed in big and deep like she was doing a line of coke. Except it wasn't coke she was inhaling, but that familiar, cool scent Carter seemed to naturally exude. She wanted to push her nose into his chest and rub it all over her. He smelled like air smelled the morning after it snowed.

She crossed her arms, squishing her seat belt into the crevice of her boobs, feeling dank and musty in her day-old T-shirt with the red wine stain. It would've been nice if she had brought a jacket with her, but the weather had been wonky in Charleston.

"Congrats on the settlement." Carter's eyes flicked to her, his large hand resting on the console between them as he drove. "Big personal win for you, right?"

It had been. In fact, Perdie had received an email from her managing partner, Frank, requesting to set up a meeting with her on Monday. "Good news only," Frank had said.

Perdie had her hopes up. She tucked her hair behind her ears and caught a glance of herself in the side mirror. *Shit.* She smoothed down the errant hairs on the crown of her head. "Yeah, on my side of the table, we only eat what we kill. We don't pump our clients for hours and then walk away with a fat check even if we lose."

A puff of air escaped his lips. "I guess we're not all natural born killers. You think maybe I could learn?"

She pushed her head into her hand against the passenger window. "Not a chance."

He laughed. "Well, tell me how you really feel."

She narrowed her eyes. There was levity in Carter's voice, but people often said that to her as if she was *too honest* with them. What they really meant was *stop telling me how you feel because I don't like it.* But it did make Noah's words ring in her head. Holding in feelings wasn't only bad for the soul. It was bad for the body too.

"Why're you here?" She turned her head to get a good look at his profile offset by the white-blue Charleston sky whipping by them.

His smile faded and he scrubbed his hand down his mouth. "One a scale of one to ten, how irritating would it be to say I couldn't tell you?"

She pursed her lips. "I'd say you're gonna need a bigger scale."

He chuckled. "Would a lie suffice, then?"

His large hands slid up to the smooth curve of the steering wheel, as they merged onto the Ravenel Bridge, its flared white rib cage swallowing them whole.

"Okay, man of mystery. I can take a hint. None of my business." She worried her bottom lip with her teeth, gazing out the window, his reflection visible against the glass. It surprised her when the next sound was her own voice. "The blonde woman though."

The sides of his eyes crinkled, but he seemed to suppress a smile. "Yes. Aubrey."

"Aubrey doesn't care that you left her hanging to drive me home?"

His eyes flickered over to her. "Oh, I see. You're jealous."

Like a reflex, she went to deny it, but then she stopped herself. For weeks she'd been thinking about this man, and then he finally appeared in the flesh right in front of her like some kind of dark apparition. She wouldn't waste this moment on plausible deniability. "Honestly?" She shrugged, letting her hands fall together in her lap. "Yeah. I am."

That earned her a double take from Carter.

Ah-ha. "You're shocked I'm admitting it? I'm a big enough person to admit that I'm jealous. Like it's a big deal? Everyone gets jealous." While it might not save her pride, sometimes taking an opponent off guard was the best strategy of all. And sometimes honesty was the best policy. Inwardly she nodded at that. *What a wholesome thought, P.*

Carter didn't respond for a stretch of time, until the motion of his hand sliding down the console in between them and over to her lap caught in her periphery. Her breath hitched at the unexpected contact, his hand smoothing over her thigh. Then easy as a beach breeze, it slipped in between her own hands, his large, rough fingers interlacing with hers in a warm, soft grasp.

"What's this? What's happening?" she sputtered.

He drew their hands away from her lap and pressed them to the hard surface of his chest, his pulse barely detectable against the skin on the back of her hand.

"There's more than one way to be honest." At her dazed expression, he smirked. "Like it's a big deal?"

He let their hands slide down the plane of his abdomen, finally resting against one of his jean-clad thighs. She stared at their shared clasp. *Well, hell.* She wasn't the only one wielding the element of surprise.

With his available hand, he turned the car off the Sullivan's Island connector and into the gated community where she lived. They slowed to the keypad at the entryway.

"Gate code?"

She was so mesmerized by the fact that they were holding hands that she didn't answer right away.

"Perdie?"

"Huh, *oh*." Her voice came out breathy. "Sixty-nine, sixty-nine."

For a second Carter stared, then he let out a crack of a laugh. "Noted," he mumbled as they passed through the entrance and into the small, well-landscaped community.

His phone GPS led them to her condo. He pulled into a parking space in front of the white building, putting the car into park. Perdie's eyes shifted from their hands to the door lever then back to their hands.

She bit her lip, assessing the evidence. Carter Leplan was here, in Charleston, the place where she, Perdie Stone, also was.

And he wouldn't tell her why.

And a beautiful blonde woman called him darling.

And the beautiful woman had asked him to go into a house with her.

And he had said *in a minute*.

And then…

And then he was holding Perdie's hand. Holding her hand like it meant something. Like he wanted to press it against his heart so she could feel it beat for her.

Oh gross. Oh god. What was she doing? She had to

let go. She had to get out of the car. She didn't even like holding hands.

"So," Carter spoke softly. "We're here."

She lifted her head. "You wanna come in?"

His chest deflated with an exhale. "Shouldn't. But I'll walk you to your door."

The snap of the seat belt release brought Perdie back to the present. Finally she dropped Carter's hand, unbuckled, and opened the car door.

There was a tension between them now, a quietness lingering, but she couldn't quite pin it down. He walked close to her but didn't touch her as they made their way up the creaky wooden steps to the hidden overhang at her front door. Her condo, while on the second floor, took up half the building, and below them was her private parkway.

But then they were at her door, her feet catching on her Come As You Are welcome mat.

She turned around to speak, but he'd already caught her by the waist, hauling her up against him then slowly stepping them back until her heels touched the ridge of the entryway.

She thought from the heated look in his eyes that his mouth might come down hard onto hers and they'd push against each other in some kind of manic, frantic desire for connection.

But none of that happened.

Instead he lowered his gaze to her hand, took it in his own, and lifted her palm to his mouth. She regarded him with curiosity as he held her hand gently at the wrist, then kissed the sensitive center of her palm with an open mouth, his tongue lashing at the flesh.

She gasped. It was positively Victorian.

Then he turned her hand to the side to expose the thin skin of her inner wrist and applied the same treatment, kissing it, letting his tongue slide across the ridges of her veins, then his bottom lip dragging along. His eyes were stormy. They'd never looked darker, all hints of green vanished.

"You're being weird," she whispered, her breath coming fast. She was watching him intently.

"You like it."

Her eyes shuttered as his mouth closed in on her neck.

"You smell so good," he said. "Like oranges."

"It's pineapple." She could barely get the words out. "Or maybe tequila."

The flat of his tongue touched the smooth, taut column of skin on the side of her neck, her head tilting from the sensation, a groan escaping her lips. He kissed her there, slow and hot, his hands trailing up from her waist to crisscross around her back so that their bodies pressed together.

When he broke away, her lips parted, anticipating the inevitable kiss. But he pulled back from her instead, his lids heavy, the color heightened on the crests of his cheekbones, and his hair tousled.

She licked her lips and swallowed. He snaked his right hand up the front of her shirt, and she tensed, waiting for the next swell of sensation which came at the pull of his index finger hooking into the center of the vee on her T-shirt. The stretchy fabric slipped down on one side, revealing the tops of her breasts and the bisecting black line of her bra. A strained groan escaped him at the sight of her sheer bra, sending a thrill up her spine.

"You're so sexy," he said, his voice a low growl. "Do you even have any idea?" He leaned his forehead against her sternum, then messily rubbed his hair against the sensitized, exposed skin.

She let out a giggle at the rough sensation. "What the hell are you doing?"

He looked up, hair a mess, lips swollen.

His gaze made her smile drop. "You're so—" She began, but her words were cut off by the soft, lazy contact of his lips on her own.

"Mmm." She grabbed the nape of his neck, pulling his head closer to her, her hands threading into his hair, tugging at the soft waves.

But he kept her at bay even through her frantic grasps. He lazily licked into her mouth, letting her lip catch with his, swirling their tongues together in a slow, intoxicating dance. Her head moved with the kiss, catching his rhythm, their mouths open, tongues sliding in and out, heat building low in her belly, nipples beading into hard points.

She dipped her hand in between them, letting her fingers latch at the waist of his jeans, fiddling with the metal button. His muffled, low growl reverberated against her mouth.

Encouraged, she let her fingers slip down farther, gliding to the hard protrusion in his pants, and then grasping its full heft in her hand.

He broke the kiss, his hand enclosing her own, dragging it back up between them. "Wait."

Her eyes shot wide. "I'm sorry, I thought you wanted me to…"

"No, no. It's not that." He closed his eyes, his brows knitted together. "That thing I can't tell you about… It's… I need a little time. For your own sake really."

She cocked her head. *Excuse me?* "What the hell is

that supposed to mean? Don't act like you know what's best for my sake. I'm a fully grown woman."

He nodded. "You're right. I want to make sure everything is clear between us before we move ahead. Physically or otherwise."

Presumptuous. "Is this about that Aubrey woman?"

He ran his hands through his hair, then looked back up at her. "Can you give me a little time?"

"Well, exactly how long will you be here?" She shuffled to the side, away from the heat of his body.

"Not sure." He shifted his weight. "But if there's a chance I'll be here for a while, will you see me again?"

This fucking guy. She shook her head slowly. "You're fucking with me. You know that, right?"

He rubbed his hand against his brow, then scrubbed it down his mouth. She was annoyed with him, but still painfully attracted, and that annoyed her more.

"I'll make it up to you. Soon. I promise." He reached out for her, fingering the hem of her shirt, a puff of laughter coming from him at the sight of the stain. "Give me a chance?"

She narrowed her eyes but was acutely aware of the tickle of his index finger against her stomach. Her whole brain zoomed in on that tiny little sensation like there was nothing else in the world. She let out a huff. "Maybe."

He gripped the hem of her T-shirt, exerting pressure to draw her near again. "I'll take a maybe."

"But you're being fucking weird."

He nodded, wrapping his other arm around her back, closing the rest of the space between them. "Understood."

"And I don't like being—" But her words died off at the touch of his lips. He kissed her long and relaxed, his hand cupping her jaw.

"I don't like being left in the dark," she said dazedly.

He let out a long breath of air. "I should go."

Perdie wanted to stamp her feet and throw a tantrum, demanding he stop being so goddamn cryptic and take her inside her house and fuck the hell out of her.

But instead she shrugged. "Okay."

He turned to leave, made his way back down the stairs and into his big Southern SUV, and finally drove off out of sight. She leaned against her doorframe, her body slack but overly stimulated and aching. *Carter Leplan has ruined my pussy, and I'll never forgive him for it.*

She fished her keys out of her pocket. Dammit, her car was still at the taco joint.

Chapter Seven

Lucille whistled. "Wow, you look fancy like a TV lawyer. But show me a little more leg, sweetheart."

Perdie whisked past her in search of her favorite coffee mug that read Will Provide Legal Advice For Tacos.

"How dare you objectify me, *creep*." Perdie hiked her skirt up, exposing a slit of thigh, then let the material drop while rummaging around the kitchen cabinets.

Lucille let out a hoot. "That's what I'm talking 'bout, baby."

On a clear morning, the wall-length window overlooking the Atlantic Intracoastal Waterway was drowned with sun, and out the window, the waves were a crisp greenish-blue, the clouds thin and still above the reflective horizon. Bananas snored quietly in his plush bed pushed against the sunny window.

As if from nowhere, Lucille procured Perdie her mug, already filled with a blond roast.

Perdie smiled. "I take it back, you're a real American hero."

"So you think they'll really do it today, then? Partner you up? Make an honest woman out of you?" Lucille sat at their kitchen table, and a rectangular glass vase filled with white amaryllis partially obscured her face. She stirred her chai latte, appearing a little distracted as she tapped at her phone.

Perdie took in the view over the water, sipping her coffee. She nodded. "Yep, big settlement under my belt, meeting with Frank at the end of the day—I've been there way longer than required for partnership, and I picked up this dress from the tailor's yesterday afternoon." She swept away an invisible speck of dust near the split neck of her knee-length red sheath. She paired the dress with nude pumps, but her red gel manicure matched the fabric, and beneath the dress she wore matching red undergarments.

Matching bra and panties was the true sign of having one's shit together, everyone knew that. And a rare fucking occurrence for Perdie.

Lucille frowned, her head bent over her phone.

Perdie narrowed her eyes suspiciously. "You got any big plans for the day?"

Lucille shrugged. "Taking Bananas to the flower shop around eleven. Hope all the wealthy neighborhood housewives are really into daffodils this week because I accidentally ordered four times the usual amount. Then, oh, who knows. Gem is working the shop all day. I'll see where the wind blows me. Free like a bird."

"No Hampton then?"

Lucille sighed, leaning back in her chair. "The fucker ghosted me again. He totally bailed on Bananas's vet appointment. I was using that appointment as a test, like a trial run. You know, for kids? Whatever. Doesn't matter. He's not returning any of my texts anyway. *Again.* At this point, I'm used to it." She tossed her phone onto the table. "Don't say I told you so. Ugh, but you know what? You did tell me so."

"It's okay, we all mess around with men we shouldn't."
Like men who leave us wet and wanting on our own door-steps. Perdie tapped her fingernails against the ceramic of her mug.

"Nope, I'm calling it. I, Lucille Knox, of sound heart and mind, declare *this*—" she gestured up and down her body with a swirling motion "—a Hampton-free zone for the rest of my days on this green planet. Perdie, you need to hold me to it. I'm done chasing his dopamine-hoarding ass around."

"That's not how dopamine works, but yes, I fully support you."

Lucille slapped her hands on the table and rose, her canary-yellow robe bright against the wood. "I wasn't going to shower this morning I was feeling so down, but fuck it, this calls for a shower."

"A moving-on baptism." Perdie lifted her mug in a toast.

Lucille sauntered up the stairs. "Good luck today. You look hot."

Perdie settled into the seat Lucille had vacated, taking a moment to let a touch of excitement flow through her limbs. They would tell her they were making her a partner today. That meant prestige. Respect. Money. Validation that she was good enough. Perdie Stone from Greeneville, South Carolina, a big-shot lawyer. And who wouldn't want those things?

A faint buzzing caught Perdie's attention from Lucille's lit phone, a new message alert on the screen.

Hampton Calhoun: BABE. Come over and watch The Holy Grail tonight? I'm trying out a new grapefruit high gravity.

Perdie rolled her eyes. Of course Hampton would come back to Lucille as if nothing had happened. They'd played this game before. And things were looking on the up-and-up for Perdie and Lucille, so this timing couldn't be worse.

Lucille joked about messing up her flower orders at her shop, but Perdie organized all the paperwork for Lucille's proprietorship. That little flower shop tucked away in a wealthy corner of a Charleston suburb was doing gangbusters. Lucille had quickly gained a reputation as the best florist in the Lowcountry. No small feat when the city was a popular wedding destination.

Perdie was proud of her, and Lucille didn't need this lowlife slowing her down. She deserved better. She'd asked Perdie to hold her to it, after all. And sometimes…

Before she could stop herself, Perdie picked up Lucille's phone, unlocked the screen—*six, nine, six, nine*—and deleted the message before promptly returning it.

Another message from Hampton popped up.

Raw dog tonight?

Ew. Perdie almost retched. "Go raw dog a fucking Pringles can, you dumpster fire." She deleted the message, then paused, her finger hovering over Hampton's contact info. She tapped a few times until she found the blue rectangle *Block Caller*. She set the phone down and shut off the screen.

Her lips pursed together in a smile. It was in everyone's best interest, really.

Frank Stetsel was still on the phone when she arrived at his fifth-floor corner office. His white hair was side-parted with a swoop and his free hand was clutching the lapel of his navy blazer, scrunching against his black-and-white checked pocket square. At the sight of her, he waved to the leather wingchair in front of his desk.

Seated, she regretted not wearing shapewear, as the material of her fitted dress was folding at her waist and riding up on her thighs. She tried her best to shimmy her skirt down without drawing attention, but she caught Frank's eyes wandering to her lap. The apparent distraction of her body, however, wasn't enough to make him hang up the damned phone.

She cleared her throat to get his attention, and his eyes finally flicked up to her face.

"Okay, I'll be home soon. Tell the kids that I won't be there for the soccer game on Saturday… Gotta go… Mmm-hmm. Okay…"

She leaned forward in anticipation. But he leaned back in his chair again.

"I have golf scheduled with a new client… Yes, it has to be me. I'll make the next game… It won't be like last time… It's my job to entertain clients. Look, I gotta go. June, I'm hanging up now. June…bye, June." Finally he pulled the phone from his face, tapping the red button with his thumb. "Wives." He rolled his eyes. "A burden, but I promise you, not worth the alimony."

She forced a smile. "Ah…ha-ha."

When he spun around on his chair to grab a pen, she quickly yanked the hem of her skirt down to her knees.

He spun back, his hands templed together on his desk. "So, Perdie, Perdie, Perdie. Per-di-ta." He tapped his fingers on the surface. "You've done some great work this past year. I feel like a proud father."

She clenched her hands together. "Thank you. I'm proud too."

"I mean, wow, this last settlement." He gave her the A-OK sign, making a clicking sound with his mouth. "A real feather in your cap."

She offered him a tight smile. "Mmm-hmm."

He nodded. "That's why I wanted to be the one to give you the news. Hear it from me as the managing partner of the securities group." He held up his index finger. "I believe that Joy and Schulz should be a place of great opportunity for all of our associates..."

She nodded along with his speech, adrenaline bubbling in her system. *Blah, blah, blah, say it already, Perdita Stone, we're making you partner. Finally, after all these years.*

There was a quiet knock on the door.

Frank stopped talking, his eyes lighting up. "Ah, right on time. Speaking of opportunity, there's the man of the hour." He gestured. "Perdie, you know Carter Leplan."

Perdie froze in her chair. "Carter Leplan?" she asked, craning her head to look towards the doorway.

Frank waved him in. "Well, time to be out with the good news. Carter has agreed to come on as a partner at Joy and Schulz. Signed his offer over the weekend. Took some convincing, but we won him in the end."

Perdie's eyes went wide. She couldn't believe the way Carter strode into the office as if it were the most normal thing in the world. She closed her jaw before it could drop, her teeth clacking together. "That's...that's great. Great for the firm." Her words stumbled.

And her gaze climbed up his body despite herself: leather Prada loafers, fitted gray pants, and a thin black cashmere sweater stretched over that perfectly sculpted chest.

Dammit, Carter Leplan.

"Frank." Carter inclined his head, "Ms. Stone." He sat in the chair next to her, long legs spread wide, one arm relaxed over the top of the chair.

Frank looked pleased with himself. "He even agreed to join the securities group." *Her* practice group.

Perdie's stomach flipped. "I don't mean to be glib, Frank, but how exactly is that good news—" she glanced at Carter "—for me specifically?"

Frank tilted his head and huffed. "The Fletcher Group has agreed to sign with Joy and Schulz because of Carter. That's a heavy hitter of a client, Perdie, and a step in the way of diversification. I thought this would be a chance for you to learn from the best, hone your skill. You told me last month that you were ready for new opportunities. You said you'd do whatever it takes, or did I misunderstand your commitment to this firm?" He leveled his gaze on her.

Carter cleared his throat. "I know from personal experience, I have plenty to learn from Ms. Stone, as well." He pressed his lips together, catching her eye. "She was more than a worthy opponent a few weeks ago. A force to be reckoned with."

Perdie failed to smile.

"Yes, our Perdie has been a great help to us," Frank said. "A feisty one."

Perdie tucked her hair behind her ear and forced the words from her lips. "You're right, Frank. I look forward to this…new…*opportunity*."

Frank rubbed his palms together. "That's the kind of team spirit I like to see out of you. We'll announce

Carter's hire tomorrow at the attorneys' meeting, so try not to let the cat out of the bag before then. I wanted to let you in on some insider information." He winked at her. "But you know how the girls love to gossip around here."

Perdie braced her hands against the armrests of her chair. "Thanks for prioritizing me in regards to such important news. My lips are sealed. If you don't mind..."

"Oh yes, please." Frank waved his hand towards the door. "Free to go. Enjoy your evening. Great news, right?"

"Great news." She grimaced as she walked to the door, the sharp points of her heels digging into flat carpet.

Behind her she could hear Frank's voice. "So, I'll be seeing you on the golf course? Better bring your A-game, I've been taking lessons on my swing..."

The passing hallway became a blur as her eyes threatened to spill, but she sniffed away the burn. Perdie Stone did not fucking cry at work. And Perdie Stone would not be defeated by that traitorous, pompous, conceited, privileged-ass motherfu—

The soft thud of footsteps followed behind her, "Perdie, stop." Carter's voice was quiet. "Perdie."

She spun on her heel, "You have got some fucking nerve."

He halted in the hallway, shoving his hands in his pocket. "I know how it looks. I get it. Can we go somewhere to talk?"

But Perdie was having none of it. "This, *this* is what you couldn't tell me?" she whisper-yelled. "No wonder you didn't want to come inside the other day. You stole my chance. You knew I'd be fucking my own fucking boss."

Carter looked in disbelief. "Stole your chance? What?

Perdie, no. You don't understand. They weren't ever planning on *giving* you a chance."

Perdie's face dropped, hands clenched. "What?"

Carter glanced behind himself, making sure no one else was around before opening the door to an empty conference room at the end of the hall and motioning for her to enter.

She glared before stomping into the room, the *snick* of the door sounding behind her.

She jabbed her index finger towards his chest. "How could you possibly know that they weren't considering me?"

"Look, after our..." he stabbed his hands through his hair, tousling it "...night together, I couldn't get you out of my head. You're so talented and smart and funny. I felt like it was a real injustice that you weren't being taken seriously. Our conversation...it stuck with me. I know you told me not to, but I rang up my friend Ferris Joy. And he told me they *were* looking to fill a partnership position, but your name wasn't even on the short list. He said they wanted someone with established clients to bring with them; they were trying to poach a guy out in New York. I know the guy. He's a real piece of shit, sexual harassment lawsuits out the ass. I thought, wouldn't it be better if it were me instead of him? I would go to bat for you, Perdie. I could help you."

"Yes, how brave of you to volunteer as tribute. The lesser of two evils still means you're evil. You know how fucking paternalistic you sound right now?"

Carter shook his head. "I didn't volunteer. He asked me if I was interested. I had to make a choice."

Perdie fumed, her breath coming fast. "It's absolutely stalker behavior to join this firm because of me."

"They offered me double what I was making."

Her jaw dropped. "You've got to be shitting me. I'm still paying off my student loans." Sure, she could buy expensive things now and again, it was all part and parcel of the role she played as an attorney, having to look the part, but she still had a fat student loan bill due at the start of every month. Joy and Schulz associate bonuses and salaries were good, but they weren't partner good.

He looked at his feet, rubbing the nape of his neck. "It's not entirely that either. I've been following the safe path my whole life. Yale, Harvard, then a respectable defense firm in a big city. A part of me wanted to do something impulsive. Shake things up. Move across the country. Learn something new. They gave me an offer I couldn't refuse. Would you turn down double the money?"

She squeezed her eyes shut before answering. "It doesn't help when you keep saying that."

Chapter Eight

Carter scrubbed his big hand down his face, the motion catching Perdie's eye. He looked frustrated and kind of sad. Still she had to clamp down a shivering memory of that very hand tugging the vee of her T-shirt on her front doorstep. *Careful, P.*

"I can make this situation better. For you. Help you get what you want."

Only a few feet of space separated them. He was propped against a corner of the long conference table, one hip on the edge, arms crossed against his chest, magnifying the appearance of his biceps. His lips were wrought in a hard line. Serious and concerned.

He'd been salivatingly hot in a T-shirt and jeans. But in front of her in a soft sweater and pair of slacks...he made business casual look like one of the Seven Deadlies. This man was so irritatingly handsome. Agh, she could murder him.

"You can't make this situation better. You're the one who made it bad in the first place. Why do you even care what I think? You're my boss now. Everything has changed, for the both of us. Not that there ever was an... an us."

Carter shook his head. "You're looking at this all

wrong. You're seeing an obstacle where there's really an opportunity. I can have your back, Perdie. Give me a chance."

"You begged for a chance a few days ago as well. Look where that's gotten me. I think I'm about out of chances for you, Carter. Sorry, Mr. Leplan, my lord, your royal highness, my most esteemed legal partner."

"Okay, well, now you're exaggerating. You shouldn't let the perfect stand in the way of the good. I know you didn't get what you wanted, but having me on your side is a great step in the right direction. I can be very influential, you know."

Perdie scrunched her face. "Ugh, stop. Forget it. Forget about being some kind of white knight. Forget it all. Forget about the hooking up. And—and…forget about ever making out with me on my doorstep ever again."

Carter paused, brow furrowed, but he straightened up to a full standing position. "Okay, I didn't think that was going to be a—"

"Or seeing my bras…you can't see them. Anymore." She smirked.

A questioning look crossed his face, his head tilting. She wanted to stop but her words kept tumbling out like ice cubes from a freezer.

"*Or* using my vibrator like a weapon against me. Like some kind of vibrator magician, like…*like a vibrician*. You'll definitely never, ever, *ever* get to do that again."

He squinted his eyes like he was trying to make out a complicated math equation. "Perdie, are you—?"

"And no more orgasms with you." She brought her hands down in a swiping motion. "Absolutely none. Never again. Not even a handful. Not even so much as one little gasp."

Her breathing was coming fast, her eyes on him.

He didn't move a muscle.

"That—" She held up a finger to punctuate. "*That*, my friend, is finished. The final straw. Forever." She was breathing heavy now, heat flushing her chest.

When he spoke, his voice was soft. "How about going down on you in a conference room?"

She narrowed her eyes at him. "What?" she hissed.

His gaze pierced her, his voice even softer now. "How about me getting on my knees right here in this conference room and licking your clit all over until you scream my name. How about that? Is that allowed?"

"How *dare* you. How dare you say something to me like that after what you've done."

"Perdie." Her name came out of his mouth like a warning.

She squeezed her eyes shut, clenching her fists at her side. "What?"

"Would you like me to do that to you?"

"Fuck. You." She whirled around and stomped towards the door, aware that his gaze was following. She paused with her hand on the knob, gulping in air. "Fuck you, Carter, and fuck the white fucking horse you fucking rode in on." She let out a huge breath.

And then, with a slow rotation of her wrist, she flipped the notch on the handle, locking them both inside.

Her heart pounded. *This is a huge mistake.* But she couldn't be in the same space as this man without growing hot between the legs. She couldn't resist him, and his BVLGARI ad face. *Pathetic.*

She turned on her heel, her eyes down. When she lifted her gaze to him, the darkness in his eyes sent a familiar shiver down her spine.

This was a bad idea. A *bad, bad* idea.

But…on the other hand…

Hadn't she worked so very hard? Hadn't she busted her ass for Frank and all the other top dogs at this firm? Hadn't she sacrificed every morsel of free time and social life for this place? Late nights and early mornings and salads eaten on messy desktops? For a job that didn't even really want her?

"Is that a yes?" Carter asked her under an unwavering gaze. "Yes or no. Tell me now."

"Goddammit, you know it's a yes." She strode towards him. "But let's get one thing straight: after this we're not friends. We're not even acquaintances. We're nothing. Colleagues and distant ones at that."

He grabbed her hips, blunt fingertips digging in soft flesh, and turned her around and pushed her up onto the surface of the conference table. Then he dropped to his knees in front of her. There were no internal windows for stragglers to peek in; they were tucked away in a locked, soundproofed, hidden corner. "I'll be anything you want if you pull your skirt up."

With frantic hands Perdie fisted the material and shimmied it up to the tops of her thighs, revealing her red silk panties.

"First things first." Carter hooked his fingers underneath the thin bands at either side of her hips and then yanked the underwear off, garnering a small yelp from her, the scrap of fabric tangled around his wrist. "Let me get a look at this pretty pussy. Here, lift your leg up over my shoulder, just like that…mmm, that's right." He pressed his hand to the outside of Perdie's thigh, the one now wrapped around his neck. Her other leg hung off the table, her knee fallen open, her heel dangling from the ground. She lay back, propped up on her elbows, a front row seat to Carter's performance.

He groaned, sliding his thumb up her exposed slit, as he brought the thumb to his mouth and licked the side of it from the base to the tip. "Jesus Christ, you're wet. I should've known. Bad Girl gets wet when she's angry, doesn't she? She needs me to lick it and make it all better. Isn't that right?"

She fisted his hair hard procuring another groan from him and pulled his mouth to her. "Why are you such a tease?" The words came out strained, she was already undulating her hips, letting her movements intermittently slide against his tongue. "Oh god..." The words came out of her like a whisper.

Then he nipped at the vulnerable, soft flesh at the inside of her thighs. "I'm a tease because it makes you so angry."

He leaned in closer and pressed an openmouthed kiss to the center of her, letting his tongue lightly flick over her clit.

"Yes, mmm-hmm..." she breathed, moving her hips.

He sucked lightly, pulling another moan from her, before dragging his tongue in a circle around the sensitive bud.

She threaded her fingers through his hair, grasping, holding him there so he couldn't tease her like he did in the hotel room. "Carter, please..."

"Keep your hand there. I like when you do that." His words were interrupted with dizzying, circling licks.

She complied, fisting and pulling at the thick hair on his head, holding him to her so he couldn't slip away.

As she held on to him, he closed his mouth over her clit and sucked hard, his mouth seamless against her body.

Then he lashed his tongue in the same, sensitive spot. This time he meant business and Perdie could feel that familiar well of piercing pleasure stabbing inside her. His licking became rhythmic, steady and fast, her hips moved in tandem.

"Do it harder." She would've begged him for it, pleaded; a jolt shot through her when he applied more pressure with his tongue. Her head lolled, and ridiculous sounds were coming from her again. She should be embarrassed, have some sense of decency. But she didn't. Couldn't find the control within herself.

He squeezed the outside of her thigh, almost painfully. There would be a bruise there in the morning but the squeeze only served to heighten the hot, wet experience of his tongue.

"God, I'm so close…" Her leg was vibrating now, the sound of her heel clacking to the floor happened in a distant haze in a distant world. His tongue was relentless, zeroing in on her clit like a sniper, then circling and circling. He wasn't teasing this time, he was *strategically targeting*. A bubble of a giggle welled up in Perdie's chest at the technical thought, but it died in her throat when she heard the zipper of his pants.

She lifted up her head, his head still moving between her thighs, the area drenched and soaking. His hand was also moving beneath him now. Another wave welled up inside her at the sight of him masturbating in front of her, her orgasm threatening to spill over, when he lifted his head.

"No, don't—" she started to whine but stopped dead.

He fisted her underwear in his hand. With his eyelids heavy, he brought it up to his cheek, rubbing his face against it, then scraping it down his abdomen and lower to his exposed cock. She panted, her mouth opened as he stroked himself with her red silk panties.

The look in his eye could have knocked her dead.

His voice was hoarse when he spoke. "You call me a Pretty Boy, but deep down I'm nothing but a filthy fucking animal. And the things I want to do to you aren't even a step above carnal."

With their eyes locked, he rubbed his cock while using his free hand to stroke at the soft folds of her pussy, the callused, rough skin on his fingertips igniting her flesh, bringing her near a peak again. She let out a guttural yell when he pushed his index finger inside her.

"Hold on for me, baby. Hold on for just a few more minutes…this shouldn't take long."

He lowered his mouth to her, his finger still inside her. His other hand still working himself, the red silk of her panties wrapped around his hand, stroking off his big, hard cock. The sight of it was too much—forbidden, naughty, but deeply hot.

"I'm coming. Carter, I'm…" The orgasm shot up inside her, rocking into her hips first, then spreading to her fingers and toes. She rolled against him, mewling and moaning, as it passed through her, tumbling down her body like a landslide. Her bones went slack.

"Carter, oh, god…wait…" He was still working away at her and himself.

"Once more, okay? For me. So I remember it." His words came out heavy and labored as his hands and mouth moved faster on her, harder this time, wet, slapping noises filling the room, both his hands working steady rhythms against their bodies.

She shook her head, "Not gonna happen…there's no way I can… Oh *fuck*." The second orgasm came out of nowhere like a surprise crash symbol in the cacophony of her body. Her eyes fluttered shut, her jaw clenched, and her legs kicked against Carter's shoulder. At the same time, she could feel and hear his groan, muffled by her own body, but she knew Carter was coming, his strokes becoming erratic, messy, wild.

With one loud grunt, he fell forward on her, resting his head against her stomach. Both of them sweating and out of breath.

"I think I'm dead." She pushed him off her and pulled down her skirt. "I think you killed me. Death by orgasm." When she lowered herself from the table, she landed unevenly to the floor. "Where's my shoe?"

In lieu of her body, he leaned his head against the leg of the table, grappling on the ground until his hand discovered the stiletto. He passed it to her. "Cunnilingus casualty," he said. He sounded drunk.

She smoothed her hair and straightened her dress, panty-free now but no worse for the wear. It had already been closing time when they stepped into the conference room, so there would be few people on the fifth floor, most likely no one else at all. But still, it wouldn't do them any good getting caught. The weighted realization of her actions began to sink in.

He appeared boneless against the table, his mouth swollen, his hair ruffled, fly undone. She wanted to package him up and take him home.

Perdie knelt next to Carter and tucked a finger into his pocket, where a hint of her red panties stuck out. "Stealing these from me?"

Carter's head lolled to the side. He reached out a hand, letting his fingertips glide from the hair by her cheek then sweep down to the divot in the split collar of her dress.

He pulled her towards him with his finger hooked in her top and kissed her on the mouth.

"Damn right," he said, his mouth still mere centimeters from hers.

She leaned back, putting space in between them. "They were expensive."

"Send me a bill." There was a glint in his eyes. "Better yet, let me buy you new ones." He went to hook his index finger into her cleavage again to draw her in for another kiss, but this time she whacked his hand away.

"Don't remind me that you're rich." She got back up to her feet, dusting herself off. "I almost forgot for a minute. Made me forget everything."

He stood up too, buttoned his pants, and ran his hands through his hair.

Perdie shook her head at the sexed-up sight of him. Devastating. If anyone caught sight of them together, it'd be a dead giveaway. "Okay, I'll leave first. Stay here ten minutes before you go. Frank won't still be here, but if he is, he'll have his door closed with Steely Dan playing so loudly he won't know any better anyway."

Carter shook his head. "Wait, you're leaving me?"

"What do you mean? Jesus, for a smart guy, you sure are a bad listener."

He sat on the table, legs spread. "Look, I respect the fact that you're mad at me, and I deserve it, and I'm willing to leave it all up to you. But you're in denial if you're trying to tell me there's nothing between us. Because you know as well as I do that there is."

A staccato laugh erupted from her high in her chest. She waved a finger. "Oh no. No, you don't. You don't get to make me out to be the bad guy here. When we walked in this room together, I told you *exactly* what you could expect out of me, and that's what I've delivered. It doesn't matter if there's something between us. Because lines have been drawn. With a cement truck." She flipped the lock on the door and took a deep breath before she uttered the next words, watching a cartoon version of herself hammer a nail in her own coffin. "Why don't you find a nice, blonde Southern girl anyway? Someone a little more your style. Maybe someone named, oh, I don't know, *Aubrey*."

He scratched the side of his face, his nostrils flaring. "You're being cruel. You know that?"

Perdie shrugged and smiled a cold, hard smile. "See you at work tomorrow. Partner."

And she shut the door behind her.

Chapter Nine

Perdie whapped her vintage Louis Vuitton briefcase onto the kitchen table and kicked her heels off as she made her way to the fridge. She bent over in search of something sticky or salty or sweet or any combination of those things. Ravenous. *Ah yes, this glass container of salted caramel topping will do.* She shoved the spoon in her mouth, caramel sticking to the roof.

Footsteps neared from above, and Lucille's very off-tune rendition of Clairo's "Pretty Girl" echoed in the staircase.

Lucille halted at the bottom of the steps, Bananas trailing at her feet. She spied Perdie in the middle of the kitchen.

Perdie shrugged, spoon in mouth. "Wha?"

"You had *sex*," Lucille gasped, her voice loud. She yanked out her earbuds and scuttled over to Perdie, Bananas's nails clicking on the hardwood behind her. "Wait a minute, but with whom?" She tapped a finger to her chin and circled Perdie's body, eyeing her suspiciously. Perdie pulled the sticky spoon from her mouth, chewing on the caramel. "Did you have sex with Frank because he gave you a promotion? You know you're not supposed to do that, right? He doesn't pay you enough.

Jill worked as a dominatrix in college and she made way more money than you."

Perdie swallowed hard and let out a sigh. "I didn't get the promotion, Luce."

Lucille's mouth dropped. "*What?* But your thing with the settlement, and all those hours you bill, and what about how they promoted Bill Wagner last year and he'd never even argued a motion in front of a judge before."

Perdie frowned. "Wow, do I talk about work that much?"

Lucille nodded. "Yeah, and *that's* how I know how shitty this is." She opened her arms and stalked into Perdie, squishing the sticky jar between them, Perdie's body stiffening in the embrace. "I hate those legal fuckers. You want me to put poison ivy in their offices? I can send it in a mixed bouquet."

"I thought that settlement was going to see me to the next level but turns out it still wasn't enough. It never feels like anything I do is enough. They wanted someone who could bring in big business. How am I supposed to bring in big business if I'm not a partner?"

Lucille rested her head on Perdie's shoulder, rocking them back and forth together. "Remember I used to help you study during law school and it all seemed so impossible because you could barely keep your eyes opened? You figured out a way then. You'll figure out a way this time too."

"If by study you mean steal Adderall for me, then yes. But thanks." Perdie extracted herself from Lucille's embrace. "You've always supported me the best."

"I know." Lucille placed her hands on Perdie's shoulders. "I don't have any Adderall, but I have edibles. We could brainstorm a new plan?"

* * *

Perdie, Lucille, and a snoring Bananas sprawled on the overstuffed leather couch together in the open space of the living room. Large feathered throw pillows piled between them and the biggest bowl of cheese popcorn rested on Lucille's lap.

Lucille shoved a fistful of popcorn into her mouth, the errant kernels tumbling down her Solange nightshirt. "Okay, okay, okay. Here's what you should do." She chewed loudly and pointed a wobbly finger at Perdie. "Quit the firm, burn the building to the ground, walk away like Angela Bassett in *How Stella Got Her Groove Back*, and work at the flower shop with me. I'd give you a million promotions, and I'd only ogle you a little bit." She tilted her head. "You do have great tits though, so it's not like it would be my fault."

Perdie had changed into flannel pants and a tank top before she and Lucille each consumed a weed gummy. They'd considered splitting one until Lucille insisted that the only feminist choice was for each of them to take a full dose. "It's what Susan B. Anthony would've wanted," she'd said as they unwrapped jumbo gummy bears from individual plastic packages. "Although, contextually speaking, Susan B. Anthony was pretty problematic."

Perdie pulled at the topknot on her head, snuggling deeper under the faux-fur blanket with Bananas tucked into her armpit.

"I can't quit the law." Perdie stroked the soft, smushed folds of Bananas's face, marveling at how many silver furs had infiltrated the canvas of his once all-black muzzle.

"Why not?"

Perdie sighed. "Because I'm good at it." Bananas

inhaled a loud snore in agreement. "Plus a fuckton of student loan debt. I gotta keep you in Solange shirts somehow."

Lucille nodded. "When she's right, she's right. Next idea." She tapped the top of her head. "You *could* sleep with Frank in exchange for partnership. Fuck your way to the top."

Perdie huffed, warranting a glare from Bananas. "Gross. He's a total misogynist."

"Ah-ha. So, it wasn't Frank you had sex with. Are you going to tell me who it was? I know you did something with someone, Perdita Stone. I haven't been your best friend for twenty years for nothing." She coughed after shoving too much popcorn in her mouth.

A vision of Carter Leplan kneeling between her legs and stroking himself off with her red silk panties flashed before her eyes, making her stomach flip. She didn't want to cry right now, and she really didn't want to tell Lucille.

Lucille's snapping fingers appeared before her eyes. "*Hello, hello*, Ground Control to Major Tom."

Perdie shook her head, but before she could say anything a peal of maniacal giggles escaped her. Damn edibles. She started wheezing in between giggles before answering Lucille. The words came out in a jumble. "I let Carter Leplan go down on me on a table in a private conference room after finding out they hired him on as a partner instead of promoting me." She blinked up at Lucille.

Lucille gulped her popcorn, eyes wide. But then puffs of laughter escaped. "Hold the front fucking door, *what*?" She started laughing too, until the two of them were both giggling on a couch together.

When their laughter died down, Lucille caught her breath. "How? *How?*"

Perdie waved a hand. "Doesn't matter. But he's at Joy and Schulz now, virtually my boss, and *I* am fuuuuuuuuucked. In so, so many ways."

Lucille shoved her hand into her silky black hair. "That's so much worse than I thought."

"Thanks."

"Hey. Light bulb." Lucille pointed her index finger in the air. "Brilliant idea by Lucille, you're welcome. Call up that Noah guy? He seemed to like you. Wasn't that the plan to get over Carter anyway?"

"Wasn't exactly sparks between the two of us. *But* he could have a potential case for Joy and Schulz."

"Holy shit, you didn't tell me that. What are you waiting for?"

"He has my card. He hasn't reached out. Don't want to be pushy about it." Perdie shifted under her blanket. "These kinds of things require finesse. Professionalism." Forget the fact that she'd passed out drunk on his couch.

"Are you kidding? Time is of the essence. You've gotta take the bull by the horns. Take the snake by the rattle. The balls by the dick—wait, no…maybe not that last one. Anyway, what've you got to lose? You're already pretty much rock bottom."

Perdie chuckled. "You have such a delicate way with words."

Lucille peered beneath long, dark lashes. "Besides, I thought he was kinda sexy."

"Oh really?" Perdie raised an eyebrow. She thought about it, reaching for her phone. "Okay, Noah it is then."

To her surprise, Noah texted in less than a minute, or at least what felt like less than a minute to Perdie. She sent her best argument via text why he should come see them to talk about his potential patent lawsuit when she received another text from him.

Noah: Is Lucille there?

Perdie clapped her hand over her mouth. She glanced up at her friend, trying to sound nonchalant. "You haven't heard from Hampton recently, have you?"

Lucille laughed a little too hard. "Nah. Not a peep. I'm an emancipated lady. Good riddance."

Perdie held up her phone camera. "Smile for Noah, Luce."

Lucille flipped the bird to the camera, yelling, "I don't smile for no man." Then she fell back, laughing at her own joke. "Ah, I'm really high."

Perdie sent the picture with their address.

Perdie: She's here.

Typing bubbles appeared. See you in twenty.

Perdie woke up late to the frantic buzzing of her alarm clock, her heart pounding, and hair in a frazzled topknot, but it didn't matter because she had a plan. Perdita Stone was a new woman, reborn, and with her eyes opened.

She reviewed the notes she'd taken on her laptop from the night before from her meeting with Noah. To Noah's disappointment (and Perdie's too), Lucille had shuffled off to bed as soon as Noah arrived, announcing she was too high for public consumption. Whatever that meant.

Luckily, Noah had still been nice enough to talk business with Perdie anyway, laying out all the specific, science-y details of his patent case. She could piece together the legal end. They would probably have to hire an expert witness or two to solidify their case, but Perdie had a good hunch about things. Real good.

No time for a red dress and matching bra and underwear today, Perdie yanked on a pair of black cigarette pants with a white button-down and silver smoking shoes. She left her hair in the topknot, and threw on her glasses.

She refused to let the presence of Carter Leplan influence how she dressed. She absolutely did not care what he thought of her one bit.

She arrived at the attorneys' meeting right on time, rushing to find a seat in the enormous room. Joy and Schulz was one of the biggest plaintiff's firms in the country, and there were well over two hundred attorneys shoved into the downstairs event room of their office building. After the general attorneys' meeting they would break off into smaller practice group meetings. That's when Perdie planned to pitch her case to Frank.

The attorneys were in a titter today. She took a seat next to the two other women in her practice group, Jennifer and Sophia. They were both a few years younger than her.

They gave Perdie slight, distracted smiles and Jennifer whispered over her shoulder, "Perdita, did you see the new guy?"

A chill ran through her. "No, who is it?"

Sophia leaned her head closer to the conversation. "We don't know yet, but he's got to be an attorney."

Jennifer shook her head, clicking her teeth. "If I weren't a married woman, I tell you what…"

"That man makes Chris Hemsworth look like my seventy-year-old gastroenterologist," said Sophia.

"You're divorced, right, Perdita?" Jennifer asked.

Perdie tried not to read anything into the slight tinge of her voice. "Nope, never married." She pulled out her phone in distraction. "I'm sure I've told you that before."

Jennifer shrugged. "Oh, well, no offense or anything."

Sophia waved her hand, shushing them. "Look, there he is sitting next to Ferris Joy…he must be someone important."

"That's Carter Leplan," Perdie said.

Sophia narrowed her eyes, nodding faintly. "He's that hot defense attorney out in San Francisco. What's he's doing here? Perdie, didn't you have some kind of depo out there?"

Perdie swallowed hard. "Something like that."

Her phone lit up.

See something of interest?

The message came from a new contact. She sneaked a peek at Carter to find him deep in conversation with Ferris Joy. He was dressed positively Charlestonian in dark denim with a forest green V-neck sweater with a blazer. One side of his sleeve had been hiked up so she could barely make out the dark beginnings of the tattoos on his arm. Her knowledge of his hidden tattoos flagged as intimate and forbidden. She quickly averted her gaze, typing on her phone.

I don't think Interest is the word I'm looking for.

Sure enough he slipped his phone from the inner pocket of his blazer, not missing a beat in his conversation. Her phone lit up.

What word are you looking for?

She glared at him from a distance, but he was still talking. She typed.

Disdain.

This time when he removed his phone from his pocket, he frowned at the message. She waited to see if he would text again but nothing. A secret part of her was disappointed. For a moment, guilt trickled into her conscience. True, she was pissed at him, but there was no reason to be overtly hostile in the workplace.

That was unnecessarily rude. I'll endeavor to be more professional next time.

Typing bubbles appeared on the screen.

Speaking of professional. Your shirt's buttoned wrong.

Her gaze shot down to her chest. *Shit.*
Another text appeared.

It's okay, buttons are hard. Would it make you feel better if I buttoned mine wrong too?

Despite herself, she laughed.
Jennifer scrunched her nose. "What's so funny?"
Perdie scratched the back of her head and shrugged. "Twitter."
She sneaked a peek at Carter, but he was already look-

ing at her this time. Wasn't she supposed to be furious with him? Yes. Yes, she *was*.

And then…he winked.

Chapter Ten

Perdie held Carter's eye. Agh, fuck her weak will. In a slow deliberate motion she stood, making the smallest inclination with her head towards the door.

"I'll be right back," she murmured to Jennifer and Sophia.

"'Kay." Sophia's eyes were transfixed on her phone. "Charles Joy is always at least twenty minutes late anyway. Imagine if we acted that way…" She shook her head.

Perdie walked out of the room, adrenaline pumping in her veins. She didn't have a plan, but whatever naughty game she was about to partake in wouldn't stop her from pitching her case in her practice group meeting today.

So, what the hell, why not have her cake and eat it too?

In the hallway his footsteps clipped behind her. She ducked left into the bathroom, shouldering open the swinging door and then pushing her back against the closed stall, her heart thumping.

She waited.

A moment later, the door swung open and his tall, masculine form appeared. *Fuck*, he was hot.

"Hey," she whispered.

He strolled towards her with a casual gait, his hands in his pockets. He stopped when they were standing almost toe to toe, the tips of her silver smoking shoes against his brown suede chukka boots.

"Hey."

"We don't have much time," she said, suddenly paralyzed, frozen against the stall door.

"Don't need much time."

A cold thrill ran through her. The conference room after work had been one thing, but a bathroom before a meeting?

As always he kept her guessing what he would do next. She was so curious, she didn't even reach for him. She wanted to watch. What kind of show would he put on? She might become addicted to the suspense.

His eyes smoldered. With a deliberate motion, he shrugged his arms out of his blazer, tossed it onto the marble counter behind him, revealing the green cashmere sweater smoothed over the hard expanse of his chest. She fisted her hands to her sides to stop herself from grabbing at him like a feral animal.

With the blazer off, his eyes reflected green, except for that one little corner of blue. But she couldn't get lost in that blue spot, because his hand had reached behind his neck to pull his sweater off over his head. Now clad only in his fitted white button-down, he shook out his hair and tossed the sweater. Like the sexiest business casual matryoshka doll in the world.

When he reached for her, her heartbeat jumped into her throat.

But she didn't break contact, not for one second. Excitement pebbled her skin. He gently fingered one translucent button at the top of her shirt, where the off-kilter button-up job was most apparent, then with a flick of his thumb and index finger, the button popped open.

He followed the same path down several more buttons, revealing the peaks of her nude T-shirt bra, briefly letting his thumb slip beneath the inside edge of her bra cup to stroke the soft skin beneath. Her breath hitched; he was so close to her nipple, a push to the left and he'd be there, a rough thumb over that delicate, aching skin. He'd never even touched her nipples before. Suddenly it was all she could think about.

He pulled the shirt out from the waist of her pants and continued unbuttoning, until it was divided in two vertical planes down her body, the round swell of her cleavage visible in between. He ran the rough flat of his hand along the inside hem, tickling her skin with the sweep of his fingers, her chest heaving with breath.

"There are so many things I want to do to you right now." Voice deep but quiet, he gazed at the open space of her shirt. She blushed at the thought of a few things he might be talking about. "How am I supposed to work all day with this in my pants?" He brought her hand to his erection, the large protrusion, hot and pulsating against her palm. "All your fault."

Her hand moved, stroking through the soft material, his eyelids heavy. But he captured her hand again and brought it to the top button of his own shirt. Taking his cue, she flicked the button open, her fingertips gliding over the skin at the hollow of his neck. He rolled his head and groaned softly. She continued down the rest of the shirt.

Following his example, she pulled the shirttails from the waist of his pants, finishing with the buttons, parting the white material, letting her nails scratch at the dark line of hair that trailed from his belly button, the muscles there lean and bunched like cords, and on the sides carved in like a vee.

Perdie bit her lip at the delectable sight. This man must live at the gym. She didn't even know where to find one. Her eyes moved to his face and his gaze flickered up to meet hers as well.

"I'm going to stroke myself off to the thought of this tonight. Alone in my bed. How desperate is that?"

Before she could say anything, he fisted the bottom hem of either side of her shirt and gave each a harsh yank until the bottoms lined up evenly. She yelped in surprise. And like that, his large but nimble fingers were buttoning her in.

"Wh-what are you doing?"

"Attempting to torture you. Is it working?" He smiled. "And fixing your buttons."

"But I thought we were…"

"We will."

She tilted her head, his hands working fast to button her up all the way to the top. "But why unbutton yours?"

"So I could do this." He pulled one side of the hem on his shirt down so that it was uneven with the other. He then proceeded to button up his shirt as well, purposely leaving it off by a few.

Once finished, he retrieved his sweater and blazer, folding them over his forearm. She gawked at him, his perfectly cut abdomen now adorned ridiculously in a crooked shirt. "You can't go out like that, you're going to be introduced in front of the whole firm in like ten minutes."

He grinned. "Oh, but I can." He ran his hand over the scruff on his laser-cut jaw. "Don't you know the benefit of having a Hollywood face? I can get away with pretty much anything."

She glowered. "Rubbing it in, of course."

"I thought you'd love to see me a little humiliated."

"It's not that. I can't handle the secondhand embarrassment." She covered her eyes with her palms. "Don't go out there like that."

He leaned in close to the side of her face, so close she could smell that pepperminty fragrance, so close she shivered at the breath wisping the shell of her ear. "Watch me." He left, the bathroom door swinging shut behind him.

Perdie stood in front of the mirror, her buttons put to rights now. She shoved her shirttails into her pants forcefully, catching a glimpse of her face in the mirror. Her skin was glowing like a summertime lightning bug. *Dammit, Carter.*

"A not-so-friendly reminder that the annual winter holiday party is in two weeks." Charles Joy stood in front of the room in a charcoal Armani suit with a hot pink shirt, his thick salt-and-pepper hair gelled in a side part. His accent was drawling, a backwoods Southern boy done good for himself. "Don't roll your eyes. I expect all attorneys present and dressed with appropriate consideration to the formality and festivity of the event. I don't shell out for top-shelf liquor for y'all to be a bunch of sticks in the mud. And Rita doesn't work her dang butt off for y'all to show up in no damn blue jeans. But more importantly, it's your job to give good face to the staff. Keep morale high."

He cleared his throat, scrolling through the agenda.

Behind him, Raymond Schulz dozed on a chair, his balding head leaned to one side. He was a behind-the-scenes kind of guy while Joy handled all the face time with clients, attorneys, and staff, being the younger and more gregarious and wild of the two longtime named partners. Joy often had some of the more senior partners on his yacht for blowout parties where much cocaine was sniffed off many bare breasts. Perdie had never been to one, but rumors circulated.

"We have a new face in the crowd, so I'll get on with the introductions," Charles Joy continued. "We take great pride in being a firm of diversified legal pursuits, and we are more than pleased to announce our newest member, Carter Leplan. Carter brings the Fletcher Group with him, so when your bonuses come out with an extra zero next year, y'all can send your thank-you cards his way… Kidding, you know I sign the paychecks around here."

The crowd of attorneys in the room craned their heads. Knowing what was to happen, Perdie's blood pressure spiked. Inwardly she cringed, keeping her eyes straight ahead so they couldn't wander over to Carter.

Charles Joy waved Carter forward. "Carter, come on up here, boy. Give us a few words."

A smattering of applause punctured the room as Carter made his way to the front, confident as ever. Charles Joy went to shake his hand, giving his misbuttoned shirt a cursory double take with a furrowed brow, but he stepped back as Carter began to speak.

Carter stood with the ease of a motivational speaker. He opened his hands towards the crowd, giving full view of his shirt, his mouth upturned and relaxed. "Thank you so much. It really is a privilege to work with you all. I know from firsthand experience the level of talent at this firm. And I look forward to learning a great deal."

Then he straightened up, appearing solemn, his mouth in a straight line. "As I'm sure you can tell, I'm a very important person." He gestured to his mismatched shirt. The crowd tittered, the other attorneys clearly taken by his easy charm. "But uh…sorry, I was a little distracted this morning." He rubbed his hand on the back of his head, his eyes fluttering to Perdie and then back. Heat crept up her cheeks. "But I promise you that my brief-writing skills are better than my shirt-buttoning skills."

Perdie couldn't believe it when the attorneys laughed. They laughed.

He lifted his hand to tip off a wave. "Find me on the fifth floor. My door is always open. Oh, and I have a bar in there fully stocked with whiskey, so…" He winked, earning a laugh from Charles Joy and another laugh from the crowd. From somewhere, someone even whistled. Carter gave an incline of his head and another smile. "Thanks so much, everyone. I truly am humbled to be here. If you'll excuse me, I'm going to go fix my shirt now." Applause and laughter broke out as he made his way back to his seat.

Charles Joy returned to the helm. "Thank you, Carter. I'll be sure to check out that whiskey selection shortly. Onto our next order of business…"

Perdie's phone lit up.

How'd I do?

The other lawyers whispered and their eyes darted Carter's way when it hit her: none of them stood a fucking chance against Carter Leplan.

* * *

The day dragged with meetings until Perdie sat down at the conference table with the securities group. Her left leg bounced and she twirled a pen in her hand. Jennifer sat next to her, giving her the side-eye. Perdie stilled, tucking her hair behind her ear.

Frank Stetsel led the meeting, running down current cases and workloads for each attorney. Carter sat to his left, his brow furrowed, tapping studious notes on his tablet. Perdie struggled to keep from staring at him. Behind him, the long windows of the office overlooked the harbor and off in the distance the Ravenel Bridge stretched across the horizon. A picture too perfect.

"Let's talk new business," Frank said, and Perdie's ears perked. "We are lucky enough to have Carter on our team, so we'll get some of you assigned to the Fletcher Group shortly. Any other leads worth sharing?"

Perdie cleared her throat. Now was her chance. "I've got something, Frank."

Frank's eyebrows went up, and he nodded. "All right, Perdita. Let's hear it."

She smiled. "In the spirit of bringing new business to the firm, I have a potential patent case with the medical university against the Zelen Corp in regards to a children's seizure drug—"

"Zelen Corp the pharma company?" Frank interrupted.

Perdie nodded. "That's right. It's a small company so it's not the usual monster conglomeration. The plaintiff is someone I know personally. He's sharp as a tack, would do well under scrutiny or even in front of a jury…"

But her voice trailed off as Frank crossed his arms, shaking his head. "Nope, nope. I'm telling you we won't get anywhere with a patent case. And against big pharma?

I don't see how we could possibly invest the time right now. But I like that fighting spirit, Perdie." He turned to face Bill Wagner, who had his pen in the air. "Bill, whatcha got?"

Before she could even process what had happened, Bill was already leaning forward, his fingers steepled at the table. "Two words for you Frank: Whistle. Blower."

Frank nodded. "You have my attention, Bill. I've been wanting to get a good whistleblower case under our belts over here. For the publicity. Makes us look good. Like we're in it for the cause."

"That's one word." Her voice cut through the room. Everyone turned to her.

"Excuse me?" Frank raised an eyebrow.

"Whistleblower is one word. Or at the very best, it's hyphenated. Hard to write a complaint if you can't spell it." A fire burned inside her belly at Frank's easy dismissal, and the humiliation was even worse with Carter right there. Still, she kept on. "How can you possibly think a whistleblower case is a safer bet than a patent case when you don't know anything about either? That's, pardon the pun, patently poor judgment. This case is at the very least worth following."

Frank let out a big sigh, rolling his eyes. "Look here, I've been around the block, and I know what I'm talking about. At the end of the day, we have limited resources and labor force. Now, if you want to challenge my judgment—"

"I'll help on a patent case," Carter interrupted. All eyes turned on him. He smiled and shrugged. "I've been on the other side of it many times so I'm able to test its temerity. I think, if nothing else, we can do some investigation. I'm happy to put in the hours and earn my place here."

"Me too." At Jennifer's voice, Perdie almost jumped out of her chair. Jennifer nervously glanced at Carter. "I'll help too. I've got extra time."

Frank gawked at them for a moment but then waved his hand dismissively. "Fine, fine, if you want to invest your time. Go for it. Don't let it interfere with your billing hours for the Fletcher Group." He turned. "Now, Bill, what's your timeline on your whistleblower...do you think we need to get the news involved?"

Perdie leaned back in her seat, eyes down as she pretended to write notes on a pad of paper.

It wasn't how she'd wanted her pitch to go down, it wasn't fair, and it certainly wasn't how she'd pictured bringing in her first client. But it was a start.

Chapter Eleven

Perdie spun a pen in her hand, feet propped up on her desk. She'd finished her work for the day. Long ago, the sun had set over the harbor outside the window.

After the meetings, time had flown. She was busy devising a plan to best streamline her prospective case with Noah while also keeping her billables high for her new assignment with the Fletcher Group. *Carter's big client. Ugh.*

The fact that she couldn't get interest in her case until she was supported by a man in the room was not lost on her. But that wouldn't stop her from using opportunities when they arose. And that was the best she could tell herself for the moment.

She rolled her head on her neck and switched off her computer screen. Still she grabbed her tablet to check her email one last time before closing shop. It wasn't out of the ordinary for her to continue answering emails late in the evening on the couch at home, Lucille clanging pots and pans in the background yelling at her to come eat dinner.

This firm wouldn't be happy until they worked her to death.

Bring the Joy to Joy and Schulz
Annual Winter Holiday Party.

She clicked the evite, revealing a twinkling white animated card:

December 23 7pm
Enjoy drinks and heavy hors d'oeuvres
at the Atlantic Theater
Dress to Impress in Formal Attire,
Old Hollywood Glam

Great. A theme.

Perdie tapped off the screen, removed her glasses, and rubbed her eyes. Attorneys and staff were allowed plus-ones to the winter holiday party. Perdie was in the habit of bringing Lucille, sparking the rumor for years that the friends were lovers, much to Lucille's delight.

But Lucille refused to attend anymore. Two years ago a senior partner in a different practice group had slapped her ass at a nearby bar. Perdie felt horrible about it, but they had little recourse. Needless to say, she wasn't exactly excited about this year's party.

Her ears perked at a soft knock on her door.

"Slumming it on the third floor, I see?" she asked Carter without moving. His image reflected in her tablet.

"Are you some kind of witch with a magic third eye?" he asked, stepping past the threshold.

"Think you know the answer to that." She dropped her tablet before spinning her chair to the front of her L-shaped desk. And then she had to bite down hard against her cheek at the sight of Carter in her doorway. Would this effect ever wear off? Could she maybe not be in awe of his face and body and masculine presence for five fucking minutes? It was proving a major distraction. "Come on in."

He strolled inside, closing the door behind him. *Real subtle.* A five o'clock shadow darkened the line of his jaw, and he was only in his button-down again, the top buttons undone and the sleeves rolled up on his forearms. She could barely glimpse the precipice of ink crawling up his left arm.

When she involuntarily licked her lips, he smirked, scraping the chair in front of her desk and taking a seat.

He gestured at the large whiteboard hanging on the wall behind her, where she had mapped a communications plan for the patent case. "That appears very thorough. And colorful." His mouth lifted in a half smile.

She shrugged. "It's the only way my brain can organize information. I used to draw on the walls a lot as a kid. My mother said I lost her every deposit on every apartment we ever lived in, but at least I learned to write before kindergarten."

Carter chuckled. "I'd guess you were a gifted child."

"Gifted in talking too much in class. Gifted in teaching the other kids how to swear."

"My mother would, on occasion, slip in my finger paintings at her gallery showings."

Perdie bit back a smile. "Did anyone buy them?"

He nodded. "Let's just say a Carter Leplan original is prominently featured in the living room of a very snobby Silicon Valley art collector."

Perdie laughed, the moment lingering. The warm residue of their early-morning lust glowed like embers.

His voice cut the spell. "You like donuts?"

Perdie raised her brow. "Does my third eye keep a watch on my office door?"

"I'll take that as a yes. There's a twenty-four-hour donut place near my rental."

She tilted her head. "Where are you renting?"

His hands casually threaded through his hair as he talked. She had to blink to keep from being mesmerized. "Upper peninsula. Temporary. My real estate agent's working overtime though. The prices out here are peanuts compared to San Francisco. Feel like a kid in the candy store except all the candy is four-thousand-square-foot colonials with a marsh view."

She snorted. "So relatable. So humble."

He relaxed his arm over the backrest of the chair, his thighs outstretched. He smiled unabashedly. "I know."

As if that smile weren't enough, her eyes trailed to the wide, empty wedge of space between his legs. She shook her head snapping back her focus but it was too late. He'd caught her.

"We don't have to get donuts, you know. We could finish other more pressing business." His voice was soft.

She met his gaze, calm but intense.

From her periphery, a warning flash of light from her tablet reminded her of the hours and hours of work ahead for the two of them. Together. As a team. A work team.

Already the sexual chemistry sparked unbearably, and it was only escalating with their interactions. Interactions like these. She couldn't let it spiral out of control. Hell, she'd been ready to fuck him in a bathroom that very morning. Unwise when so much was on the line. What had she been thinking?

She was dick-drunk.

She scratched at the wispy hair tickling her forehead.

He drove her to distraction. She'd given in too many times already. She would put an end to it.

A small smile played upon her lips as she stood, winding around her desk towards him. She leaned over, close to his ear. "What kind of business could you possibly be referring to?"

Her hand wandered to a button on his shirt, index finger dangling on its edge. She smirked inwardly at the sight of his right hand clenching the armrest of the chair.

"Seems that you're already demonstrably aware." His voice was strained.

She lifted her knee, resting it between the gap of his legs, bringing her other hand to his shirt button. From the corner of her eye, his Adam's apple worked in his throat.

Then with slow attention to each one, she buttoned him up all the way to the juncture at the top of his neck, patting the spot there.

"Turnabout is fair play." She let her fingertips glide over the arch of his shoulder as she turned to leave. "See you in the morning."

But he caught her by the wrist, drawing her near so she bent down to him, face-to-face, her palm pressed against his chest. His pulse steadily thudded beneath the material.

Her own chest clenched.

"This isn't a game you're going to win." His voice sent goose bumps up her arms.

She wanted to kiss him. Of course she wanted to kiss him. Who wouldn't want to kiss this man? A nun would be hard-pressed to turn him down. She wanted to give in to every reckless impulse. But she pulled her hand from his grip and smoothed the wrinkles at the front of her shirt.

"Watch me." She snatched the handle of her briefcase off her desk and walked out the door.

Perdie didn't sleep well the next several days, but work managed to overtake her every waking second anyway. She played a game with herself: for each day she managed to avoid a sexually arousing encounter with Carter, she marked a little yellow star on her whiteboard.

Because today made three in a row, Lucille gave her a gift, a boat-shaped white vase teeming with lilac, dogwood, and tulips, to reward Perdie for being "so pure and chaste like a well-behaved Regency period lady."

Perdie placed the fancy flowers on her desk with a self-satisfied smile, but after a few hours the massive arrangement began to overwhelm her. Her desk was being swallowed up by an elfin forest.

"Sorry, Luce. But this guy needs a new home." She lugged the arrangement to Jennifer's office next door. Due to Perdie's patent case, she and Jennifer had also been spending quite a lot of time together. "Knock, knock." Perdie leaned against the doorframe, inching her way in.

When Jennifer looked up, the perfect S-shape of her bright blond ponytail bobbed. And the enormous diamond ring on her left hand flashed in the midday light. Jennifer had married rich apparently. "What in god's good name is that?"

"A gift, but I don't have room for it in my office. I thought maybe you might like it right here?" Perdie set the flowers on an empty table near Jennifer's window. Then she stepped back to admire Lucille's good work.

"Oh, from Carter?" Jennifer pursed her lips but said the words casually, patting the curl of her ponytail.

Perdie froze in place. "From my friend Lucille."

Jennifer nodded. "That's right, your friend with the flower shop. What's that place called again? Pricks? Edgy for a florist. Do you think she could help with a baby shower I'm planning?"

Perdie's eyes narrowed. "What did you mean *from Carter*?"

Jennifer paused, her hands hovering near her keyboard. "Oh, come on, Perdita. He hasn't even been here a month but it's so obvious the way he's been trailing you around. Do you think he really needs to be on the third floor twenty times a day?"

A cold wave of anxiety flooded Perdie. "Of course he's around a lot. We're working two different cases together." She folded her arms. "Our relationship is purely professional." Or at least it definitely would be now...

Jennifer shrugged. "Well, my advice to you? Be careful. People talk."

When Perdie returned to her own desk, a large rectangular box had replaced the flowers. She lifted the edge of the lid to reveal a dozen gourmet donuts.

You gotta be fucking kidding me. The timing couldn't be worse. Had Carter slipped in and left her fucking donuts right after Jennifer warned her people were getting suspicious?

It wasn't good.

She closed the door and sat down and picked up her desk phone to heighten her feeling of professionalism. She dialed Carter's extension.

"Carter Leplan."

Despite the closed door, she cupped the receiver, her words hushed. "What the fuck are you doing?"

He responded in a similarly hushed tone. "Writing a brief. What are *you* doing?"

She straightened up in her chair. "Um, hello, the donuts?"

"I thought a dozen would be enough for one woman, but Jesus, I guess I should've gone with twenty-four. Did you try the vanilla glaze? Highly recommend. They use real vanilla bean."

She scoffed. "Carter. Are you kidding me? You can't leave me gifts. People are starting to talk about us. You know, *in the office*." She awaited his shocked response.

Carter chuckled. "Maybe people wouldn't talk about us *in the office* if you'd let me take you somewhere else. Like, say, outside of this building?"

She leaned back in her chair, frowning. "I don't understand what you want from me."

"I like you," he said plainly.

Her arms shot up in the air. "Ugh, you're the most confusing person I've ever met."

"Nobody at Joy and Schulz is going to care if we date. There's more important stuff going on. We are two consenting adults. We can sign a contract with HR."

"Correction. Nobody will care what *you* are doing at Joy and Schulz. You're a partner, AKA a person in a position of power over me—"

"Thus a contract."

"You think a contract fixes this?"

He laughed. "You don't think a contract fixes things? Wait until I tell you about this fun job called being a lawyer..."

"That's not how shit works for me. I've explained this to you before. I'm judged by a double standard. Besides, I thought you wanted to help not hurt my chances at making partner."

At that, Carter sighed. "Okay, fine. You're right. What do you want me to do?"

Perdie had been prepared for another round of jokes but found herself deflated at Carter's quick agreement. But that's what she wanted, wasn't it?

There was a moment of silence while she drummed her knuckles on the smooth desk surface. Then she pushed out a big breath. "Act like there's nothing. Like I said before. Colleagues. Okay?"

His voice was resigned. "Colleagues it is. But, Perdie?" He paused. "If you change your mind, I'm not going to be around forever, you know?"

A tiny twinge poked in her chest, but she ignored it. "Yeah, I know. Nobody is." Then she gently placed the phone into its receiver.

She let her head fall back over her chair and groaned in frustration. *Fuck.* Why was it when she got what she wanted it still wasn't what she wanted?

With a huff, she flipped opened the box of donuts, grabbed a vanilla glaze, and shoved a huge bite into her mouth. Instantly, she moaned. Who knew vanilla glaze could be so damned good?

Carter.

Annoying. How right he was. How easily he had agreed to drop things with her. She bit into the yeasty donut again, chewing with zeal until she stopped herself and tossed the remaining half in the box.

These would have to go out into the kitchen. But then she stood and faced the whiteboard behind her desk. With small upward brushes, she erased the three yellow stars.

Chapter Twelve

Perdie awokc in her bed, mouth dry, and a dull headache nudging her left eye. She pushed up on her elbows, grappling around on the nightstand for the two aspirin she'd left there the night before. Her hand bumped the glass containing last night's wine.

She brought it to her nose and gave it a whiff. *Malbec, still good.* She popped the two pills, gulped down half the glass, and wiped her mouth with her hand. She needed all the courage she could drink before she lit up her phone screen to check her notifications.

The last few days might've had her in a spiral. That's what Lucille called it, at least. They'd stayed up late Friday night recapping each other's lives.

Perdie grabbed her phone and squinted at it. Zero messages.

Actually, that wasn't accurate. There were twenty-seven work-related messages. Zero from Carter.

He'd behaved irritatingly professional with her the whole week after their phone conversation. She'd requested he treat her like nothing but a colleague, and well, by fuck he had been doing exactly as she requested.

And it was driving her out of her goddamn mind.

She clicked off her screen and rolled over in her bed, a wave of dizziness overtaking her vision.

Okay, well, maybe hair of the dog hadn't been the wisest choice.

There was a quiet knock, and Lucille peeked her head through the crack of the doorway, her topknot poking into Perdie's room before the rest of her. "Hello, my beautiful baby birdie. How are we doing this morning?"

Perdie's body was a sweaty and tangled lump in her bed-sheets, encased in nothing but an oversized T-shirt with the emblazoned movie title *Earth Girls Are Easy*. She stretched her arms out above her. "*Aaaaaghhhhhhhhh.* It's been seven hours and four days since I told Carter to go away."

Lucille tiptoed inside. "Okay, Sinead, I think it's time to get out of bed. And if you're going to drink wine at ten in the morning, at least let me know so I can join you, yes? Now, why don't you say we make this thing official and go to brunch?"

Perdie groaned. "I can't, I have all this work to do, and I have to get in touch with Noah about our discovery process."

"Invite him along. He likes hanging out with us. Isn't that basically why he agreed to be your client in the first place?"

Lucille's words didn't betray any extra emotion, but Perdie hadn't forgotten the way she'd called Noah *sexy* a few weeks ago. And she'd been thriving without Hampton around.

Perdie scratched her head. "Yeah, I suppose I can."

"What's *really* wrong with you? Can it really be all about this Carter guy? I've never seen you like this over anyone."

At Perdie's silence, Lucille's eyes went wide. "*Wow,*

talk about role reversal. For once you're the one hung up on some loser and not me."

Perdie rubbed her face. "Yeah, except he's *not* a loser. He's…" She gulped. Then whispered, "He's nice."

Lucille cupped her ear and leaned forward. "Sorry, didn't catch that?"

Perdie rolled her eyes. "He's *nice*. And not like a nice guy who's actually a creep. A nice guy who's actually… good."

Lucille laughed. "Plot twist. A nice guy. Who could've seen that coming? Well, why don't you text him then? Why even put on this facade. Maybe he's right. You're two consenting adults…"

"No." Perdie shook her head. "I have to show *some* level of restraint. You should've seen the judgment in Jennifer's eyes."

Lucille crossed her arms. "Okay, but she always looks like that. And since when you do you give a fuck? She hired me for a baby shower so she can't be all bad."

Perdie could feel her insides simmering to a roil, so she swung her legs over the side of the bed. "I need to hold strong."

Lucille stepped forward and planted her hands on Perdie's shoulders. "I mean this from the bottom of my heart. Text the guy already."

Then she spun around to leave, turning back with a bright smile that showed off her dimples. "Brunch at eleven with Noah. Should I wear my new red sweater? Never mind. It doesn't matter. I'll leave the details to you. Be back soon, so hurry up and get ready."

Perdie collapsed onto her bed, spread like a starfish. She clicked the button on her phone one more time.

Zero messages.

Okay. Enough of that. Up again, she wobbled to the bathroom.

After a steaming hot shower renewed her spirits, she wrapped herself in her silk robe with thick velvet cuffs and collar that made her feel like some kind of sexy old-timey movie star.

No more obsessing over Carter. Rebirth.

She held that conviction for about five more seconds until she checked her phone again.

One message from Carter.

Her heart raced, or maybe it was the residuals of a hangover.

50,000 digital documents received at 9:42am. FYI

Her heart sank. Oh. Completely professional. What else would it be? The fact that she was hoping for any-thing else was lunacy.

She froze in place as a wicked thought crossed her mind. She could take a sexy pic and *accidentally* send it in response. Hadn't Lucille used that ploy with Hampton to much success in the past? She could pretend it was meant for someone else. Some fictional man who was also drop-dead gorgeous and also into her very much but whom she hadn't basically told to fuck off and treat her like a sexless gnome.

After all, there was no better time to send a dirty pic than when one was flushed and supple right out of the shower.

She sat back on her bed, a splash of water from the ends of her hair hitting the glass. No, of course, it was too desperate. Too obvious.

Sighing, she picked up her phone to text Noah.

Got the digital docs right on time. Any interest in brunch around 11 for discussion? Mimosas on me. And by me, I mean Joy and Schulz ;)

She hit send, the curiously sharp feeling in her sternum for Carter beginning to dissipate along with her hangover. A little work and play could distract her now.

Her phone lit up.

Golf with Frank and the Fletcher Group people. Didn't know mimosas were on the list of permissible colleague activities. What other "colleague" activities am I missing out on?

Perdie clapped her hand over her mouth. She had sent the message to Carter instead of Noah. Talk about her subconscious working overtime. Freud would have a field day.

P: Sorry, meant to send this to our patent plaintiff.

C: Mimosas with your client?

Was he jealous?

P: Golf with YOUR client.

C: AND Bloody Marys.

The next message made her heart thud in her chest, a selfie of Carter, Bloody Mary in hand, the sprawling green-and-blue backdrop of the manicured golf course behind him.

The subsequent thought that popped into her head was a naughty one. One she shouldn't act out. One she should thoroughly resist. It could only serve to complicate a friendly and normal situation. The selfie Carter sent her was completely innocent. It could only stand to tangle her into a weird, sexually charged workplace-web of which she had purposely extricated herself.

Still, she reached for her half-full wineglass. She raised it to her lips, squeezing her cleavage together, peering up at her lens under dark lashes and snapped the selfie.

The Fates intervened that day because usually Perdie had to take at least seventeen selfies before she could pick a suitable one for public consumption. But this time, with the morning light streaming into her bedroom, the luxe velvet trim of her robe, the moisturized and flushed skin from her shower, she looked good. She also looked like a woman who wanted to get fucked.

An invitation kind of pic.

The Fates left her no choice. A selfie like this didn't come along just any millennia. And who was she, a mere mortal, to tempt the wrath of the selfie gods by throwing out a perfectly good celestial gift? The karmic and cosmic risks were too great.

She sent the picture. She had no other options really.

P: How about wine with myself?

A minute passed. No response. Another minute. She began to panic. She threw her phone onto the bed. She would forget she sent it, she would put it out of her mind. They would act like it had never happened.

At the office, she'd done her best to keep her distance, and she'd withdrawn all outward indicators of flirting. And he'd followed her lead. Maybe he was already over the whole thing. He said he wouldn't wait around forever…

Her breath hitched when she flipped her phone back over to find one new message from Carter. She bit her lip and unlocked the screen.

C: You're being a very, very, very bad…colleague.

Delight and relief rushed through her. He was flirting.

She mentally slapped herself: she was playing games, and she couldn't stop herself. The worst part was her nipples were getting hard from one little suggestive text. What would it have been like to have his mouth on them? She never did find out, a tragedy now.

Emboldened, she let her robe slide off the slope of her right shoulder so the tiniest slip of nipple showed and a whole hell of a lot of cleavage. As her damp hair fell over one eye, she snapped another selfie. Before she could think twice, she hit send.

She squeezed her eyes shut but this time the screen lit up quickly.

C: You shouldn't play with fire if you don't want to get fucked, Bad Girl.

Welp, he was definitely still interested. The corners of her lips curled up despite herself. But this was his warning, wasn't it? Her chance to back off.

She dipped her left shoulder allowing the robe to slide off the other side as well. Heading into big-league territory now. Her breasts were exposed, her silky robe hanging loosely from her upper arms, her hair shedding droplets down her bare skin. She raised her phone to snap the pic—

"P, where did you decide— Oh, heyyo. What's going on here?" Lucille had elbowed her way into the crack of the doorway.

Perdie snatched up her robe in a hurry. "I…just got out of the shower… I'll text Noah right now." She tightened the robe.

Lucille's eyes narrowed. "Uh-huh." She slowly backed out of the room, latching the door shut.

Another text appeared on her screen.

You know if you need help taking nudes, I'm here for you.

It was from Lucille.

The interruption had been for the best, slowing Perdie's roll before she did anything even more rash.

She texted Noah, extra careful to select the right contact, and they set up a time and place for brunch. *Lucille's coming,* she added for good measure.

Then she leaned against her headboard and stared at the ceiling, her skin still tingling from her hot shower. Or maybe from her texts with Carter.

Once again, she let the top of her robe drop, her own fingertips traveling to the sensitized peaks of her nipples. She turned her head to the side with her breasts exposed, save for her long hair tumbling around them, her fingertips trailing over the tightened tips, and held up her phone. *Click.*

She hesitated only briefly. He was out golfing with her bosses. Clients. She shouldn't do this, it would only fulfill a brief surge of lust. And was lust worth it? On the other hand...

She sent the picture.

P: Your move, Pretty Boy.

Instantly her phone lit up. Carter was trying to *call* her. And like any other time someone tried to call her, Perdie's first instinct was to decline.

Who actually talked on their cell phones in this day and age? The thought of it freaked her out. What did he want to have a discussion about—her half-naked picture? Why couldn't he send a dick pic in return like a normal man?

Perdie tentatively lifted the phone to her ear, and her voice croaked when she answered. "Hello?"

She could hear Carter's labored breath on the other end, probably from jogging away from the other lawyers on the golf course. The thought both embarrassed and thrilled her.

"Go out with me tonight."

At his words, she sharply inhaled. She didn't know why it surprised her so much; after all, they'd been sexting moments before. *She* had been doing most of the work too. But that was sex. And what he was asking was something other than sex...

Her fingers trailed north against her headboard. "Go out where? Your place? My place? The backseat of that big old SUV of yours?" She twirled a lock of hair on her finger.

"Perdie." His voice sounded like a warning.

"What, Carter?" She feigned innocence.

"I'm talking about a proper date. And the SUV was a rental."

She fiddled with the trim of her robe, her index finger gliding up and down the naked skin of her breast. "Best I can offer you is more sexting."

Carter chuckled. "I'm not a pawn shop. I'm a real person. I know that you like playing this game with me, but is that *all* you like? Because I don't believe it."

Her hand stilled and her words came out small. "I don't know."

"Well, why don't you give yourself the chance to collect more evidence?"

She let her thumb scrape across the puckered skin of her nipple and shivered at the idea of Carter's tongue there instead. "Okay, fine. I'll *meet* you somewhere. But it has to be later because I'm not going to cancel my brunch for you."

"I would never dare ask a lady to cancel brunch."

"*And* you have to send me a dick pic."

He sounded surprised. "What?"

She cleared her throat, straightening up on the bed. "You heard me. Those are my terms."

"Okay…"

"It's for collateral. Your face has to be in it. You got a dirty pic of me. I get a dirty pic of you. Fair's fair. Them's the rules."

"I'll do it on one condition."

She lifted a brow. "What's that?"

"You have to answer a few questions."

Her curiosity piqued. "Ask away."

Men's voices called in the background, rustling Carter's phone. "No, I'll text you later. I have to get back to the course."

She shook her head. "For someone who appears so incredibly normal, you really are the weirdest person I've ever met."

"You like games? We'll play a game."

She shrugged. "Fine, and Carter?"

"Yeah?"

"Make it a good pic."

Chapter Thirteen

Lucille and Noah were drunk, and they were two of the happiest drunks Perdie had ever seen in her life. The trio was seated in a corner booth of one of Perdie's favorite brunch spots on the main strip of Sullivan's Island, the Smokewood Café.

Perdie was packing away her stacks of color-coded notes from her discussion with Noah as a server came out with tin trays of burnt ends, barbecued chicken thighs, smoked pork shoulder, homemade sweet pickles, fried okra, cheesy grits, and deep-fried mac-and-cheese balls. On a crisp, chilly afternoon, Charleston comfort food simply could not be beat.

As was custom for Perdie and Lucille, they'd started with many rounds of drinks well before ordering food. This gave Perdie and Noah ample time to discuss the case. Although only Lucille and Noah were partaking in the drinks, since Perdie was acting as designated driver. Oh, and hired legal counsel, of course.

Noah was a surprisingly easy client in terms of communicating complicated material, and this was a huge asset in Perdie's eyes. He had a serious yet concise way of describing the most esoteric concepts, even while he was sucking down the Smokewood Café's famous frozen pineapple and bourbon drink, the Mind Melder. Perdie was lucky she got what she needed before he and Lucille were both inevitably too drunk for coherence.

She'd also been furtively checking her phone the entire time, but Carter hadn't texted since they'd hung up. It was probably for the best as she'd needed to concentrate on Noah anyway. But they were done with business stuff. Now they were onto barbecue stuff.

"So, Noah." Lucille stabbed a fist-sized chicken thigh with her fork. "How'd you get into neurogenetics anyway? You always dream of being a neurogenitician when you were a little kid?"

Noah's eyes were heavy, his long, dark lashes lowered from so much alcohol, and his lips were curled faintly upwards. He gazed up at Lucille. "No, I don't believe I knew what neurogenetics were as a child. I never was allowed a wide scope of exploration when I was young."

"No? That's so depressing." Lucille twirled the little hairs sticking out of one of her space buns. With her shiny jet-black hair, the spray of freckles across her nose, and the bright red wool crewneck sweater fitted on her petite body, Noah didn't stand a chance.

Then Noah's voice surprised her. "I grew up in…well, something similar to a cult."

Perdie choked on her sweet tea.

Lucille's eyes went wide. "Oh my god. Was it a weird sex cult?"

Perdie rested a hand on Noah's forearm. "As your acting counsel, you don't have to answer that. Lucille, *shut up*."

Noah shook his head and waved a hand. "No, it's fine,

I don't mind talking about it. It was very rural. There wasn't a lot of opportunity for conducting scientific research, which is why I only discovered my life's passion later on in life. After breaking away."

Lucille frowned. "Breaking away? What about your family?"

Noah methodically sliced through a fried mac-and-cheese ball before answering. "We don't speak anymore. It's unfortunate but inevitable. I pursued my education, which I wouldn't have been able to do otherwise. Sacrifice is a part of life, and we don't get to choose into which family we are born." He forked a chunk of mac and cheese into his mouth before continuing. "I have a very skilled therapist."

Lucille hiccupped. "I sell flowers," she blurted out.

Perdie's head was ping-ponging between them, interested in what might happen next.

A slow smile spread across Noah's face. "A florist? Why did you choose that profession?"

Lucille leaned in close with a somber air. "Because I hate everything else," she whispered. They both stared at each other before breaking into laughter.

Perdie laughed as well. It was cute, but it was like she was in the middle of weirdo mating season. She took the distraction to check her phone.

P: Waiting on you, Pretty Boy...

C: Heading home from golf now. How's three o'clock at Palmetto Coffee?

P: You know my price of admission. One dick pic, please.

C: You owe me some answers first.

P: I know your full set of terms and as discussed, I have agreed. Proceed with your questions and I shall provide you with answers. Then you're gonna send me a you-know-what of your you-know-who.

C: Unlimited questions?

P: I'll give you three.

C: Deal. But you have to be honest. I'm almost back.

Perdie rubbed her hands together in anticipation, and looked up to see both Lucille and Noah staring at her. "What?"

Lucille nodded. "This is about Carter. She's got it bad."

Perdie's jaw dropped. "Lucille."

Noah was unperturbed. "He's assigned to my case as well, correct?"

Lucille slapped him on the arm. "That's right. It's like one of those legal dramas where everyone is super sexy."

Noah nodded sagely. "He does indeed look like a movie star."

On a reflex, Perdie snapped, "Oh fuck off." Then her eyes went wide. Noah was her friend, but she would be wise not to push the boundaries of civility directly after he had signed on as her client.

But Noah wasn't offended. In fact, he laughed, shaking his head. "Can I confess something to you both?" The color in his cheeks was high from the liquor, and merriment danced in his eyes.

Perdie shrugged. "Of course. Just nothing illegal, okay? I can't know about that stuff. I'm not that kind of lawyer."

Noah leaned back in his chair, setting down his utensils. "You're the first friends I've made since I moved here two years ago."

Perdie's face softened. Noah was kind of a teddy bear deep down.

Lucille reached out to rub his arm. "Aww, sweetie, that's so nice. But sad. But nice." Her hand went from rubbing to squeezing in a matter of seconds. "Wow, do you work out?"

Perdie shook her head at her friend's shamelessness. "You don't have roommates or anything, huh? Why'd you buy such an enormous house?"

Noah glanced down, blushing, as he rubbed his eyebrows. "Call it optimism. I've always wanted a big family."

Perdie raised a brow. "In like a culty way?"

"No, in an I've always wanted to be a dad kind of way."

Lucille was staring at Noah with an inscrutable expression now, but she quickly turned her gaze, grabbing a drink menu. "Another round?" she asked, her voice high.

Perdie's phone lit up. She pushed out her chair, grabbing the phone. "If you don't mind, I have to check something for work. Going to run to my car for a few. Order as much as you want…on me. Get the banana pudding, you won't regret it."

Perdie shuffled off through the gravel parking lot to wait on Carter. Ridiculous to sneak away but also she was grateful she'd parked in a lonely corner facing a wall, so no one could see her.

Why are you so concerned about being seen, P?

She blushed as she seated herself in the driver's seat. What kind of salacious things would he ask her? He had a penchant and, *let's be honest*, talent for dirty talk. Her stomach flipped in anticipation, and she retrieved her phone from her bag to text him.

C: You there?

P: Waiting...

Her phone lit up. A video call. Again she panicked. A regular phone call she had come to terms with, but now a video call?

Something new every damn time.

She checked herself in the rearview mirror first. Her hair had dried in natural dark waves and she'd donned a tight, thin turtleneck tucked into a pair of black skinny jeans.

With a big inhale, she accepted the call and had to blink twice when the sight of a live action Carter appeared on her screen.

"Are you in a parking lot?" he asked as he made his way through a modern apartment, opening the door to an enormous white bathroom.

"Are you in a bathroom?"

"I'm all sweaty." He reached behind his head and pulled off his long-sleeve shirt, his broad but sculpted chest completely bare. She could see him working off his out-of-picture pants as well.

"Oh my god, we're getting right down to business aren't we?"

He flashed a smile, speaking casually. "So, I used to surf a lot…"

He stepped into the shower, and suddenly her view of him expanded so she could see his entire naked torso. He had set the phone on a shelf in the shower.

"What are you doing?" she mumbled.

He turned the silver faucet handle, sending a stream of water over his head. "Which is why I have a water-proof phone case."

"You're joking. You can't shower right now." She bit her lip and craned her head in a futile effort to see past the dip of his hips cut off by the black frame of her phone screen. "That is so rude."

"A rinse. No big deal. I have to look pretty tonight for our date."

"Don't call it a date. Date sounds so…" Her words trailed off as she caught sight of him wetting his hair, his biceps flexed, and the length of his happy trail bobbed lower on the screen. He turned his head to the side under the stream of water and chuckled at her entranced face.

"See? I have to use all the tools in my arsenal to keep you honest during our impending interrogation."

"If you show me your tool I'll be as honest as you want." She stared unabashedly, but shook her head, snapping herself out of it. She waved her hand. "I only have a few minutes, so hit me with it."

She struggled to keep her eyes on his face when he grabbed an expensive bar of soap and began rubbing it over his forearm, then moving up the length of his biceps and over his left pec muscle.

"My first question is a tough one, so it's okay if you

crack under the pressure. I'm an extremely skilled litigator." He scraped a hand through his hair, letting the water rinse out the shampoo. They weren't even physically together, but the experience was acutely intimate. Even through the screen she could see the playful glint in his eye.

She cocked her head. "I can take it, Counsellor."

"What is…" he paused, rolling his neck so a stream of water could run down his shoulder "…your favorite color?"

Perdie let out a laugh. "*That's* what you want to ask me?" She looked up at the ceiling of her car, then back to Carter. "Okay, I actually *do* have one."

"And?"

She lifted a shoulder. "It's fuchsia."

"Fuchsia?"

"You know, like a saturated, bright pink?"

He stretched an arm behind his neck. "Like the color of your toenails the first night we met?"

Perdie's jaw dropped. "You absolute freak. How do you remember that?"

"I'm smart. I went to Harvard."

"Oh fuck off. Next question."

"And Yale," he muttered, wiping water from his eyes. "Fine, the first one was too easy. But I've lulled you into a false sense of security. Next one is really tough. Ready?"

"Carter."

He smiled. "If you were an animal, what animal would you be?"

Perdie giggled again. "Wow. So easy. Bananas, my pug, of course."

"Learning something new. I didn't even know you had a pug. Does he snore?"

"Is that your third question?"

"No, it's an addendum. Question 2b."

She bit back a smile as she let her eyes trail over the hard lines of his body, the carved vee of his lower abdomen. "Yes, he snores like a buzz saw. I share joint custody with my roommate, Lucille."

"And you have a roommate." He caught sight of her gaze and scraped the soap down his happy trail, rubbing the washboard of his abs with his hand.

She let out a huff of air. "We can't all buy four-thousand-square-foot colonials on our own. Lucille…she's my best friend. Sister, really. Soul mate. Love of my life. I'd live with her no matter how much money I make. And I'd gruesomely murder anyone who hurt her. Seriously. Decapitation."

He nodded gravely. "Now I know who I have to impress. And who not to piss off."

Carter reached to turn off the water, and then suddenly came into close view as he retrieved his phone and stepped out of the shower, toweling his shoulder and neck before tucking the towel low on his hips.

Perdie bit her lip, only getting a partial view of his actions, her brain filling in the blanks.

He hopped up onto the expansive white marble counter in his bathroom, the image of his torso obscured by the steamed-up mirror behind him. She wished it would clear up so she could admire the 360-degree view. And also those tattoos…

His voice brought her back to the task at hand. "Last question."

"Last question, and then you drop the fucking towel." Her words came out terser than intended.

A smile played on his lips. "And then we go on a date."

"Ugh, leave it to two lawyers to construct such complicated rules of engagement."

"Last question." He ran his fingers through his hair, then shook it into place. He leveled his gaze. "Why won't you admit you have feelings for me?"

Perdie's eyes widened and she opened her mouth to speak but no words came out. Then, thinking fast, she gave him a sultry look. "I do admit to having feelings towards you. Sexy ones. And steamy ones. And naked ones."

"Objection, your honor. Illegal wordplay."

She paused and laughed a little to herself. "Fine. I can't admit that I like you because…" She glanced out the window. "Because… I think no matter what, once you really get to know me, I'll do nothing but disappoint you." The words startled even her.

His eyebrows knitted together. "Why would you think something like that?"

Despite herself, she thought about the last few days ignoring Carter and the relief when he'd responded to her texts earlier. Her heart thumped. "Because it's thrilling chasing someone. And it's thrilling sneaking around in the office. And it's thrilling playing these games. But at the end of the day, I'm a flawed person like anyone else. Except I'm not willing to change. People find it very frustrating about me."

He rubbed his chin. "Nothing about what you're saying scares me."

She leaned back, pushing against the seat of the car. "Look, my mom wasn't around very much when I was a kid, and when she was, she wasn't about to waste her time on me. I was messy and disorganized and overly sensitive."

"Sounds like a normal kid," said Carter.

Perdie sat in contemplation. "You wanna know why my favorite color is fuchsia? When I was eight years old my mother trained as a personal color consultant. Do you know what that is?"

Carter shook his head.

"It was this popular thing in the eighties where a consultant would drape you with different colored fabrics to see which colors suited you best, and then the grouping of those fabrics determined your 'season.'" She held up her free hand to make air quotes. "Well, my mom got into it late. And she did my colors."

He laughed. "Don't keep me in suspense. What's your season?"

"Bright winter, but that's not the point. The point is, it was one of the few things she did with me. I never forgot it. Afterwards she gave me a swatch of my best colors. And thirty years later, I *still* only wear the colors on that swatch. I have it in my purse right now." She dug into her handbag and pulled out the tattered packet of colors. "This is how little I'm willing to change. Completely unadaptable. Stuck in my ways, and I didn't have anyone to teach me how to be any better than that. So…"

"You think that's going to scare me off?"

She sighed. "You said so yourself. You're a rule follower, Carter. You followed the yellow brick road and it took you to Yale and Harvard and a white-glove defense firm. I barely graduated law school. Half the people at Joy and Schulz can't even stand me. They think I'm a huge bitch. And you know what? They're right. I'm fighting tooth and nail for a sliver of recognition that maybe I don't even deserve. Everyone likes you a hundred times more than me already, and you barely even had to try. You naturally give people what they want. It's like your secret talent or something. Your secret weapon. God knows it's working on me." She lowered her lashes at that last line. Her heart was beating fast after sharing so much about herself. She wasn't used to doing that with anyone but Lucille.

His voice was quiet. "Is it? Is it working on you?"

She bit her lower lip, breathing in deep and silent for a long stretch. But the silence between them was loud. She lifted her gaze. "It's time."

He tilted his head, face innocent. "Time for what?"

She stretched her free hand over her head grabbing onto the headrest and smiled. "Time to fulfill the second clause of our oral agreement."

The side of his mouth curled up. Then he gave a brief incline of his head. "Lift up your shirt first and give me a peek. I wanna put forth my best showing and I need some encouragement. Are you going to screenshot this?"

"Maybe." She glanced out both side windows, ensuring privacy, before pulling up the hem of her shirt, revealing one side of her lacy fuchsia balconette.

His breathing grew more ragged. "Pull it down, a little bit…do it for me…show me a little bit more…"

Her finger climbed up the lacy top line, and then she hooked it into the bra and yanked down the material to expose her nipple. The crisp air in her car heightened the intense tingling of her skin.

Out of view of the camera, she could tell his hand was starting to move in his lap, his lids growing heavy. When she flicked the taut point of her nipple with her finger, he let out a groan, his hand moving faster.

"Carter…"

But he was staring at her too intently on the screen to respond.

"Carter."

"What?"

She licked her lips. "Angle the camera down."

"Oh…"

Her chest went tight when the camera lowered to his leisurely stroking hand, a thick, heavy cock encased inside. Of course it was huge, she'd touched it before, but it was also so perfectly formed. Mostly straight but with a slight curve and well proportioned, pink but ruddy and swollen with blood, one vein trailing up the shaft, similar to the veins crawling up Carter's muscular forearms. He stroked it slowly, patiently…in no rush at all… Her mouth began to water.

Could a dick be sexy? Like *really* sexy? Because somehow Carter's dick managed it.

She swallowed, attention glued to the screen. "Okay, amendment to the second clause. Will accept the real thing in lieu of dick pic. Later today." A thrill ran through her at the thought.

Carter lifted the screen, his hand still working below. She almost protested but kept her mouth shut. "I am… agreeable to this amendment."

With the realization that her shirt was still up, and her hand was hooked into her bra, she slowly tugged the hem down, clearing her throat and straightening up. Jesus Christ she had really forgotten herself in the moment.

She almost jumped when a message popped up on her screen, pausing her view of Carter.

L: OMG P, HAVE YOU BEEN ABDUCTED BY ALIENS? PS
WE ATE ALL THE BANANA PUDDING PPS I ORDERED
MORE BANANA PUDDING

She closed out of the message, returning to Carter. "Shit, I lost track of time. I've got to get back to brunch." She let her head fall against the headrest in pure frustration, but then she straightened again. "I will see you *very* soon."

He gave her a nod. "See you soon."

When Perdie returned to the inside corner booth to collect whatever was left of Noah and Lucille, her insides were thrumming. It was like she could feel the endorphins coursing through her veins. She might actually feel something for Carter. And he might actually feel something for her. Or at least, it certainly appeared that way. And they were going to do…*something* about it tonight.

She approached the table, where Lucille's head was resting against Noah's big shoulder. "Come on, kids. Mom's going to drive your day-drunk asses home." She helped Lucille up, and Lucille grabbed Noah by the hand, pulling him up as well. Even while drunk and with Lucille's erratic yanking of his arm, Noah was completely steady on his feet.

"Here, Mom, take this." Lucille pushed a brown paper to-go bag into Perdie's chest. "It's the second round of banana pudding. It defeated us." Lucille's words slurred.

"I'm so sorry to hear that," Perdie said soothingly, as they trampled their way out to the gravel parking lot and into Perdie's vehicle.

Noah settled into the passenger seat, his long legs

still cramped even though the seat had been moved all the way back.

"I'll bring you to yours, Noah. You were great today."

He rubbed his eyes a little, a drunken laugh escaping his mouth.

Lucille called out. "Noah's not going to his place. He's coming to ours to watch cult documentaries with me."

Perdie lifted her brows, but Noah was nodding along. "S'true. I've got insider knowledge."

Perdie shrugged. "Great, sounds like a plan."

The drive home was quick, and Perdie's adrenaline was pumping. She'd be happy to get the two drunks settled into the house so she could get ready for Carter. She found herself nibbling on the edge of her thumbnail as she pulled into her private parking spot next to Lucille's thirteen-year-old Prius.

"Hurray. We made it," Lucille cheered from the backseat. "Hey, I changed my mind about that banana pudding, can you pass it to me."

Perdie laughed. "Yes, as soon as you get out of this vehicle and safely into the kitchen, consider the banana pudding all yours."

"And Noah's," Lucille said.

"And mine" came Noah's deep, serious voice.

Maybe Perdie was still riding high from her video call with Carter, but she laughed again, feeling giddy and excited.

But when they all tumbled out of the car, Perdie heard a familiar voice. It was a scream really. An annoying, desperate yell. The voice of the last person she ever wanted to hear from again.

"Lucille Renee Knox, I fucking love you so fucking much!"

Perdie's heart dropped into her stomach as she spun around. Lucille's mouth was agape. Noah's eyes tracked the figure coming towards them in the distance.

Fuck.

Hampton had returned.

Chapter Fourteen

"Hey, so now might be a bad time to tell you something…" Perdie muttered, wringing her hands.

"Lucille." The voice cut through the empty parking lot.

"Is that Hampton, or am I drunk?" Lucille asked, rubbing her eyes.

"Unfortunately—" Perdie gritted her teeth "—both."

Perdie futilely clutched the banana pudding close to her, irritation pricking at her skin at the sight of Hampton's messy blond hair, long beard, and black beanie coming into clear view. He beelined it to Lucille, pulling on the strings of his striped wool hoodie, silver rings glinting from his fingers.

"Babe." He dropped to his knees in front of her and wrapped his arms around her legs, causing her to wobble off balance.

"Hampton? What's going on?" She wiggled, but he held fast, squishing the side of his face against her shins. "What are you doing? It's freaking me out."

"Baby, I've come to apologize, I've learned my lesson."

"What lesson—"

"Um…" Perdie cut in. "I really have to tell—"

"Where have you *been*?" Lucille's eyes were wide. "Oh god, I'm too drunk for this shit."

"I'm here for you now, I'll never leave again." Hampton kissed her knee, looking up to her pleadingly.

Lucille reached below and fisted the back of his shirt, prying his leeching body off her. "Am I in opposite land? Here for me? You bailed on Bananas's appointment and then you ghosted me, like you *always* do."

"It's torture without you. I can't eat, can't sleep. I can barely drink my own microbrew creations." Hampton straightened, grasping her elbow with one hand, the other hand trailing to Lucille's cheek.

She craned her head away. "You could've just texted." Lucille's voice was exasperated.

He dropped the hand at Lucille's face and cocked his head. "It's okay, I get you've been ignoring me. I knew I had to come in person, that there was no other way. I did you wrong. But I'm here to make right. Now, what's it going to take to win you back? It's like that saying, *you don't know what you've got till it's gone.* L-Bomb." He caressed her once again. "Tell me what to do. Anything."

"I can't watch…" Perdie murmured to herself. Cringeworthy. Noah appeared in her periphery. *If Lucille ditches Noah because of this embarrassing display…*

"Those other women don't mean anything to me…"

Lucille pushed against him hard with her palms. "Other women—what? *Ugh, gross.* This isn't funny."

"I think you need to leave." Noah's stern voice popped in.

At that, Hampton's eyes darkened. He brought his fists together to crack his knuckles and stalked over. "Who are you?" He spat out the words and turned his head to Lucille, his finger jabbing into Noah's chest. "Is this your new guy? Is he the reason you've been ignoring me? Fucking *Lurch* over here."

Noah's jaw flicked but he stayed put. "Your behavior isn't welcome here."

"What are you gonna do about it?" Hampton faked a lunge at Noah, but Noah stood like a tree trunk. "You wanna go? Because I'll take you out. You see what I'll do for you, Luce?"

Perdie shook her head; she had to end this. It was too hard to watch. And there was no way Hampton could take Noah in a fight. It'd be an instant knockout. "Hampton, back off. I'm the one who blocked you on Lucille's phone, and that's why she's been ignoring you. She had no idea. If you've got a problem right now, take it up with me. And for your own safety, leave Noah out of this. Use your eyes, he's *huge*."

Lucille's eyes snapped over to her. "P, what were you thinking? Look what you did."

Perdie mouthed back, "I'm so sorry, talk later?"

But Hampton was fuming. "What the hell? I always knew you were some kind of fucking meddling *bitch*."

Perdie reached into her handbag, searching for her phone. "I'm calling the cops."

"No cops…" Lucille whispered. But Hampton was on the move.

He stalked over, face-to-face with Perdie.

With her hands shaking, she snatched her phone from her handbag.

"Hey!"

Before she could unlock the screen, Hampton grabbed it from her, threw it on the ground, and stomped on it with his boot. "How's it feel to have someone interfere with your personal shit, huh?"

"Hampton, you can't just do that to people's phones!" Lucille exclaimed. "People store pictures of their dogs on those things."

Oh hell no. The crushed glass and metal on the ground had Perdie's adrenaline pumping. The right thing to do would be to walk away, to shuffle off and ensure everyone could get inside safely. The *peaceful* approach. Maybe even let Noah handle it. He was big and strong, and clearly capable. That would be the right thing to do. Swallow her pride.

And with that reasonable thought in mind, Perdie yanked the flimsy cardboard box of banana pudding out of its bag. "Oh, you messed with the wrong meddling bitch today."

She cocked her arm and shock crossed over Hampton's features as she smashed the box square against his face, the paper crumpling, viscous yellow pudding exploding from every seam, splattering his beard, hoodie, hair, and beanie, and then dripping onto black pavement. He stumbled, bent over after for a moment, stunned from the hit.

"Holy shit. P, I can't believe you did that." Lucille clapped her hand over her mouth.

Time stood still. The collapsed box hit the ground. Hampton shook banana pudding off his sleeves, wiping it from his eyes.

And then without warning Perdie burst into laughter at the sight of him, peals of laughter ripping from her chest. He looked so *silly*. She wished she had more pudding to throw. You could never go wrong with banana pudding…

"I think it's time for you to go," said Noah.

"Fuck *you*, buddy." Hampton spit pudding on the ground.

"No." All heads turned at the snap of Lucille's voice. She stood arms akimbo. "*I* get to tell him. I'm the one who gets to tell him to leave. You don't get to steal my thunder. Just because you're big and strong and serious." She pointed her finger at Hampton. "I lied. You never *once* gave me an orgasm. And dopamine doesn't work that way." Then she smiled and waved. "Goodbye."

This time Noah had to smother a smile.

"Oh you think that's funny?" Hampton asked. Without warning, Hampton took a swing at Noah's face. *Sucker punch.* But Noah ducked with ease, the momentum causing Hampton to spin in a circle.

"Shit, Noah, watch out!" Lucille yelled.

Perdie yanked Lucille by the sleeve to move her out of harm's way.

Hampton geared up for another punch but like a flash, Noah snatched Hampton up by the collar, holding him out like a rag doll.

Noah's voice was deadly calm. "My moral code compels me to inform you that while I might be inebriated, I have four consecutive bareknuckle boxing titles from the greater New York City area. I want you to carefully evaluate this data set before I release my hold on your collar. Consider your odds of survival at this juncture. Once you have reached the only logical conclusion, then consider the fact that when released, the only way you leave this property unharmed is if you walk without so much as one more word to either me or these two women ever again."

Hampton's breath was heavy, and banana pudding remnants gunked off his face. He turned his head to spit pudding out onto the pavement. "Whatever, man. I don't need this shit anyway."

Noah leveled a stern glare, relaxing his grip on Hampton's collar, letting Hampton crumple.

Hampton glared at all three of them, wiping his face with the hem of his hoodie, before turning around. Perdie tracked his movements until he jumped into his white Range Rover and peeled out of the neighborhood, flipping them the bird out the window.

They all stood in a moment of silence.

"Thank god he's gone. Lucky no one got hurt." Perdie pushed out a huge breath.

"Are you really a bareknuckle boxer?" Lucille asked when they finally made their way to the wooden stairs.

"In another lifetime." *Creak.* *"Ugh."* Noah halted on the stairwell, and Perdie bumped against his back.

"What is it?" Perdie asked.

"I think I've stepped on a nail. Actually, I don't think it. I know it."

"Shit." Welp, she'd spoken too soon about no one getting hurt.

With painstaking slowness, Noah lifted his foot to investigate. A large, rusty nail protruded from the sole.

"Whoa." Lucille rushed up the stairs and pushed Perdie aside. "That looks bad."

Perdie attempted to disguise her horror. She was *very* squeamish. "Noah, we've got to get you to a hospital, quick. Here, grab onto our shoulders and we'll guide you down."

Lucille put her head in her hands. "I think I'm drunk and sober and hungover all at once."

"Too bad, get in the car."

It took both Lucille and Perdie shouldering Noah's body to get him to Perdie's car, and folding him into the backseat.

Brunch was officially over.

* * *

Perdie and Lucille sat shoulder to shoulder in the hard plastic chairs of the emergency room. They'd waited for over two hours before a doctor finally could see Noah. And now they were waiting longer while Noah got an emergency tetanus shot and his foot examined.

Lucille, anxious and a little drunk, had burst into tears at the news, but Noah had been stoic as ever, explaining to her calmly that a nail in the foot was nothing compared to a boxing match.

"Are you furious with me?" Perdie asked, staring at the vending machine against the wall in front of her. She wrung her hands in her lap, her ankles crossed. "I shouldn't have interfered with you and Hampton."

Lucille rested her head on Perdie's shoulder. She sighed. "No... No, I'm not mad. I mean, what you did was wrong but... Okay, I have a confession to make. That guy Michael from, like, two years ago—"

"The bass player?"

"Yeah. That's the one. Well, I *may* have texted him on your behalf saying you moved to Alaska."

"You can't be serious. Who would even believe that?"

"He didn't know Taylor Swift."

"Excuse me?"

Lucille dramatically rolled her eyes. "Okay, so he was waiting for you in the kitchen one time and that 'Look What You Made Me Do' song was playing over our speaker system, and granted it's not from the greatest era of Taylor's music, but still he said 'Who sings this?' and I said 'Taylor Swift' and he said 'Who's that?' And, Perdie, I can't abide by the elitism, I just can't. Imagine a musician not knowing who Taylor Swift is! I gave him a preemptive strike. It was wrong of me though. And

Michael probably wasn't even half as bad as Hampton. Not even a tenth as bad. I don't know what I was doing with Hampton, anyway. It was like I was under some weird spell."

Perdie pursed her lips, then sighed. "How about we admit that our intentions are good, but our boundaries aren't always great. So, we need to respect boundaries a little better. Deal?"

"Deal." Lucille rested her head against Perdie's shoulder again. "I'm lying. I might do it again. I'd probably do a lot of things. I couldn't stand to see anyone hurt you. Or Taylor." She sniffled and rubbed her face.

Perdie rested her head on top of Lucille's. "I know, Luce. Me too. And don't even get me started on what I'd do for Rihanna."

"But next time let's get a handyman. And some pepper spray."

"Really? I thought the banana pudding worked fine."

Lucille laughed. "Maybe now isn't the best time for me to leap back into the dating pool. I think I need a little time to myself."

"Oh?"

"And…speaking of the dating pool, you gonna 'fess up about those dirty pics you were sending this morning?"

A cold wave washed over Perdie. "Carter. Shit. *Shit.* What time is it?"

"Six fifteen?"

In the midst of panic, time slipped away from her. She cursed herself and her abnormal brain. Perdie reached for her phone— *Shit.* No phone. "Quick. Give me your phone."

"I thought we were setting boundaries?"

"Lucille!"

Lucille dug her phone out of her handbag and handed it over.

Perdie couldn't call or text Carter because she didn't know his number. The best she could was try his office phone, but he wouldn't be in the office. She let her head drop back in the chair. She'd have to email his work address. *Ugh, HR better not find any of this.*

As she was typing, a sinking feeling festered in her stomach. Surely he would understand why she had waited to contact him. Her phone was broken after all. And an ex-boyfriend had attempted to assault a friend of hers. And their client had stepped on a rusty nail due to her homeowner negligence. It wasn't like she had *purposely* stood him up…

At the end of the message, she left Lucille's number, asking him to contact her there. She returned the phone to Lucille. "Hey, this is important, are you sober now?"

Lucille tilted her head, considering the question, then nodded. "Feels like it. Why, do you want to get a drink? Honestly, I could use one."

"No, pay attention. If you get a text from a number you don't recognize, let me know right away, okay?"

Lucille saluted. "Aye, aye, captain."

By the time Sunday afternoon rolled around, Perdie's sinking feeling had grown to the size of a black hole.

Noah had been all patched up—hopefully he wouldn't suffer any infections—and he'd stayed with them overnight. She'd woken to find him splayed out on the couch, legs dangling off the end, with Bananas sleeping on his chest as if it were an enormous dog bed. *Both* were snoring.

Coffee mug in hand, Perdie picked up the faux fur

blanket that was hanging off the side of a cushion and pulled it over Noah and Bananas so that Bananas's little head was poking out beneath.

Lucille would die if she saw this.

Carter had never texted, nor had he emailed. Nor did he attempt to reach out in any other way. She did get about fifty-seven emails from Jennifer regarding Noah's case after Perdie sent her notes along. And wasn't it going to be *so* much fun following up on all that work.

She meandered into her bedroom and stared at herself in the vanity mirror next to her dresser.

Her mouth was wrought in a tight line, her skin sallow, hair half out of a ponytail, and she was wearing a ratty sweatshirt that Lucille's father had given her ten years earlier. Knox Family Christmas it read with a now peeling, ironed-on picture of the then family dog Oscar wearing a Santa hat. The Knoxes were nothing if not dog people.

After a soft knock on her door, Lucille peeked inside. "Hello, my lovely little blue jay. How are we feeling this morning?"

Perdie pointed to her face. "As I look."

Lucille inched into the room, tightening her canary-yellow robe around her waist. "So, now is probably a bad time to tell you that I have to drive home for Christmas. I was planning on leaving Friday. They asked if you were coming."

Perdie rocked back in her chair. "Too much on my plate right now. As much as I want another Knox Family Christmas sweatshirt."

"Don't worry, I'll bring one back. My dad already had it made for you." Lucille toyed with a glass container of perfume on Perdie's vanity. "Also, I asked Noah to come."

Perdie raised a brow. "Thought you were hopping out of the dating pool."

"As *friends*. He doesn't have any family, so…" She lowered her gaze. "And did you see how flippin' cute he looks out there sleeping with Bananas?"

Perdie pointed a finger at her. "Bananas stays here. Don't try to haul him away."

Lucille gave a small smile. "I am a little worried about not being here with you over the holidays. And I don't feel entirely sure Hampton won't try to come around…"

Perdie waved a hand. "Eh, we have bigger fish to fry than that." Although inwardly she was worried about the same things.

Lucille patted Perdie on the shoulder. "Maybe when I return before the New Year, you'll even let me meet Carter." She padded out of the room, closing the door behind her.

And the black hole inside Perdie threatened to swallow her up.

Chapter Fifteen

Perdie waited at the entrance of the elevator on the fifth floor counting backwards from ten. She smoothed out the sleeves of her cobalt blue blazer and checked the collar to make sure the tag wasn't sticking out. In a surge of optimism, she'd donned matching white lace undergarments too.

She had been issued a new firm cell phone that morning. Luckily, not many questions were asked by the IT department as more than a few attorneys had been known for breaking phones in much more nefarious ways. Still, Carter wasn't returning her texts and was only responding to impersonal business emails.

Perdie silently swore at herself. What did she expect? They worked together, and he was senior to her. The possibility of this kind of awkward scenario had loomed and she'd gone ahead and let her feelings rear their ugly head anyway.

But it was wrong that he would be so avoidant of her under such unfair circumstances. She couldn't have eschewed standing him up. It wasn't like she'd planned for an awful ex to show up at her condo and her friend (and client) to step on a rusty nail.

But also she wasn't exactly blameless for the whole

scenario going down either. Her actions *had* pushed the dominos into motion.

The timing couldn't have been worse.

At any rate, she was prepared to be the bigger person and apologize which was *not* typically her MO.

She made her way through the winding hallway and knocked on Carter's already open door. He was turned partially away, facing his computer screen, in a soft gray button-up. His hair was tousled, like he'd been running his hands through it, a tic of his, and his face was more darkened with stubble than she'd ever seen. Sexy as always, effortlessly, irritatingly so. But more than all that, he appeared tired as hell. A pang of guilt stabbed her sternum, not that she had any reason to believe his tiredness had something to do with her.

She swallowed hard but stepped past the threshold of the door. "Are you avoiding me?"

His gaze flitted from his computer, eyebrows raised, turning in his chair to face her. She resisted the urge to smooth down her hair or straighten her blazer.

She bit her cheek, but after a moment he answered. "*Avoiding* would be the wrong word."

The answer lit her up. Perhaps they were falling into old habits quickly and there wasn't anything else deeper or darker behind Carter's sudden radio silence. She smiled, setting into a seat in the chair in front of his desk. "What's the right word?"

He sighed, smoothing his thumb and index finger over his eyebrows. "You know what? I'm not in the mood to play games with you right now."

Her throat tightened. Words bubbled up and over. "I wasn't playing games. I swear to god. It was a freak accident, and as soon as I could, I tried to get a hold of you.

If you hadn't ignored me you would know how much I wanted to see you that night. I would never stand you up on purpose."

He rocked back in his chair and put his hands out like he meant to soothe her. "Okay…okay. It's okay." He took a breath, letting his chair drop. "I'm sorry. I was ignoring you, and it wasn't right. And I agree. Your behavior was reasonable given the situation. Necessary even. It's just…" He shifted in his chair, considering his words. "You hurt my feelings. I wouldn't have *forgotten* about our date until several hours later. That's so…"

She waited for him to finish as his words trailed off. She couldn't ignore the heavy pit in her stomach from seeing him this way. She felt bad. Guilty.

He closed his eyes with a slight shake of his head. "It's more than that. I'm a sensitive person. I'm beginning to feel like a fool chasing you around. And one minute I think it's exactly what you want from me and then the next minute you're giving me a totally different message. Been this way since moment go. And at some point, I have to ask myself: Am I the asshole here? Am I pushing you into something beyond your emotional capabilities? Look, I'm not completely ignorant. I know the effect my physical appearance can have on people. I've been benefiting from it my whole life. But I don't want to push you into something because of how I look. I was really trying to…make a real relationship happen between us."

Perdie's eyes went wide and a reflexive panic set in her chest. "Whoa, whoa, a *relationship*? We barely even know each other. I thought we were going on a *date*. That's what we agreed to. A date with maybe some extra-curriculars afterwards. You can't pretend like I'm emotionally stunted when I agreed to the terms you yourself laid out."

He shrugged. "I'm a guy who wants a real connection. But not at the expense of what someone else wants. I can't be your go-to sex guy. It's not in my DNA."

Perdie let out a breath, her eyes closing. "It's not fair to expect something out of me that I'm not ready to give."

"That's why I'm staying away. It's not the fact that you stood me up that hurts. It's the fact that you barely even tried to make things better. You could have at least called on Sunday. It might be nice to know that you care... like...a little bit."

"Are you kidding? You ignored my emails. Ghosting someone is a pretty clear sign that you should leave them alone, and you ghosted on me. I'm not trying to be some kind of stalker." Perdie was so used to such emotionally stunted men that she couldn't even call them twice in a row without getting called *crazy*. And here was Carter, asking her to try a little harder.

"Stalker? You avoid me half the time. Can you blame me if I might need a little more convincing that you really wanted to see me? You pointed it out yourself: I can persuade you with sex or games or whatever else but that's wrong. I'm not in the business of tricking someone into intimacy. Or at least, I really don't want to be. And I can't pretend it's only sex I want. And you can't pretend it's not. I think that has become pretty clear. But bottom line, I wish you'd have fought for this. At least a tiny bit." He regarded her steadily. "We're at a stalemate."

That wasn't entirely true. But the situation was messy enough having to work together. There was no challenge in his voice but there was *something* in his eyes. Like he was waiting for her to object. Waiting for her to tell him he was wrong.

Dammit, fight for him, Perdie. Do it. Do it.

But he was breaking off more than she could chew. So, instead, she choked.

She nibbled on her lower lip, mind uneasy. Finally, she cleared her throat. "I sent you the first draft of that complaint for the Fletcher Group. I'll be on the lookout for your notes."

Carter steepled his hands on his desk, resting his chin against them. "I expect we'll be making a few trips out to San Francisco after the holidays to meet with them."

"Well, at least it's better than North Dakota." She regretted the words as soon as they slipped from her lips.

Carter stared at her for a long moment. "Right."

Perdie scratched the top of her head, voice quiet. "I should go." She braced her arms on the chair to leave but Carter's words made her pause.

"I want you to know, I still have your back at work. This personal…stuff between us doesn't change anything. Okay?"

She stood, pulling at the cuff of her blazer. "Ah, thanks. I guess I'll—"

"See you Friday?"

"Friday?"

He gave a small smile. "The holiday party."

Shit. It'd slipped her mind. And she wouldn't even have a date to take along. Her stomach lurched. "Yeah, should be really fun."

She turned to leave as Jennifer and Sophia were entering the room.

"Oh, Perdita." Jennifer's tone was harsh, but her mouth was curved in a smile. "Fancy seeing you here."

"I was leaving, actually."

"Did you get a chance to read the memo I sent around—"

"I'll get right on it as soon as I get to my office." Perdie brushed by without so much as a glance over her shoulder.

"Wow. She looks like hell." Sophia's voice carried into the hallway.

"Stop being so damned stubborn and let me do the damned winged eyeliner on you." Lucille chased Perdie from the living room to the kitchen island, wielding her Marc Jacobs black eyeliner like a weapon. They squared off, the island acting as a barrier.

"I'm skipping the party," Perdie declared dramatically. She posed like a *Street Fighter* character, ready to jolt. Her winter-white beaded scoop-neck shift dress shimmered beneath the light fixture.

She juked left but Lucille's reflexes proved quick, anticipating Perdie's moves. Lucille jumped left too, snatching Perdie's forearm before she could flee her fate.

"Lies," Lucille declared. "You care too much about your career to skip the holiday party. Now, let me make you look nice."

"Don't you have to leave?"

Undeterred, Lucille dragged Perdie to the couch and yanked her down. "Knox Family Christmas can wait. Now, look up. No, *with your eyes*. Jesus Christ, sometimes I wonder about you."

Perdie sighed, giving up the fight, and lifted her gaze to the ceiling as Lucille's hand closed in on her face, gliding the liner over Perdie's eyelid in a tickling sweep. Lucille had already finished most of Perdie's makeup— the foundation, the contrast, the highlight, the falsies, the shimmer. She'd also put Perdie through an hour of hair curling to produce a perfect Old Hollywood S curl.

But for some reason, the longer it took, the more anxious Perdie became.

"Now use the brilliant berry liquid lip with a high-sheen gloss," Lucille advised like a very stern professor. "You can carry bright colors like nobody else I know, and it would be a tragedy for you to miss out on an opportunity to make Carter Leplan eat his own self-righteous words."

Perdie tried not to blink as Lucille added finishing touches. Then Lucille gently placed the lipstick and gloss inside Perdie's vintage silver clutch.

Perdie fluttered her eyes, adjusting to the heavy makeup and lashes, then examined her face in Lucille's little hand mirror. "You really are good at this."

"And *you* look like a perfectly sharp, murderous, little Christmas icicle." Lucille pinched Perdie's chin, moving her face a little to the left and then right. "Just like I wanted you to be." She booped Perdie's nose with her index finger.

The tune of the doorbell caused Bananas to let out a few muffled *whou-whou*s before the door quietly cracked open.

"I brought champagne. Does your family like champagne?" Noah stepped into the living room, his tall form holding out two cardboard carriers of champagne in offering.

"Everybody loves champagne. But I don't think we'll need twelve bottles. Actually, on second thought..." Lucille jumped up and caught Noah in a big hug. His eyes widened at her embrace. She quickly dropped her arms as if caught in the act of a crime, took a carrier from

Noah, and set it on the coffee table. "Doesn't Perdie look amazing?"

Noah bent down to scratch Bananas on the head as he nodded. "Yes. Amazing." But he was staring at Lucille the whole time.

Lucille picked up her paint-splattered leather duffel and rummaged in the closet for her coat and scarf. "You sure you're going to be okay without me?" she asked over her shoulder.

Perdie sat primly on the couch, careful not to disturb dress, hair, or makeup. "Believe it or not, I'm capable of being on my own for a few days. Besides, I'll have Bananas."

Lucille walked over and kissed Perdie on the cheek. "Text me, call me, telegram me, smoke signal if you need anything." Then she turned to Noah. "You ready to blow this joint?"

Noah gave a slight bow. "Yes, I look forward to the new experience."

Lucille grabbed him by the arm, pulling him out. "Buddy, you are gonna love the laid-back, crunchy lifestyle of Asheville. Be safe, P. Have fun tonight. Don't do anything I wouldn't do…" And she closed the door behind them.

Chapter Sixteen

Perdie balanced on one foot in front of the entrance to the Atlantic Theater to fix the strap of her heel. The chilly winter air licked her bare legs, and the enormous old-school marquee blared bright with the festive message: *Happy Holidays from Joy and Schulz.*

Perdie wasn't experiencing much joy though. For one, her silver stilettos were already threatening bodily harm, her toes scrunched and smarting in the ungiving leather. And the butterflies in her stomach were attempting to escape by way of her mouth. *Oh good god, don't puke.* She tightened the belt of her white faux fur coat. The coat was *extra as hell* according to Lucille but also *necessary in these trying times.* If nothing else, Perdie was certainly following the Old Hollywood Glam theme of the night.

She hated walking into places alone, especially formal events like these. She was accustomed to the care-free comfort of Lucille for most gatherings, or at the very least a date she'd scrounged up elsewhere. She hadn't been doing much swiping on the dating apps the past few weeks, that went without saying. But she had to reject her own cowardice. She'd have to face Carter one way or another, and if she did it alone, well, she was woman enough to stand in front of a Joy and Schulz partner with whom she'd almost had an illicit affair and eat shit like a pro.

Enough stalling, walk your ass inside that door, big girl.

Perdie headed in through the heavy glass entrance.

Rita from event planning greeted her at a check-in table. "Oh, Perdita, don't you look lovely tonight," Rita chirped, tapping at the laptop. "You're all set. Coat check is to your left."

Perdie experienced mild panic at the thought of removing her coat, stripping away a layer of protective armor, and serving herself up on a white shimmery platter to the rest of the lawyers. But she shook away the fear— no more dramatics. It was just a party, and she was just a person. She'd have a few drinks, shake a few hands, and get out of there, spending the rest of the night on the couch with Bananas, eating panettone out of a box.

She headed to the coat check, undoing her belt. As the coat slipped from her shoulders, a familiar voice surprised her.

"Wow, I've been out of the Charleston office for far too long. When did they start hiring models as lawyers?"

A small smile flitted over Perdie's face. The voice belonged to Max Goodridge, a friend who worked in the Joy and Schulz satellite New York office. From anyone else, she would've found the line cheesy at best and sexist at worst. But they were pals, so to speak, and had possibly engaged in some innocent flirting before. Nothing serious, as Max had been married then, and Perdie wasn't in the habit of hooking up with married men *or* coworkers. Or at least, she hadn't been at the time. But she wasn't going to let her mind wander to Carter...

"Flatterer." She moved aside as Max leaned over to

hand his coat to the coat check, the velvet of his navy tuxedo jacket brushing against the bare skin of her arm.

He flashed a bright white smile. "You can flatter and speak the truth all in one."

"And what's your truth, exactly? Still mixing your Glenlivet with ginger ale?"

He lifted a finger to his lips. "Shhh, don't let my secret out. You'll compromise my manhood."

"Forget about your manhood, in some countries you could be arrested for such an offense."

"Good thing I know an excellent attorney."

She raised an eyebrow. "And a bunch of shit ones."

Max chuckled as they made their way through the lobby and into a swarm of decked-out, mingling people, sequins and jewelry glittering under glass chandeliers.

"That's why you're my favorite one here." He swooped two coupe glasses from a flowing champagne pyramid centerpiece and handed one to Perdie.

"Why's that?"

"Because you don't fake anything." He winked when she playfully whacked him on the arm with her clutch.

"Not that you'd have any idea what I do or don't fake."

"You don't seem like a faker to me," he said with a naughty smile on his face as they neared the main room.

The jazzy, smoky tones of a popular Charleston cover band floated through the air. They only played K-pop covers, which Perdie knew well thanks to Lucille. Even so, if she wasn't at a work event, the whole thing might feel a little magical, romantic even.

But Max was handsome, wasn't he? His dense swath of hair was a deep auburn and a little on the messy side, and his thick matching beard contrasted nicely with his pale skin. He wore a tartan bow tie with his tuxedo, har-

monious with his overall style. Lumberjack meets Lux-
embourgian prince meets big-city attorney? Perhaps not
Perdie's usual type, but his confidence and charm sold
the whole package well. Maybe he wasn't Carter Leplan
handsome, but then again, who was? Either way, Perdie
was sure Max wasn't wanting for attention.

Perdie sipped from her glass, the effervescence tickling her nose. She was going to be okay. She smiled and
let out a satisfied sigh, letting her eyes wander the room,
the silver and gold tables stacked with mountains of fancy
hors d'oeuvres and desserts. There was an espresso station in the corner and several bars scattered throughout with people already lining up behind them. Joy and
Schulz didn't play when it came to alcohol distribution.

She and Max said cordial hellos to fellow partygoers
as the large stage came into view, the band dressed in
black suits and sequined dresses.

But as soon as a modicum of ease settled over her, she
spotted Carter across the other side of the large ballroom.
Dammit, Carter. It only took a glimpse of the back of his
tall body smoothed in a crisp midnight tuxedo to ping
her radar. Quickly, she averted her gaze before she could
register any details. Regular, everyday men could turn
out damned good in a tux. Lord only knew the kind of
psychic damage Carter could inflict all dressed up like
James Bond.

Perdie mentally swept the room, targeting who she
would have to rub elbows with for a few minutes before
she could jet. But in the meantime…

"So, Max, where you staying? You in town for long?"
Perdie absently swirled her champagne.

He scratched the back of his neck. "Staying at the
Wentforth. Can't beat the location."

Perdie nodded. "Ah, very old money, very old lady chic of you. I'm convinced that place is haunted."

His eyes glimmered. "Don't try to scare me, or I'll show up at your doorstep towing ghosts."

At that, Perdie's stomach blipped. Did she really want to be flirting with Max right now? Maybe it would have been fun last year. Although familiar and pleasant, it felt far less fun than it should have.

Max cleared his throat. "You probably already heard about Kathryn and me."

She nodded. She'd gathered through the grapevine that Max had divorced. "Sorry to hear."

He shrugged. "I'm not. We grew apart like adults tend to do when they get married too young and barely know themselves yet. Hadn't been happy for a long time. At any rate, I'm a free man now..." His gaze flickered over her.

It was an opening, and if she wanted to, she could spend the whole evening with Max by her side. He was handsome, funny, smart. He could distract her from her feelings, from work, from the fact that she would spend the holidays alone. Hooking up with someone at a satellite office was way more inconspicuous than with someone on the fifth floor. But...

Stop. Thinking. About. Carter. Ugh, but she couldn't. Suddenly, she needed to escape.

"Sorry, I, uh..." Perdie pointed to a corner. "Frank. I have to... I have to talk to Frank about a deadline. I'll see you in a bit, okay?"

"Sure, of course." Max's eyebrows went up, but he downed his drink and straightened his bow tie. "I should do some hobnobbing with the rest of the Charleston folks anyway. Don't want them to forget my face."

She gave a smile, squeezing his shoulder. "Nobody

could. I'll see you later." She rushed off to a crowded corner beyond the stage, offering polite *hello how are you Merry Christmas Happy Hanukkah Joyous Kwanzaas* to the other attorneys and staff along the way.

Phew. She sidled up to a corner bar with only a few people lingering in a makeshift line. She knocked back her champagne and plunked it onto an empty tray next to the bar.

"Dirty vodka martini, please." She leaned against the counter, scoping the room as the bartender mixed her drink. Frank at her nine o'clock, Charles Joy to her right, managing partner Minnie Martinson beyond the third bar, and Jennifer and Sophia hanging on the arms of their boring husbands on the perimeter. Drink in hand, she fished out the toothpick, scraped the olive off with her teeth, and took a big pull from the wide-rimmed glass.

Right, time to rub elbows.

On her way, the dessert bar caught her eye. *You weakwilled woman*, she chastised herself as she shoved a pink macaron in her mouth, coupling it with another big swig of her martini. Not the greatest combination of flavors of all time. As she chewed, she spun around and—

Smack. "Whoa…" Her mouth was full. Her martini wobbled as she teetered on the points of her heels from the impact. A hand shot out and caught her elbow so she could recover her balance. She barely avoided a spill down her cleavage.

But then she swore to herself as her gaze slowly ascended up the body in front of hers to the familiar lasercut jaw and kissable lips. Her brain zeroed in on that hazel eye with the little blue patch in the iris. She gulped down the macaron as his hand trailed from her elbow to her forearm and then dropped to his side.

"Hey, you," she eked out. Carter's shawl-collar tuxedo was crisp, black, and perfectly tailored to his muscular and tall form. He might as well have been accepting an Oscar.

And he wasn't alone. The pert blonde in a red off-the-shoulder bandage dress was the same one who had called him *Carter darling* outside of a large house on a sunny winter day not so long ago.

Aubrey.

"And…and hello, you," Perdie stammered out, nodding towards Aubrey.

Aubrey smiled brightly, her voice laden with a Charleston lilt. "Oh, I'm sorry, have we met before? This is my first time at one of these, meeting so many new people. I swear I forget everyone's names as fast as I learn 'em."

Aubrey tucked her hand into the crook of Carter's elbow, and a wave of nausea swept over Perdie.

She closed her eyes for one brief moment. *Doesn't matter. He's not yours.*

Carter straightened out his arm, dropping Aubrey's clasp, and cleared his throat. "Perdie, I should properly introduce you—"

Oh hell no. She couldn't stand there in front of them for one more second. "Ah…sorry…gotta Frank, I mean catch Frank…" She gestured with her martini glass towards a spot in the distance, as if Frank were an elusive gazelle. "Have a deadline…so…yeah…" Her voice trailed off and as she brushed past them, Carter craned his neck to watch her go, brows furrowed. *Nope, not tonight, Pretty Boy.* She couldn't pretend to be friends *right now.*

Perdie trotted away, cheeks hot and chest tight. If she

could physically distance herself, she could neutralize her memory. Tame the feelings.

She elbowed her way through the crowd when she spotted Frank in a navy and black suit with Ferris Joy. Frank spotted her too, winging an arm to invite her into the circle of conversation.

"Perdie, good to see you looking so…well…" His hand landed on her lower back and she forced her face to remain fixed in a smile. He turned to Ferris Joy. "Perdie here has been a busy little bee with your good friend Carter. Got herself a little patent case to work on."

Perdie grimaced at the condescending tone—how *did* he always manage it, like some kind of special skill. But no matter, she could small talk with these two men for a few minutes at least.

"Yeah, Carter's been busy lately. House shopping and all," said Ferris, shifting his eyes back and forth, sniffing and rubbing at the bottom of his nose. *Oh great, he's coked out.* His eyes darted around the room for more important people to talk to. He sipped from a tumbler of scotch. "You in the market for a house? Lots of houses for sale right now. Lots and lots of houses."

Perdie scrunched her nose in question. "I've got a condo off the Sullivan's connector."

Frank clapped Ferris on the shoulder with a nervous laugh. "He's asking because his sister recently got her real estate license. Always a good networker, this one."

Perdie inwardly rolled her eyes. Frank was such a kiss ass, never forgetting for one moment that Ferris Joy was the son to Charles Joy.

"Let me introduce the two of you, she's at the party. Nice to make friends, isn't it?" Frank said. "And you never know when you might need to upgrade that living situation of yours. Kids and marriage and all that. Can't put it off forever. May as well help a fellow attorney out too. Kill two birds with one stone. Ferris, we'll catch up at the after-party." He grabbed Perdie's elbow and led her towards the bar.

"Let me give you a little advice." Frank spoke close to her ear. "If you want to stay in good with this firm, you gotta do business with its family. You'll thank me later."

With that, Frank pulled Perdie through the large ballroom. The band played a jazz cover of BLACKPINK's "How You Like That." A chill prickled her skin. Frank was *returning* her to Carter and Aubrey.

Oh no.

Just as he'd done with Ferris, Frank clapped a hand on Carter's shoulder, turning Carter around to their attention. "Carter, my boy. Came by to introduce our Perdie here to your lovely date. We were discussing the importance of *networking* at our firm."

Perdie attempted a smile. "Oh, we've met—"

Frank placed a hand on Perdie's shoulder. "Perdita Stone, Aubrey Joy, Ferris Joy's sister and *hopefully* our associates' new go-to house shopper."

Carter nodded, keeping an eye on Perdie. "Yes, that's right. Aubrey is my real estate agent."

Aubrey swatted Carter's biceps. "Well, I'm your *date* too, sweetheart."

Carter smiled tightly, running his hand through his hair, one lock falling errantly in his eye.

Perdie clenched her fist to her side. When Aubrey laughed, Perdie's proverbial vampire fangs sharpened to deadly points but she endeavored to keep her cool. "A real estate agent. Fun. How's business?"

Aubrey adjusted the cleavage of her dress. Perdie

watched both men to see who was creeping. Frank, of course. But Carter's eyes were straight ahead, drilling into Perdie's soul. She forced herself to pay attention to Aubrey.

"Well, it was real scary at first, but when Ferris told me Carter was moving here, I was so excited because I knew he could be my first big sale. This guy's not hur-tin' in the wallet department if you know what I mean." She elbowed him playfully. Perdie avoided his eyes. "And well, now I want to be the number-one real estate agent in the Lowcountry. Put my picture on a bench for people to sit on. I just think that'd be great, don't you? Ferris isn't the only talented Joy kid!"

Despite herself, Perdie kind of liked Aubrey's exu-berant optimism and her guileless lack of self-awareness over the idea of people sitting on her face on a public bench. And she had to hand it to the girl, she wasn't afraid to let her feelings show. Carter might like someone like that. Perdie regarded the two of them together. Like two bright, shiny ornaments glimmering on a tree.

"I'm sure you'll do very well here. Sorry to tell you I'm not in the market." Across the room, Perdie spotted a dash of red hair. *Max*. She needed him now, she needed him like a shield. Luckily, she caught his eye. When she in-clined her head like *get over here right now*, he lifted his glass in her direction and headed towards her. *Thank god.*

"Perdie's neighborhood is very quiet," Carter said, his gaze challenging.

"Oh, you've been before?" Frank's voice cut in. "Why, I don't believe I've ever gotten an invitation."

Max arrived, saving Perdie the necessity of explana-tion, elbowing his way in next to Perdie, flashing those bright white teeth. He held out his hand to Carter and then Aubrey. "Max Goodridge. We haven't been formally introduced."

Perdie let out a sigh of relief. Max was an ally. Someone who liked her. He'd keep her from falling off the deep end with Carter and Aubrey.

The group settled in and chatted, the conversation shifting away from house shopping and Perdie's condo.

As the conversation inevitably turned to work, Perdie didn't dare glance at Carter. Instead she made eye contact with Max. A smirk played on her lips as he raised his glass of what appeared to be scotch. He smothered a smile at her knowing wink and then passed the glass over. She sipped from it, confirming the evidence of the ginger ale.

A laugh escaped her as she passed the drink back.

"What's so funny?" Aubrey asked with an expectant smile. "You two sharing an inside joke?"

With the direct question, Perdie was forced to acknowledge Aubrey and Carter. Carter's face was tense and he was staring at her with more scrutiny than made her comfortable. But it gave her a small thrill, the idea that he might be jealous. Also, it irritated her. He was the one with the date, not her.

"It's a secret." She smiled. "I can't tell you or it would permanently alter your perception of Max, and I'm not that kind of friend."

Max winked at her and the muscle of Carter's jaw tightened.

That's what you get.

"Secrets. Secrets are no fun." Aubrey laughed nervously, her eyes darting around the three of them.

Perdie allowed the lingering silence before speaking again. "I'm heading to the bar." She tipped back her drink, a lipstick stain on the rim.

"I'll join you." Max smiled and rested his hand on her lower back. This time, she liked it but not for the right reasons. She willed herself not to throw a glance at Carter as she and Max walked away together. *Eat shit, Pretty Boy.*

She twisted the empty glass stem as they walked, watching the rotating bright pink marks smudging the rim. *The lipstick.* Probably a mess on her face after two drinks. God, she hoped she hadn't looked sloppy in front of everyone. She touched Max's arm. "Hey, I'm going to run to the bathroom to fix my lipstick. I'll meet you at the bar."

"Don't be too long. You're a vision of perfection," Max said, making the uncertainty in her chest grow.

Perdie peeled off, escaping into the bathroom past the hallway. Once there, she leaned close to a large mirror, inspecting her face. Okay, all things considered, but still she followed Lucille's directions. First the lip color, then the gloss. She gave a few puckers and turned to leave, walking into the hallway, the stream of music and lights creeping in from the opening and closing gala doors.

She took a deep breath, the vision of Frank and Max and Carter and Aubrey still fresh in her brain. It made her hot and foggy. She didn't want to go back. Not yet. Instead, she turned around and walked out the back hallway exit.

Chapter Seventeen

The winter air soothed Perdie's heated cheeks as she click-clacked to a small hidden alcove behind the theater. She leaned against the brick wall of the building, mesmerized by the twinkling shrubbery in front of her. The Christmas lights had grown slightly hazy due to the drinks she'd consumed. Above her, the sky was dark and clear, her breath sending forth a billowy cloud. She set her clutch by her feet—she'd been keeping it squished between her side and upper arm the whole night. Then she rubbed the tops of her bare arms, soothing the goose bumps as a sharp breeze forced a shiver through her bones. She should've collected her jacket too but she needed time to herself.

The back door opened with a heavy, decompressing sound.

"Are you cold?" Carter asked her as his large frame stepped into view. He strolled towards her, then shrugged out of his black tuxedo jacket. From beyond the door the dulcet tones of a Got7 cover floated outside, "Aura."

"Are you a stalker?" A small part of her that had expected him to show danced with glee. The other part panicked. She reflexively jerked away when he reached around her shoulders, but then caught herself when he rested the jacket around her.

"Thanks." She burrowed into the silk-lined coat, begrudgingly grateful for the extra layer.

Somehow Carter looked even better without his jacket, with his hands shoved in his pockets, intimate, like he might remove more layers. Perdie inwardly cursed her dirty mind.

"So, you and that guy have a thing?" he asked casually, his eyes turned up to the night sky.

She kept her face forward too. "Do you and that woman?"

He shrugged. "Like I said. She's my real estate agent."

She couldn't stop herself from scoffing. "You might've mentioned it earlier."

"I don't see why someone like my real estate agent would require a special mention." His tone was teasing, but it made her roll her eyes.

"Come on. You could've mentioned who she was the day you drove me home. You know, when you kissed me on my doorstep."

One side of his mouth curled up. "You were jealous."

"So why didn't you explain yourself then?"

He looked at her for a moment, incredulous. "Did you really think I would openly bail on a woman I was seeing to drive another woman home with every intention of kissing that other woman boneless?" He cocked his head, waiting for her answer.

Perdie's mouth dropped open. "Don't act so innocent. It was a reasonable assumption."

He elbowed her side gently. "You really do believe the worst about me, don't you? And here I thought you were reaching for excuses not to like me."

Her eyes narrowed. "Carter, *any* woman alive would've made the same assumptions that I did."

"Then why'd you let me kiss you?"

The words irked her, and she almost lied, but then gave up with a sigh. "Because who in their right mind wouldn't?"

He paused. "Okay, fine. Of course I liked that you were jealous. I admit it. I'm sorry. But I didn't honestly believe you thought there was something going on with Aubrey and me. I thought you and I were having a little fun. Playing games, like we do." He pulled at the French cuffs of his sleeve. "And please accept this preemptive apology because I also like that you're jealous right now."

She crossed her arms in front of her chest, the beads of her dress biting into the flesh of her forearms. "I still don't believe you're telling the truth about her."

With one swift motion he reached around her, setting her pulse off. He slid his phone out of the inner pocket of his jacket at the side of her shoulder. He unlocked it and held it out to her. "Here's proof."

The messages were between him and Aubrey, nothing more than a series of links to different houses for sale and polite lines of small talk exchanged.

"Here, take it. Go ahead. Scroll all you like. I'm an innocent man." He prodded the phone at her.

She waved a hand, pushing it out of her view. "Stop it. Stop it. This is madness. I don't want to see your text messages, for god's sake, that's none of my business. You owe me nothing. Especially now. You said we were at a stalemate. You said we should stay away."

He rolled his shoulder against the wall to face her profile, absently reaching out to thumb the hem of her dress. Her body gravitated towards his touch.

"I lied."

His words ran down her spine with a crackle.

Then, her eyes fluttered closed as his hand crept up the side of her thigh, the shimmery white material at the hem of her dress slipping over the flat of his hand. "I'm a liar, Perdie. I saw you with Max Goodridge and… How could I let you walk away? But if you tell me to go, I will. Say the words, and I'll leave you alone."

Time stood still. The glide of his calloused fingertips scraped small circles over the skin of her outer thigh.

"How much have you been drinking?" he asked. Her breath hitched as his hand swept over the top of her leg and now grazed near her inner thigh, tickling her with the same hypnotic, circular motion.

Her voice came out breathy. "Only a little. You?" She tensed her jaw, raising her chin as his hand came so close to the juncture in between her thighs. *Almost there.*

"Not a drop."

She pushed out a hot lungful of oxygen she didn't know she was holding when he leaned in next to her, his breath warming the shell of her ear, the heat from his body radiating off him and onto her.

"No panties?" he said as his touch dragged inward.

A finger slipped into the folds of her pussy, moving in slow, steady strokes. She shivered but not from the cold.

"Bad, Bad Girl. Wet already? It's like you were waiting for me to come and find you…"

"You couldn't even stay away for a week." Her words were punctuated with stabs of pleasure, her head falling back against the brick as his fingertips began their steady, confident work against her body. "Even after you swore you would…" An early wave rose up and fell, her nipples beaded to aching points, his hot touch heightened by the nip of cold air.

"I'll be around you for as long as you'll have me." He spoke easily but his thumb rubbed lightly against her clit, and she drew her knee up, resting one heeled foot against the wall, allowing him easier access. In response, he pushed a finger in deep, curling it with expert dexterity.

A moan escaped her as her hips rocked with the rhythm of his hand on the sensitive folds of her sex and clit. She was slippery and hot and he was playing her like a skipping stone over a pond.

"Kiss me," she whispered as an orgasm built inside her with each stroke of his thumb and curl of his finger. "Kiss me on the mouth."

He nuzzled the crook of her neck. "Not until you come for me."

"But I need you to…" she whimpered, gyrating. He nipped at her ear and increased the pressure of his thumb, compelling a moan deep from within her diaphragm. She moved shamelessly now, her hair catching against the rough surface of the wall, her thighs clenching and un-clenching, little murmurs of *yes* escaping her lips every few seconds until they became more and more frequent and loud.

"I'm close," she murmured. "Almost there…"

He was on her without hesitation, breathing heavily against her ear. "I want you to come fast and hard for me, got that? Tell me you will. Say yes."

"So close…"

"Say it." His tone was stern.

"Yes."

"Yes, *what*?" Without removing his hand, he shifted his weight onto her, pushing her thighs wider with his hips, as he continued to work her inside and out. The hard press of his body propelled another wave, stronger this time and threatening to slip over.

She could barely get out the words. "Yes… I'm gonna…come for you…" And then everything inside her clenched hard, her pussy grasping his finger, her clit pulsating against his stroking thumb, her stomach muscles contracting, jaw tightening. She wrenched forward, all sound taken from her voice, and pressed her forehead against his chest. Then a strangled cry escaped her as her orgasm nearly peaked.

He leaned back, his free hand prying her chin up to his own. His tongue licked at the seam of her mouth. She tried to gain hold of reality while her orgasm released over her. When his tongue slipped past the barrier of her lips, she was hit hard with a wave of pleasure, her cries muffled by his mouth.

He pushed his lips against hers, closing the gap between them, tangling them together as her orgasm crested once more and then fell again, her entire body collapsing against the wall. A whimper died in her throat.

He broke away with a harsh breath and removed himself from inside her, but continued to lazily stroke her delicate folds with his thumb.

She was panting and tired but also fiending for his body.

"Carter." She tried to catch her breath, her chest rising and falling. "Carter…fuck me. Please? Against the wall…" Her eyes closed and the words came out as a strained whine. "Just do it. Do it now…"

There was a pause before he answered her but his voice sounded tired and ragged. "Not how I wanted our first time to go…but can't change fate."

At once, both their hands went for the zipper of his pants. She got there first, fumbling with the button and reaching in to grasp the heft of the huge erection tucked inside. He groaned as she stroked him, feeling the silky skin of his hot flesh slide up and down her hand, letting out her own moan as he in turn continued to stroke her, her dress riding high on her hips.

He was pushing a finger inside her again, lining up his hips between hers, his cock pressed against her belly, when suddenly he halted, body going still.

"What? What's wrong?" She wiped her hair from her eyes with her free hand. Her skin was damp with sweat.

He let his forehead fall against the wall at the side of her shoulder before letting out the words. "No condom."

"Shit." She released her grip, and he backed up, letting the hem of her dress fall. He tucked himself into his pants with a grimace. A gust of cool wind swirled between them.

She could still smell his skin and the scent of his cologne from his jacket. A puff of laughter left her lips. His hair was disheveled and a faded smear of her lipstick stained his mouth.

With her thumb, she reached up to wipe at the skin above his lips. "You have lipstick all over you." Unable to contain her rueful smile, she swept the errant hair at his forehead she'd noticed earlier, smoothing it off his face.

He smiled, clearly liking the touch. He wiped at his mouth with the back of his hand.

"Better?" he asked.

"Good enough." She laughed, but then sucked her teeth, letting out a sigh. "People will wonder where we are. We should head in."

He nodded, his face going serious. "Okay."

She knelt to grab her clutch. She'd have to fix her lipstick again too. The constant applying and reapplying was a full-time job.

"Talk more later?" she asked in a hopeful tone.

"Definitely."

She liked the way he said *definitely* as if they were a sure thing to him. As if he had no doubts in the world. A small smile remained on her lips as she wrestled with the clutch, fishing for the pocket mirror and lipstick Lucille had placed inside. In her clumsy post-orgasm state, the small silver bag slipped from her cold hands with a soft thud to the ground.

The contents splayed between their feet.

Their eyes rose to meet each other. They spotted it at the same time.

There it lay next to Perdie's lipstick and lip gloss, pocket mirror and credit card like a Christmas present under a tree: the shiny blue square wrapper of one single condom.

Lucille had slipped it in, bless her.

Perdie's lips parted. Carter's gaze smoldered.

"Against the wall," he ordered.

Chapter Eighteen

For once in her goddamned life, Perdita Stone did as she was fucking told. Her feet tracked backwards, one unsteady scrape at a time, until her back hit the chilled brick wall. She kept her eyes on Carter. Darkness glimmered, as he knelt to pick up the condom, tucked it into his pocket, and stalked over.

His arms came to either side of her shoulders, caging her. She helplessly arched towards him, and when his mouth dropped to hers in a wet, hot kiss, a hum vibrated in her throat. The hum expanded into a moan as his tongue licked against hers. Carter was the only man who could kiss her until her whole body felt soft and lax. She needed him to hold her upright or she would melt right into the ground.

As if by command, his hand traveled up the back of her dress, squeezed her ass and then yanked her thigh up around his waist, garnering a yelp.

His mouth went to her neck, tongue sliding around the taut skin in a messy figure eight. Her head rolled, eyelashes fluttered. "Jesus, you're good at this…"

"Wish I could get this off you." He breathed into her neck, giving the neckline of her dress a futile tug. Her breasts strained against the material, feeling heavy. Her nipples ached.

"I wish you could too…"

"Your tits are like one of the Seven Wonders of the World," he said, his hand rubbing hard, his mouth dipping down to tongue the beginning line of her cleavage. She would laugh at how cheesy he was if she wasn't so completely ruined. But then her pulse went wild as he continued. "I want to grab them, lick them, fuck them, come on them…"

"Jesus *Christ*…"

Then his mouth returned to hers. "But you asked for a fuck against a brick wall, and I'd be hard-pressed to turn you down so that's what you're going to get. But only this one time."

"Yes…yes…" Her hips undulated at his voice.

"Next time I take it as slow as I want. Strip off every piece of clothing on this body of yours and spend hours with my mouth all over every inch."

She let out another yelp as he yanked her even closer. Her breath stopped as he rubbed his clothed erection against her bare pussy, the protrusion stroking right on her clit, his hips rocking against hers in an obscene fashion. Both their eyes fixated on the juncture between them where their bodies met, hypnotized at the sight. It was a carnal thing to do, absolutely indecent. Perdie should be embarrassed, or mortified or shocked. But she wasn't. Painful want coursed through her. And he was awfully clean-cut for such a filthy, fucking, dirty, wicked scoundrel.

His voice strained when he spoke. "I can tell by how wet you are that you like that, baby. But I'm going to come in my pants if we don't get this show on the road…"

He slipped the condom out of his pocket and tore the shiny plastic open with his teeth. Then with one hand, he unzipped his pants, tugged on his cock until it sprang out, so close to her own bare pussy…

"You want this inside you?" His breath was ragged.

"So much."

"Say *please*, Bad Girl. Beg for my cock."

"Please…" Her words were nothing more than a whimper. She would've said anything in that moment. Her compliance was rewarded with a hard thrust as he pushed into her. She moaned. He was big, but lord knew she was ready for it. Then he stilled, buried to the hilt, the two of them catching their breaths.

"Move…please move…"

He leaned in to kiss her, hard and soft at once while he began to thrust in earnest. "Beg for it, baby," he murmured against her mouth. He kissed her again.

She jerked up and down the wall, the skin of her back shielded by his jacket, which was hanging limply from her shoulders.

"I want it. I want it so bad…" Whose desperate voice was that? That's right, *hers*.

"This?" He rocked his hips into her, pinning her to the wall.

She wrapped her other leg tightly around his waist. She was suspended with his hand beneath her ass, her arms clinging to his neck. *"Ah…"*

Another hard thrust. "Is this what you want?"

And again. So hard she could feel a pierce of pleasure in the back of her throat, the roof of her mouth, and behind her eyes.

He squeezed her breast, pushing and kneading des-

perately with the palm of his hand. "Tell me you like it."
His whisper tickled her ear.

But her brain was frazzled. She thought she might
be babbling.

"Tell me you like it or I'll take this cock away from
you, you hear me? Don't make me punish you for being
such a bad girl. Punish us both…"

His words were a haze in the ether. "I love it…oh
god…just…keep…god, *Carter*." She was almost weeping
now. Pleasure was welling up in her, emotions swirling
at the base of her belly like a deadly spell in a cauldron.

He leaned in against her neck. "I like it when you say
my name."

"Carter…" She was panting, bouncing, writhing on
his dick. His strong hands and arms held her in place.
God, he was strong. And she was weak, as weak willed
as they came.

Another hum vibrated in her throat when his hand
came to grab her breast, then traveled to her throat and
jaw, cupping her face. She closed her eyes.

"I'm right here, baby. I'm right here with you," he said.

She was so close she could feel the orgasm igniting
but she struggled. Stuck. She needed something to push
her over the edge, a harsh shove off the cliff. "Talk to
me," she panted. The rhythmic thrusts inside accentu-
ated each breath. "Say…something…dirty."

Carter was quiet for a moment, the only sound in the
air the wet slap of his body against hers. But when he
spoke his words were dark. "Flirting with another man
right in front of me…" Another collision between their
bodies. "When you wanted my big hard cock the whole
time…" He grunted. "Only a bad girl would do some-

thing like that. I should take this cock away from you… but I know you'd do anything for it."

"It's true… I did… I would… I'd do anything for it…"

"I know. I have you begging and pleading. What else can I get you to do?"

Pleasure roiled within her, his voice stoking the flames. She leaned forward and nipped at his lower lip, their mouths frantically coming together in a kiss. Carter's breath was hot against her. He broke away but she went in again, this time, biting harder.

A harsh, guttural sound sprang from his throat, punctuated by another deep, hard thrust inside her.

It was more than she could take.

"I'm close…" she whispered, the swell of an orgasm painfully threatening to unfurl.

"Me too." He caught her mouth with his, as his strokes quickened, grew errant, and aggressive. Her body bounced wildly on his, her head nearly slapping the brick, their lips struggling to remain in contact.

And then it hit from deep within. At first, it hurt. Like pain from a needle when it punctures the most sensitive part of flesh. It punctured something within. And then it blossomed. Blossomed into her belly like a match on a gas stove, setting her whole body aflame. She let out a long, helpless, gasping cry.

"You too…" she pleaded, between gasps. "You come too…"

Her back smacked the wall as Carter pushed into her and then froze, his eyes squeezed shut. His grunts coincided with his thrusts, topping off her orgasm, as they finally came down, panting and grasping.

When it was over, their bodies stilled, chests heaving. The sound of the city echoed in the hidden alcove.

His arm pressed against the wall, his head against his arms. His coat dangled from her shoulders, shielding her from the harsh scratch of brick.

"Oh my fucking god, Perdie," he panted, still inside her, rocking in and out leisurely until finally pulling away, a hiss between his teeth. She felt empty and cold when he released her.

He gently set her wobbling feet to earth. She wavered, steadying herself with the wall.

"How do you expect me to go back to that pointless fucking party after *that*? I'm only a mere mortal." He tugged off the condom with a wince, tossed it in a small waste receptacle in the corner, and tucked himself in. It should have been awkward, watching him in the aftermath of sex. But it wasn't. Not with him.

She shimmied down her dress, smoothed out her neckline, then flicked her hair behind her shoulders, attempting to pat the thick mane into complacency. But he grabbed her hand away with a dark glint in his eye and pressed it against the white of his shirt, hot skin seeping through onto her palm. She could feel the heavy tattoo of his heart.

"You're killing me," he said. "Killing me on the inside."

Perdie twisted her hand to envelop his, thumbing the ragged calluses and ridges on his palm. She brought his hand down between them and pried open his curled fingers to examine the scrapes inside. "Did your hands get scraped up from the wall?"

His thumb in return stroked a line in the center of her palm. "A little, but they're used to it."

"From what?"

"Mountain climbing. Well, wall climbing now. Not as many big rocks around here."

She examined his hand for a moment, the scraped swath of skin. "Why mountain climbing?"

"Because I'm an unstoppable force who needs to challenge an immovable object."

And in that second, his curious expression stole her mind, a thief in the night.

And then the unspeakable.

A burning wetness sprang to her eyes. *Tears?* She shuttered her gaze, a sob fighting to escape. All the feelings stirring inside her like wet slush—emotional, physical, spiritual—were about to wring out like a washcloth in a fist. Already wrenched and ragged, she sniffed futilely to ease the tightness.

Maybe it was the bite of cold wind on her face? Maybe it was the two drinks from before? Maybe it was that Mercury was in retrograde? But tears? Where did they come from? And worse, she suddenly had the urge to bury her face into his chest and let loose a sob like a child with a skinned knee.

She bit her lip hard, stealing another glimpse. *Fuck.* A mistake. And then…just like that…she cracked.

"Oh *shit*. Perdie. Are you crying?" In a flash his thumb swiped her cheek, smearing away the hot tear.

She tried to hide her face, but he cupped her jaw, eye to eye, searching.

"Oh god, oh god. I'm so sorry." He wrapped her in his arms and pulled her limp body to his warm chest. But the tears streamed like water from a busted spigot. Pathetic, muffled sobs. "Whatever it is, I'm sorry." He rocked her gently. "Was it the dirty talk? Too much? Too far? I'll never do it again. I swear it. God I'm an asshole."

She wiped at her face and choked, shaking against him. "No, not that. I like that... I wanted that..."

"Then what? Tell me what's wrong. What're you feeling?"

But how could she find words for a feeling she'd never experienced before? It was like describing her own internal organs. Like describing the very blood that coursed inside her veins. Where to start? She pulled away, snorting and huffing, but he squeezed her gently.

"Stay," he whispered, and when she lifted her chin, his mouth turned up into a gentle smile. He stroked the exposed skin of her upper back with his thumb. "Take a breath. In and out. Nice and slow. Talk to me."

She swallowed hard. Humiliated at her breakdown. But like the tears, the words spilled too. "I don't know what I'm doing with my life," she said, her voice gurgling and uneven. "I'm thirty-nine and I don't know what the *fuck* I'm doing with my life. What's the point of any of this? Like, what's the fucking point?"

He stroked her hair, smoothing it, soothing her. "I guess I haven't ever really considered it."

She nodded against his chest. "Sometimes it's all I think about." A sob burst through again, accented with a hiccup. "And... And... *I love Lucille so much.*"

He leaned away from the hug with a questioning frown. "Lucille? Your roommate?"

Perdie nodded, wiping her nose with her hand. "My best friend. I don't know, I love her so much."

He nodded. "I understand."

"I'm feeling a lot of things right now. I think maybe it's the weather. Or the holidays. Or... I'm a Scorpio, you know."

"No, I didn't know. I'm a Leo."

His answer made her laugh, pressed hard against his white shirt. With a start, she pushed away to see the wet, inky splotch of mascara on the otherwise pristine material.

"Oh no, your shirt. I've totally ruined it. Got makeup all over you." She futilely wiped at the spot with her fingertips, then dragged her thumb under her eyes, rubbing the wet excess of makeup. "Wait, here, put your coat on. It'll hide the stain."

But he merely shushed her, rocking her, his hand on her hair, her cheek to his chest. "Relax. I'll put it on when we go in. I'm not worried about my shirt. You burst into tears after we had sex against the wall. I have different priorities at the moment. Okay?"

She stiffened a bit, but then let out a big calming puff of air.

"Let's think about good things," he said. "Tell me why you love your friend Lucille so much."

"She put the condom in my clutch."

A deep rumble of a laugh vibrated his chest. "Wow. In that case, I should send her a thank-you card. Maybe a fruit basket."

"Oh god, no. She doesn't like fruit, only chocolate." Perdie sniffled.

"Okay, I'll get on the phone with a chocolatier."

She let out a giggle. Lucille might actually really like that. But then her face fell. She wiggled hard out of Carter's arms and knelt to gather her clutch. The contents had been left splayed on the ground. Too vulnerable.

"I need to leave." She was exhausted from the crying. The sex too. "I can't be here." She opened the mirror, regarding herself in the reflection. Her eyes were swollen but she'd already wiped away most of the mascara, and by some miracle of glue science the false eyelashes remained attached. She dabbed her face, and worked to smooth her hair. Fortunately, presentable again. Wet though, in lots of places.

He scratched the back of his neck and knelt down as well to retrieve his jacket from the ground. "Let me take you home."

She clicked the mirror shut and returned it to the clutch. "What about Aubrey?"

"We came in separate cars."

"Wait, what?"

"She's my real estate agent and my friend's sister. I was trying to help her network. It wasn't a date."

Perdie pursed her lips. "She's pretty."

He cocked his head. "And?"

"And nice."

The side of his lips curled. "I don't like nice."

She rolled her eyes but couldn't hide her smile. "You're a masochist."

He reached forward, his fingertips sliding behind her knee for a fleeting moment, forcing her to shiver. "And you're as sharp as a blade."

"An icicle, would you say?" Perdie laughed.

"Too hot for an icicle." He winked. His face was boyish, wolfish, and sexy all in one. She had never stood a chance in the first place, had she? *Fuckin' A.*

She closed her eyes and nodded. "Okay." She scratched at the skin on her arms. "Make sure it's all good with Aubrey though. I don't want her abandoned at this shitshow party. Then again, I don't think someone who looks like that probably spends too much time alone. But make sure she's safe."

He nodded, as if extracting a plan from his brain.

"We'll go inside. Slip into the bathroom, get straightened out. I'll text Ferris from there." He ran his hands through his hair and then down his neck. Once his jacket was on, he was right as rain. "Ready?"

"How do I look?" she asked.

His lids went heavy, the lights hazing behind him. "Like a goddamned dream." He rubbed his brow. "I'll tell Ferris I had an emergency. He's so coked out he won't care anyway."

Perdie let out a huff of a laugh at the uncharacteristically cynical statement. "Now you get how I see them. All right then. Game on, Pretty Boy."

An amused smirk crossed his face. "You talk like that and you're asking for round t—"

His words were cut off by the decompressing door, voices following. She recognized those voices. Color drained from her face.

Carter's expression was inscrutable. "Don't panic," he murmured.

And the echoing footsteps rounded the corner.

Chapter Nineteen

Don't. Freak. Out. We're two colleagues chillin' outside who certainly did not *fuck against a wall.*

The sound of chatting and laughter neared the corner, and faced with the dead end of the alcove, Perdie and Carter had no choice but to await their fate. The flush on Carter's skin could easily be explained by the crisp winter air, and his jacket was covering the splotch of tears and mascara. The way he looked like sex wrapped up in a penguin suit—well, there was no helping that. The only thing that could betray them now was Perdie's own awkward blunderings.

We're fucked.

Sophia was the first to appear, her hair in an afro and wearing a black satin dress with a deep vee and elbow-length gloves. *How did she even own those?*

Her husband, Paul, followed, a man with thick hair and puffed red cheeks, a cigar behind his ear. *She's too good for him.* Somehow Perdie could just tell. Cupped in his hands were several plastic shot glasses squeezed together, and he walked carefully so as not to spill the liquor.

They stopped short at the sight of Carter and Perdie. Jennifer bumped behind them, steadying herself with

Sophia's arm, her hulk of a husband, Owen, in a black tux bringing up the rear.

"Oh." Jennifer cocked her head, her row of *Breakfast at Tiffany's* pearls swaying against her sheath dress. "We were wondering where you were hiding, Perdita. Been searching all over for you." She tottered towards them, her gait swaying a bit on shiny black heels. She held a cigar between her index finger and thumb. "Saw you come in with Max earlier, then you—*poof*—disappeared like a ghost."

Perdie wished she could *poof* disappear from this moment but instead forced a smile. "Too many lawyers in one room creates a lot of hot air. Needed a breather."

Jennifer unsteadily rummaged into her black envelope clutch, dangling the cigar between her lips as she procured a lighter and flicked until it ignited. Her eyes shifted over to Carter as she pulled a drag. Then she passed it off to her husband. "Hold this for me, Owen." She leveled her gaze on them. "You too, Carter? Out for a breath of fresh?"

Carter smiled, crossing his arms, cool as a cucumber. "Me too, Jennifer." Of course Jennifer wouldn't dare challenge a superior.

Perdie's eyes darted frantically around the group. "We had to…um…bang out—" *Nope.* She cleared her throat. "*Work* out…the details of an argument I've been constructing." She bit her cheek as the corners of Carter's mouth twitched. "Two bores at a fun party, am I right? Also, Carter was saying he has to return to his *date* anyway."

Perdie raised her eyebrows, hoping he would get the hint and leave. The more separation between them in front of Jennifer and Sophia, the better.

Paul wandered over to a ledge with a huge potted

bush and arranged the plastic shot glasses in a row on the surface. "Yeah, dude. I saw her, blonde in the red dress? Lucky man."

"Oh, shut up, Paul," Sophia snapped. "Nobody asked you for your opinion."

"Hey, don't get pissed at me for making an observation, babe. You're just grumpy 'cuz you can't drink, but don't worry, I'll take a shot in your honor. I brought extra."

Sophia shook her head, exchanging a knowing glance with Jennifer. Perdie had not been invited into their friendship circle, and she wasn't doing herself any favors by fucking the boss.

Perdie elbowed Carter's side while Sophia and Paul's tiff distracted the others.

Carter rubbed his hands together. "Yep. Heading in, to see my *date*."

She refused to meet his gaze.

As he turned to leave, Sophia touched Carter's tuxedo jacket. He froze in place.

"Hey, there's something on your jacket…" She plucked a tiny white opalescent bead from the stark black material and held it out in front of him between her index and forefinger. "Huh. Looks like some kind of bead."

Perdie bit her cheek again *hard*, hoping to god the expression on her face wasn't giving her away.

Carter let out a huff, took the bead from Sophia, and fisted his hand into his pocket. "Holiday decorations…a hazard of the festivities, I guess." He nodded to the group and turned to leave. "I'll see you all inside."

Everyone was eerily quiet until the squeaking hinges indicated the door closing. Perdie had to stop herself from letting out a big sigh of relief.

She almost jumped at Jennifer's voice. "Actually, I'm glad he's gone. Sophia and I did want to talk with you about something important, Perdita. About some observations we've made recently at the firm."

She went cold at the words, but then her clutch vibrated. "Hold that thought. Gimme just a…" She yanked her phone out. There was one new message from Carter. She nibbled her lip as she read.

C: Meet me by the coat check. Making sure all is good with Aubrey.

"Something work related?" she asked Jennifer as she let her phone slip into the silk lining of her clutch. Her nervous swell ballooned. Sophia and Jennifer might very well be about to confront her about her relationship with Carter right here at a work party.

Wait. Did she even have a relationship with Carter?

Both Sophia and Jennifer fidgeted, uncomfortable. "Something like that…" Sophia said. "We've been discussing our current situation and we agree that there's an issue that might need to be addressed and resolved. It involves you."

Oh god. Quick. Confuse. Redirect. Look over there.

"Me? C'mon, Sophia, do we have to do this now? Don't be a buzzkill. I don't want to get tangled up in *more* work talk. Besides, I already have Carter working me to the bone." She almost winced at her choice of words. "How about tonight we prioritize the important stuff? Until we get back in the office. Paul, pass me one of those?" She gestured towards the ledge with the potted shrubbery.

"Hell yes." Paul handed her a shot.

Expectantly, Perdie held up the plastic cup in a toast. "Shots for the holidays, anyone?"

Jennifer pursed her lips and handed her cigar to her husband as she too accepted a shot from Paul. "Fine. I suppose it can wait. I didn't hire a babysitter so I could *not* party. But it *is* important. I'll shoot you a private meeting request later."

Sophia nodded. "The three of us need to sit down and talk." She waved off Paul's offer of alcohol with a wave of disgust. "Are you serious?"

Perdie was grateful that the redirection worked. For now. But it would give her time to devise a plan about Carter. She brought the rim of her cup to her lips, and the small touch of liquid burned her sensitive skin. *Tequila.* "Bottoms up."

Everyone but Sophia tilted their heads, downing the liquid. They each tossed their cups into the trash. Perdie let the warmth of the liquor wash over her insides as Owen and Paul discussed Clemson sports and Sophia fixed errant strands fallen from Jennifer's French twist.

Perdie slipped her phone from her clutch again.

P: Sorry, Pretty Boy.

There was no way Perdie and Carter could leave together now. They'd be absolutely suspicious. Guilty, as they were. And people were drunk, but they weren't drunk enough to forget juicy gossip.

P: Looks like we'll be staying awhile.

The next few hours flew by in a hazy blur against a backdrop of glitzy Christmas decorations and jazzy cover songs. The combination was having a euphoric effect on Perdie's psyche. Or maybe it was the orgasms. Or that she'd escaped a potential conversation of doom with her colleagues. Whatever the case, she was feeling the holiday joy.

She made the rounds, joining in each intermingling group of attorneys and staff, letting Max fill up her martini glass whenever spirits ran low, taking care to limit her proximity to Carter.

Emboldened by her drinks, she dropped in on a conversation with managing partner Minnie Martinson and Charles Joy, gleaning such useful tips as "work hard, play hard" and to "keep your head down." *Original.* She was proud of herself for sneaking into their orbit at all. Although, for being such successful people, they weren't very clever. But no stress. As long as she could keep her name on their brains, she could still have a shot at partner.

While she might have been avoiding Carter, Carter had not been avoiding her. She could easily catch his eye, even now when he was talking with Aubrey and Ferris and a few other senior attorneys, including one attorney's wife, Aisha Wakely, the founder of Lowcountry Pro Bono Access. Aisha wasn't a fan of these parties but she would show on occasion, attempting to recruit volunteer lawyers. But even while he was deep in a conversation with Aisha, he inclined his head, a secret message between the two of them. He was keeping tabs, and it sent a thrill down her drunken spine.

When she made the rounds all the way to Carter and Aubrey, Max in tow, she determined that she needed to make secret amends with Aubrey. The woman hadn't even known Perdie was sharpening her fangs before, and none of Perdie's feelings of jealousy were Aubrey's fault. Besides, she actually kind of liked the woman.

Perdie waved an unsteady finger in the air. "Look, Aubrey. You seem like a nice person, can I give you some advice?"

Aubrey's eyelids fluttered, but she smiled, as if unsure and potentially a little afraid of what Perdie might say. "When you say something like that it makes me nervous."

Perdie waved her hand in the air, dismissing Aubrey's nerves. "No, no, no, no. You'll thank me. I promise."

Aubrey shrugged. "Okay, what is it?"

"You're wearing the wrong shade of red." Perdie swallowed a hiccup.

Aubrey tilted her head. "Excuse me?"

Perdie gestured at Aubrey's red bandage dress. "Don't get me wrong. You're stunning. Like a wholesome Jessica Rabbit. But this shade of red is all wrong, baby girl. Too cool, too dark for your undertones. You need something warmer...brighter. *Then* you'll really sparkle." Perdie's eyes lit up at the thought. "Like a Christmas ornament. Here..." She fished inside her clutch for her phone, dismissing Carter's waiting message.

C: Anytime you're ready to leave Bad Girl...

Her eyes only flittered to him for a second before she did a quick search and held up her phone to Aubrey's face. She handed Aubrey her pocket mirror.

"See how this color on my phone screen is *so* much better against your face."

Aubrey examined the results in the mirror and nodded her head slowly. "Wow, I never did realize." She turned to Carter. "Carter, isn't Perdie such a riot?"

"*Riot*'s not the word I would use." His mouth tightened. "On second thought, maybe it is."

Perdie smiled innocently, tugging on the cuff of Max's dark blue sleeve. "Now, this guy has it right. I can't think of a better color or style on you than this blue and this tartan, Max." She nodded approvingly, patting the velvet material at his biceps, entirely aware that the interaction would irk Carter. She peeked beneath her falsies to see his jaw tick with tension.

Max feigned embarrassment, rubbing his beard. "Flatterer."

Perdie reached up to ruffle his hair. "You can tell the truth and flatter all in one."

Her phone vibrated again.

C: We done playing this game?

Perdie smirked as she raised her glass to her lips, the taste surprising her: *Jesus*, when had she switched to scotch? She let her mind wander as Aubrey and Max discussed the ins and outs of Manhattan real estate. She assessed the crowd, everyone louder than they should be, well into their sixth and seventh rounds of drinks, and some even sloppily dancing in front of the stage. It was finally the perfect time to slip away.

And so, with a pat on Max's arm, and mumbling *I'll be back* in her best *Terminator* impression, Perdie found herself tottering right out the dining hall, tumbler of scotch in hand.

Chapter Twenty

Rita had long abandoned the check-in table, and the only sound in the lobby was that of Perdie's high heels clacking against the hard marble floor. She retrieved her coat from the coat check, tugged the sash tight around her waist, and then leaned against a wall near the door. Waiting.

When Carter appeared, striding towards her like James Bond to a baccarat table, she examined her manicure nonchalantly, fake sipping her scotch. But she tripped on her heels attempting to cross one ankle over another. *Shit.* She straightened.

"Stalking me again?" she asked, feigning boredom.

He let out a low whistle. "You're wasted, Bad Girl."

She shrugged. "So what? It's a party."

He reached out and tucked a strand of her hair behind her ear, the gesture prompting her to face him. His eyes were green under the harsh lobby light. "Time to go home, don't you think?"

"You don't tell me what you do." She turned her head away. "Besides, everything's off between us. I'm *over* this." She sneaked a peek at him.

He chuckled. "Yeah, yeah. I've heard that about a million times before."

She bit back a laugh at her bluff being called out and cleared her throat. "But seriously. Jennifer and Sophia *know* something."

"Like what?"

Perdie stiffened. "They said they needed to talk to me."

"And?"

Perdie crossed her arms tight in front of her chest, attempting to balance her drink on the inside of her folded elbow. "*And* I told them to stop ruining a fun time. I wasn't about to get called out at a party. How awkward."

The corner of Carter's mouth twitched. "I think I need to help you with your fact-finding skills."

"Psh. Stop being so good at everything."

"You don't even know half the things I'm good at, yet." His eyes glimmered. *Agh.* Sometimes all she wanted to do was fight with him. "C'mon, let me take you home."

She huffed. "You're not the boss of me."

She was aware of her juvenile reaction, but a moment of silence passed as they both processed the meaning of her words.

Carter's face softened into a gentle smile, and he rubbed his hand up and down the white faux fur of her coat sleeve. "I promise I only have the interest of your health in mind. You're gonna have one hell of a hangover tomorrow, mark my words."

"Plus, you don't want me to flirt with Max anymore. Admit it." She jabbed at his shoulder with her index finger, but his hand caught her own and held it against his body.

Then his voice dropped low and soft as he leaned in near her ear. "Oh, I *definitely* don't want you to do that anymore."

Even with her coat wrapped tightly around her, goose bumps prickled all over her arms and neck. And just like that, her tumbler of scotch slipped from her free hand— *crash!*—and exploded into shards, amber liquid snaking a path on the marble floor. Carter yanked Perdie against his chest and jumped from the wreckage.

"Okay, yeah," she squeaked. "Maybe it's time to go." She wiggled her way out of his grasp. "But you're not coming in."

If he was disappointed, he didn't let on. Part of her wished he would.

"Doorstep delivery it is."

Carter located a Slippery When Wet sign tipped up near the lobby bathroom and moved it over Perdie's broken glass. He ushered her out the door, his hand grazing her lower back.

The temperature dropped in the late hours of the night, but now it was humid too, leaving her chilly and damp. She had to concentrate while walking, her feet smarting with every step on the cobblestone street. One wrong move and she might crack an ankle bone clean in two. "Where are we even going? Shouldn't we order a car?"

"I'm sober. Parked nearby." Carter's steps in comparison were smooth and steady. She admired his gorgeous profile through her haze.

"Shit." The tip of her heel snagged on an uneven stone. She tumbled as her foot slipped from the shoe. She grasped Carter's arm on her way to wiping out face-first.

"Whoa." He caught her by the elbow, helping her upright.

"Fucking heels," she muttered while disentangling.

"Why do you always wear them if they're so painful?" He waited next to her while she unsuccessfully used him as a balance bar and attempted to wiggle her swollen foot back into the shoe.

She gritted her teeth, giving up with only one shoe on, the other hanging in her hand, and limped down the freezing ground. "Oh my god, how do I explain this? Hold on, let me pull out my dissertation on European cultural beauty standards for women. It all began in the mid fifteen hundreds when Catherine de Medici— Hey!"

Perdie's reality shifted upside down as Carter knelt and hoisted her body over his shoulder, her arms and head dangling down his back and his hand squarely pressed on her ass.

Futility, she beat her fists against the muscle of his back. "Put me down, you brute."

She let out a yelp as his hand landed in a sturdy smack against her behind. "You're gonna break your goddamn ankle."

"I'm gonna break your goddamn back. Where are you taking me?" Her head was swimming a bit hanging up-side down.

But Carter walked with the ease of a man who didn't have an entire grown woman slung over his shoulder. "Relax. We're almost there."

He led them down a quiet street with a row of parked cars. Bowing, he gently slid Perdie to the ground. When she regained composure, her head was dizzy, and not just from the drinks. She stood lopsided, holding one shoe.

In front of her was a gleaming black sports car. Carter retrieved his key fob, prompting the car to beep softly.

He really was James Bond.

She inclined her chin. "I don't know what's worse, the big-ass SUV—"

"A *rental*."

"Or this tiny-ass *Speed Racer*, James Bond vehicle."

"It's a 911."

"Can I drive it?"

"I'd prefer to *Die Another Day.*"

"I didn't mean right *now.*"

He opened the door for her, and she folded into the vehicle. "'Go, Speed Racer, go,'" she sang quietly. The door shut next to her.

Carter revved the car to life, the engine roaring like a chainsaw. His hand enveloped the silver gear shifter, and Perdie stared in fascination when he maneuvered their way out of the tiny space and sped down the empty side street, eventually exiting the peninsula and merging onto the Ravenel Bridge.

Perdie zoned out, hypnotized by the structured white beams zooming past as Carter shifted gears smooth as butter. The boat lights twinkled over the murky waters of the harbor surrounding them.

"Did you have a good time tonight?" The sides of Carter's lips tugged upwards.

She groaned. "I'll let you know tomorrow morning."

"You want to see me in the morning?"

Perdie rolled her head on the headrest. "You always talk about these games we play, but you don't really like to play games at all, do you?"

He raised an eyebrow. "What do you mean?"

"You, like…" she paused, concentrating on her words "…say how you feel."

A slow smile spread over his face. "I'd grab your hand right now, if I didn't have to shift gears."

Perdie scrunched her nose. "Never met anyone like you."

"That a bad thing?"

"Magic 8 Ball says 'Reply hazy ask again later.'"

Carter chuckled. "And you say I'm weird."

"Sixty-nine, sixty-nine," she squealed as they arrived at Perdie's gated entrance.

Amusement glinted in his eyes, and he punched the code in. "Thanks, I hadn't forgotten."

But Perdie was developing a weird feeling in her chest. The stress, the party, the sex, and most importantly all that mixed-up liquor-drinking had caught up with her. When Carter pulled up in front of her building, she hastily unlatched her seat belt and practically tumbled out of the car.

"Hey, why don't you let me walk you upstairs?"

"No." She steadied herself with both hands over the top of the passenger window. "You'll make me cry again."

Carter squinted, confused. "Perdie, I don't under—"

But she was already hobbling up the stairs of her condo. She needed water. Yoga pants. Hell, underwear. And her head was spinning. The cold wind whipped around her.

When she got to her door, she leaned against the wooden railing by the stairs, giving Carter a big wave. "Bye," she called. His expression remained bewildered but he complied, peeling slowly out of her parking lot when she opened the front door.

She stepped into the empty, dark space, a few bulbs twinkling from the baseboards, and hit the lights. *That's right. Lucille was gone.* Nobody was home. Well, except for Bananas, thank god. She called for him, clapping against her thigh until the jingle of his collar broke through the silence in the house. He stretched long and yawned once near her feet, and she scooped him up, plopped down on the couch, and tugged a blanket on top of them.

"Bananas, you're not gonna believe what your mommy did," she mused absently as she stroked his head.

The wind was picking up pace and the trees were whirring a mournful howl. She hugged Bananas, suddenly wide awake.

Lucille was worried about Perdie being alone during the holidays for good reason. Namely, the paranoia that was brewing now.

Bam.

She jerked at a tree branch smacking against her window.

Bam. Bam. Bam.

She grabbed her phone, clutching it close as she typed.

P: Creepy noises outside. Freaking out.

Lucille: Oh god, it's not Hampton, is it? Set the house alarm!

Hampton? Perdie hadn't even considered the fact that Hampton could show up at any second. What would she do if he did? She'd signed up for self-defense classes once but then no-showed because of late nights at the office.

Perdie froze on the couch, her heart thumping erratically in her chest. *Twilight Zone.* Everything glared eerily. Nothing was safe. *Dammit*, why couldn't she sober up?

She picked up her phone again, squeezing hard. Was she really going to do this?

Carter arrived in ten minutes flat. At his quiet knock, she shuffled over, still in her dress and coat, Bananas nestled in her arms, blanket tossed over her head like Darth Maul. She yanked the door open.

Carter paused in the entryway. "Ah…what happened to you in the span of ten minutes?"

"Lucille's out of town, and I freaked myself out."

She moved aside. He padded through the door, inclining his head. "Makes perfect sense."

"Here, this way to the living room. You want anything to drink?" she asked over her shoulder. Carter shook his head, and they settled into the couch, his long legs outstretched on the worn leather. Perdie curled up on a cushion, still cocooned in her blanket. She let go of Bananas, whose grunty nose began working overtime to suss out the new person in the house. The instant calm of Carter's presence almost *alarmed* her.

"So, we're not going to mention the elephant in the room?" Carter gestured towards the fireplace. With his arm raised, the space on his lap was open for Bananas to crawl in and snuggle up.

"Oh, hello." Carter stroked the dog's round head, as Bananas let out a loud snoring-sigh.

A warm feeling washed over Perdie, but she shook her head, clearing her thoughts. "Sometimes I get anxious when I'm drunk. I know I ran out of your car but—"

A rumble of a laugh came from Carter's chest. "No, not that. *That*." He gestured towards the fireplace again, and Perdie squinted.

"*Oh*. Yeah, that's a painting we commissioned. It's not that uncommon in Charleston to hang family portraits."

The oil painting featuring Lucille, Perdie, and Bananas posed Renaissance style above the fireplace mantel had been there for so many years that Perdie didn't

even think twice about it anymore. It was simply a fixture of their lives.

Carter ran his hands through his hair, shaking his
head. "Now I know you're definitely the weird one of
the two of us. Although, it's nice to see the face of the
woman I'm so indebted to."

Perdie let the blanket fall from her head to her shoulders. "I have another favor to ask you."

"Go on."

She stood, shedding her blanket and coat to the
ground, and Bananas shuffled away, disgruntled by the
disruption. "Unzip my dress?" She reached behind herself to show him the zipper. "The zipper's hidden. Always sticks right by my hips."

With her body wedged between his legs, Carter's eyes
darkened.

He brought his hands to either side of her hips, squeezing the soft flesh, firm but restrained. "Trying to kill
me?" he asked, his voice weary.

"Hurrryyy, get me out of this thing."

The blunt tips of his fingers brushed against the bare
skin between her shoulder blades, pinching the small zipper. Visceral relief pummeled down her body as he pulled
the zipper, the material slackening at her breasts and
waist. He gave one quick yank when the zipper snagged
at the flare of her hips, and then she was free to strip off
the rest of her dress.

Before she could step away, Carter's fingertips caressed the vulnerable skin of her back, gliding up and
down. A small moan escaped her lips as he curled his
fingers, the callused tips lightly scratching. She swayed
on her feet.

"No bra either, huh?"

She grabbed his wrists and spun around, his mouth so close to her breasts he could almost be touching. His gaze roved over her.

Slowly she reached up to the left strap of her dress, letting it slip from her arm. She did the same with the right. The material dropped, exposing her breasts. Her hand clasped the dress below her bust line. His eyes closed briefly, like the vision caused him a moment of excruciating pain.

Her chest fell and rose harshly as she waited for him to touch her. Her eyelids shuttered. Her nipples beaded to aching points.

"Why aren't you doing anything?" she whispered.

Hot breath fanned over her skin at the press of his forehead against her sternum.

"Carter..."

Hands came to grip her waist and he craned his neck, chin resting against her. "You're drunk."

"I'm fine." She grasped his hand, using it to palm her breast. She bit her bottom lip at the tough flesh finally pressed against her own naked skin. With her hand covering his, she squeezed, his fingers retracting against her flesh. Torment flooded his eyes. The need for more. Her unruly body swayed from side to side.

Another strangled groan from Carter. His hand slipped away. "Later," he said. "Plenty of time later. Please, I'm begging you. Go put some clothes on before you kill me dead."

Perdie took an unsteady step back as she lifted the dress to her sternum. "*Ugh*, why do you have to be so..." Her hazy mind searched for the word. "*Good.* Damn you." And she stomped off to her bedroom to change.

When she returned, after donning her velvet-trimmed

silk robe, she tossed a shirt and pair of pajama pants at
Carter.

"Here. The T-shirt's mine, but the pants belong to
some guy Lucille used to hook up with. They should fit."

Carter undid the cuffs of his shirt, his bow tie hanging
loose around his neck in a short bumpy strip. She loved
him undone like that.

He held up the T-shirt. "Earth Girls Are Easy?"

She shrugged. "If you don't know that movie, I can't
help you, bucko."

He flipped the garment over his shoulder and pointed
to the snoring dog, who'd returned to his lap. "Thanks.
Although I don't think I'll be moving anytime soon."

Perdie bit back a smile at Bananas snoozing peacefully. "Good news, I shall offer you a reprieve." She collapsed on the couch, her eyes heavy as iron. Absently she
stroked the snoring dog's head. "He has to go out before
bed anyway. He's fifteen."

Perdie yawned big as her head fell against the back of
the couch. "Gotta grab his leash and put my shoes on…"
Another yawn overtook her.

A hand squeezed her knee. "I'll take Bananas out for
the night. Where's his leash?"

She pointed vaguely towards the door. "Hung up over
there."

The weight besides her shifted, and she cracked an
eye. Carter stood, gently placing Bananas on the floor.

"Okay…" she murmured. "But you gotta carry him up
and down those stairs. He has a bad back…"

Carter's voice…footsteps…the jingle of a collar…and
then…everything faded to black.

Chapter Twenty-One

"DASHING THROUGH THE SNOW!"

"What the fu—" Perdie awoke with a start, moaning at the ear-splitting music blaring over her living room speakers. Her nose pushed into the cushion of the couch, and her back pressed hard into the hot torso of the man behind her. *Oh*, and that wasn't the only thing pressed hard behind her.

"IN A ONE-HORSE OPEN SLEIGH!"

Carter's arms flexed around her rib cage, pulling her tighter against him. *"Agh..."* He grunted, burying his mouth in the hair at the dip of her neck. "Are we being haunted by the Ghost of Christmas Past?" His voice was hoarse and he had to shout over the cheerful music.

"O'ER THE FIELDS WE GO!"

With some effort, Perdie extricated an arm out of Carter's crushing embrace, his forearm slipping over her half-covered breast. She patted the edge of the end table until she landed on her phone.

"LAUGHING ALL THE WAY AH HA HA!"

Lucille, you asshole. Lucille had remote access to the stereo system in the condo. She rubbed one of her eyes to clear the blur, a false eyelash sticking to her index finger as she tried to focus on the screen, swiping to find the icon. A text from Lucille awaited her.

L: AHAHAHAHAHAHAHAHAHAHAHA

"Make it stop." Carter shook his head against her neck. *"BELLS ON BOB TAIL RI—"*
Silence fell over the room as Perdie tapped the right button. *Phew.* She let out a big exhale, her heart pounding from the startling wakeup. Her vision mostly cleared, which gave her a view of Carter's large hand covering her left breast, exposed from the loose opening of her robe.

Then her eyes slammed shut at the piercing throb at her temple. *Oh, that's right. Hangover of the millennium reporting for duty.*

"Carter…" Perdie strained against him but only succeeded in rubbing her ass on his dick.

He sucked in hard, palm squeezing.

She struggled again, and this time, his hips rocked into her slowly, a little moan escaping from her mouth despite herself. "Hey, I gotta…"

His hips were still moving, his erection still frictioning against the silky material.

"Stay…" His breath was harsh in her ear. "Mmm…"

The opposing forces of lust and nausea combined with her entrapment-induced panic. "Hey…let me…*ahhh*…so hungover…"

"I've got a cure for that hangover." He flipped her roughly in his arms, greedy lips pressing against her sternum where the material of her robe parted. He trailed kisses between the valley of her breasts towards her stomach.

She giggled, forgetting her ailments, but grabbed his hair before he could head lower. "Stop."

He blew a raspberry against the soft skin of her belly, pulling another peal of painful giggles from her.

"Agh, god, no, everything hurts."

His voice was muffled. "Lie back, and I'll make it all better…"

She walked her fingers from his hair to his neck, fisted the collar of his shirt, and yanked his face to hers. His hair was tousled and eyes dark and hooded. *Damn you, hangover.*

"The only cure is a hot shower. And weed. And maybe some coffee." Her fingers released his collar.

He strained on his elbows, hovering above, like he might snatch her into that crushing embrace of his. But instead he leaned close and planted a feather-soft kiss against the side of her eyebrow, his eyelashes tickling her skin.

He rolled away, dropping unceremoniously off the side of the couch with a thud, groan, and a laugh. At the commotion, Bananas unfurled himself from beneath the blanket on the opposite end of the couch and jumped to the floor to investigate.

"Agh. Bananas," Carter spit out, thrashing his head as the dog stepped all over his chest, his squished snout rooting around and grunting into Carter's face.

A silent laugh threatened to take over, and Perdie squeezed her eyes shut. "Stop making me laugh. It hurts my head."

Carter scooped Bananas into his chest, cradling him like a football, then rose to his feet. "I'll make the coffee. Go shower."

With a degree of pain, Perdie stood, yanking the sash of her robe closed. She let the backs of her knees press against the couch to steady her body and jutted her hip.

Her hair fell over one eye like a model. "Still think I look like a dream?" Her voice scratched.

He chuckled. "More like a sexy nightmare."

"Hey!" She smacked his biceps. Bananas let out a *whao-whao-whao*.

"What? I said *sexy*."

She headed to the bathroom. "There's an extra toothbrush in the linen closet. Upstairs hallway to the right."

Perdie leaned against the outside glass door of the shower as steam filled the air, letting her robe fall from her shoulders and pool on the floor by her feet. She took another pull from her vape, naked now, and already growing pleasantly fuzzy from the effects. Within a few minutes, the throbbing in her temples subsided and the nausea settled, leaving her contentedly warm, swallowed up in hot mist. She was lucky. Vaping didn't always work that way for her hangovers. *Hurray for small Christmas miracles*.

She set the apparatus on the sink counter and stepped under the hot stream of water. The scent of orange and vanilla wafted through the air. She dribbled the honey-like liquid onto her palm and massaged it deep into her scalp.

Once done, she zoned out, soothing water cascading down her head and face and body like one of those dome-shaped yard fountains.

As she lathered up another loofah, a quiet knock thumped the door. She froze. Carter hadn't actually seen her body before—only flashes, bits and pieces. A graze here, a grope there. A feel, a flick. And then there were those times when various body parts of his had been fully inside various parts of hers. But still, here she was, wet, hot, and in the buff.

"Yeah?" Her voice croaked.

The door cracked, and a cool gust of dry air billowed through. His form entered into blurry view. The dripping loofah in her hand slipped foamy soap down her chest. He yanked his shirt over his head and tossed it to the ground.

Holy fuck. She was about to see him naked too.

Then his thumbs stretched the elastic band at his waist and shoved the sweatpants down, and he kicked them to the side. She bit her lip in anticipation. She could practically feel the rough scratch of his fingertips against her slippery skin. Could feel her hands smoothing over the hard jut of his erection.

The shower door squeaked open. "Can I come in?"

She gulped as her brain processed all of him at once in hard, naked flesh. His body was long, lean but cut. Hair traveled neatly from above his erection to his belly button, leading to six-pack abs, then fanning out over his chest. His shoulders were broad and veins traveled up and down the bulges of his arms.

He was a hulking mass of muscle but he wasn't a brute as she had yelled the night before. And despite the beautifully masculine cut of his jaw, and the dark furrowed arch of his eyebrows, he wasn't a Pretty Boy either, as she liked to tease so much.

Nope. Carter Leplan was neither brute nor Pretty Boy: he was simply all man from head to toe.

"Well, you're already dressed for the occasion." She stepped aside so he could stand beneath the water.

"You've been in here for forty-five minutes."

Whoopsie daisies. High times.

She shivered as his hand found her skin. He swirled his index finger on the clinging foam, spreading it over the swell of her breast, trailing it to the edge of her pebbled nipple, barely grazing the delicate pinkness. The vibrant colors and black graphic lines that decorated his left arm and shoulder in dizzying, abstract patterns contrasted sharply against her own bare skin.

"Tell me about these," she said, following a thick banded line traveling up his arm. His skin was hot to the touch.

"I don't divulge that information until after the third date."

"Third date? You've been inside me."

"And don't forget it." He rolled his head on his neck as her nails grazed the corded muscles. "But I need more…"

"More…what?"

He grasped her hand with the loofah, scraped it to his chest, the same soapy trail gliding down his body until it reached the crisp hair above his cock. She let the loofah drop, her gaze dropping with it, and she filled her hand with his erection, eyes fixated on the hard protrusion. She fisted it with long, smooth strokes, squeezing at the head.

His head fell back. "I think about you all the time," he gasped.

"Think about me? Like wet and naked?" Another smooth stroke, up and down.

"That too. But mostly, I just think about you. Everything about you."

She rested her forehead against his chest before tipping her chin to see him. She continued the leisurely pumping. "How can you admit that so easily?"

His breath grew shallow; he brought his thumb to circle her nipple until he leaned in close, drawing the tip into his mouth with a hard suck. She gasped at the sensation, a spike of pleasure stabbing at her insides, the nipple leaving his mouth with a popping noise.

"How can I admit what?" His mouth traveled to her

other nipple, lavishing the tip with his tongue before giving it a long suck again, then lapped at the water on the tip. When he spoke, it was against the swell of her breast. "That you're the first thing on my mind in the morning and the last thing I think about before I close my eyes at night?"

"You're talking nonsense." Her fingernails scraped through the wet hair on his head. "I guess you're used to everyone instantly falling in love with you."

He unfolded, nuzzling her neck, tongue and lips meeting the skin there, trailing to the sensitive folds of her ears. "Not everyone."

She yelped as he pushed her against the cold, wet tile, forcing her to release her hold on his erection as he pinned her hands over her head, holding her hostage by her wrists. He bucked his hips into her belly.

She arched her back as his free hand groped her tits hard, the flesh spilling over in his palm, the ragged calluses on his skin rough against her sensitized nipples. His voice was harsh. "We aren't fucking against a wall again, Bad Girl, no matter how hard you try to tempt me. Not this time."

A whimper escaped her as he kneaded at her flesh.

"I'm taking you to the bedroom. I'm sitting you on my lap and I'm making you ride my dick until you forget your own name and can only remember mine. You got that?"

"Carter…"

"Ah, catching on quick. I knew you would." He kissed her hard on the mouth. He tasted clean, like peppermint toothpaste. But his kiss was dirty, tongue thrusting in and out without finesse or politeness, fucking her mouth with his own. It was primal, sloppy. She met it with her own thrusts until she moaned.

The stream of water ended abruptly as he reached behind to pull the faucet handle. They were both wet and dripping when his hands jostled beneath her, cupping her ass, and hoisting her up, prompting her to wrap her arms around his neck and legs around his waist, hanging on for dear life. Frantically, he found her mouth, kissing her as he carried her out.

"Wrong way!" she yelled.

He about-faced, kicking the door open.

They landed on the bed together, Carter's back against the headboard, the mattress creaking beneath them, her legs straddling his hips, and the heat of his cock pulsating between them.

"Condoms?" he asked. She nodded to the nightstand. Reaching over, he slid open the drawer rummaging inside. He busied his other hand with her clit, collecting the moisture from her soaked pussy and rubbing it all around the sensitive bud.

Instead of a condom, his hand emerged with a silver cylindrical object. "Well, hello, old friend." Her silver bullet.

Her eyes drooped from his dizzying strokes, but she managed to pant out the words. "That's not even the good one…"

He flipped the small switch, the familiar buzz in her ears. "But we have such fond memories together…"

She shook her head. "Don't touch me with that…so close already…the second you shove…your cock in me I'll pop…" She swallowed thickly, biting her lip as her eyes rolled back in her head. His thumb pressed down in the slick moisture at the entrance of her pussy.

"Oh, you better not, Bad Girl." She moaned when he leaned forward to nip at her breasts.

Without mercy, Carter replaced the stroking of his hand with the vibrator, rubbing lightly against her.

The vibration shot from her clit and to her belly button. She groaned.

"Hold this," he said, grasping her limp hand and pressing it to the toy.

Her pussy ached so bad she almost wept. Her words breathless. "Carter, no... I'm gonna... Carter... I can't..."

"It wasn't a request." With his hand still on hers, he increased the pressure, making her squirm. He clicked the frequency up a notch. She let out a deep cry but his commanding voice silenced her. "And you better use it like you mean it. Rub that clit like you'll die if you don't."

She emitted sharp whimpers as she rubbed the vibrator to her sensitive skin, causing her body to jerk and spasm involuntarily. She didn't want to come yet—*dear god don't come yet*—not until she could feel him wedged deep inside of her. Torturously, she fought to keep from rolling her hips against the force of the vibration. She was practically weeping from it.

He was a cruel, evil man. She might even hate him.

His cock rested in between them, jutting upright. It took everything within her not to rub against it. With his teeth, he ripped open the condom wrapper, tossing it to the floor. She hadn't even noticed he'd procured one, couldn't concentrate anyway. Her eyes were heavy as he rolled the tight rubber down his engorged cock.

"Inside me. Want it *inside me*." As usual, she was desperate. Her hips lifted, fitting her opening against the head, the vibrator nearly slipping from her hand.

"Don't you dare let that vibrator drop from that swollen little clit of yours, Bad Girl. You'll make me very, very angry if you do."

With a swallow, she held on to it, short piercing sensations shooting from her clit throughout her body. And finally, she sank down, slowly enveloping the crown of his dick, her pussy stretching to make room, ready to accommodate anything he wanted from her. Anything at all.

She wanted to ease him inside but he grasped her hips and wrenched her all the way, making them both groan on impact. Once buried to the hilt, he gripped her hips; he held her in place there, unmoving. She couldn't help but peer down, her vision a blur. His eyes were lost in the heat of their moment, dark and stormy. His hands roamed up her stomach and to her tits, squeezing, holding her upright.

"Ride it."

Her eyes rolled back in her head and her whole body wavered as he jerked her with his hips. Like a marionette doll held up by invisible strings. On a whimpering inhale, she rolled her hips, his cock buried, the vibrator shooting jolts of pleasure to her appendages. She was boneless as she worked herself up and down on him, both running towards and away from the orgasm that ached and boiled within her.

He leaned up, teeth pressed to her ear. "Yes, you're being a very good girl bouncing on my cock, let's see if I can't make you bounce even more." He bucked his hips again, their bodies thrashing together wildly, her tits jiggling near his face. He slapped one lightly, sending a shock down through her then did the same to the other. "Keep those big tits of yours right where I can see them."

When he drew in her left nipple with a strong suck, a deep long moan ripped from her chest "Oh no, Carter, it's happening. It's…it's…" Bouncing with the thrusts of his hips, she came until she almost couldn't feel anything at all anymore.

"Oh fuck. You're so fucking wet, all over me. Coming so hard." He let out a strained gasp of air, his back taut like a bow. "Gonna come…come inside you…" His hands came to her hips in a vice grip, as he bucked wildly into her. "Take it, Bad Girl. It's all yours. It's all for you."

The vibrator dropped from her hand, rolling to the side, but even so, another orgasm swirled in her and threatened to break through her already busted barriers. The Kool-Aid Man of orgasms. The precipice of a giggle threatened but they were both coming now, coming together like how it happened in the movies. Two bodies straining against one another, falling without a parachute, not knowing where they might land.

When it was all over, she toppled, her wet hair fanned over his shoulder. They were breathless, sticky. He ran his fingertips from her hips up towards the middle of her back making her shiver and then came to cup either side of her jaw with his palms.

Their eyes met, chests heaving. Perdie didn't know what to say, feelings leaked out from inside of her like a half-cracked can of coke. Orgasms with him always hurt a little bit. He wanted so much of her. Everything.

Her jaw dropped open, the words almost there. She had to say something.

She cleared her throat. "I think—"

"JINGLE BELLS JINGLE BELLS JINGLE ALL THE WAY!"

The music blared throughout the house. She fell on him, laughing against his chest as he wrapped his arms around her in a tight embrace, and she let the music play.

* * *

Carter rubbed the side of his face and neck with a towel, then hung it up on the hook inside Perdie's door before stabbing his legs back into the sweatpants. The pants fit him well, slung low across his hips, highlighting the carved vee of muscle flanking his abs. Perdie dressed in an oversized cashmere sweater that fell to her midthigh, pairing it with fleece-lined knee socks.

She stood in the doorway of her bedroom, admiring him. He scratched his knuckles over his flexed abdomen, then gave a smile when he noticed he was being watched. She openly gawked as she pulled a hit off her vape.

She was comfortable in her half-dressed state, a little high again from the weed, and a lot high from the orgasm. Her body thrummed. Also, she'd cranked the heat in her condo to a balmy seventy-six. She hadn't so much as peeked out the window but so far the day had proven eventful.

Carter padded out past her, planting a kiss on top of her head. "Breakfast?" he called over her shoulder.

She pivoted on the ball of her foot to follow. "You cook?"

"Best I got is scrambled eggs. I can do a pickup?"

Instantly, Perdie's brain shifted into high gear. "Yes, there's a French place across the street. Let's do the chocolate croissants, pan bagnat, banana and Nutella crepes, half a quiche au fromage... *Oh.* Or maybe a quiche lorraine. You know what? Dealer's choice. I'm not picky. The croque madame. And some macarons too. *And* macaroons, the coconut thingies. You have to do both. Always do both. They aren't the same thing, you know?"

"Uh-huh, uh-huh, and what should I order?" he deadpanned.

She tapped his chest, thinking. "Wait one second." She ran upstairs to Lucille's room and then scurried back down and pushed a shirt into Carter's abdomen. "Here. Take this sweatshirt. You'll get cold."

"I don't think a sweatshirt of yours will fit me."

"Nah, it belonged to Lucille's dad. He's huge."

"She sure has a lot of clothing artifacts."

Perdie rolled her eyes. "Oh, Pretty Boy, you have no idea the kinds of artifacts Lucille collects."

Carter pushed against the front door, the wood scraping hard against the slats of her porch. "Whoa…"

"What?"

"We might have to do some cooking after all."

"What do you mean? Oh, ugh." Perdie peeked around Carter, the cold air nipping at her naked thighs, hands, and face. She hadn't seen anything like it in well over a decade. The entire parking lot was covered in snow. Not covered, *buried*. Charleston was not a city that prepared for snow. Everything, *everything*, would be shut down.

"We're snowed in." Her voice was a whisper. "First one room, one bed." Perdie shoved her hands in her hair. "Now we're snowed in." She spun around. "Do you know what's happening here? Do you understand the gravity of our situation?"

"It's just snow. It'll melt."

"No. It's not just snow. It's happening. The gods are conspiring." Her head dropped back as if she were conversing with the gods.

Carter's eyebrows knitted together but he followed her gaze up to the blank white ceiling. "Oh, wow, you're high."

Her face grew solemn as she clasped either side of his

face, the stubble of his jaw scratching her palms. "Yes. Very." She nodded.

"All right, I'm sold. Hand it over."

She procured the vape from the leg of her sock and plopped it into his palm. "Time to really have some fun, Pretty Boy."

Chapter Twenty-Two

Carter's dick was shoved so far down Perdie's throat it may as well have been a throat swab, and yet she dove for more, straining with alacrity to reach the root.

"Jesus, *fuck*…" Carter leaned against the front doorframe, chest bare, sweatshirt tossed over his left shoulder, borrowed sweatpants pulled around his thighs. Perdie knelt before him, her tongue and throat working in tandem, her nails digging into the backs of his hamstrings. She was determined to get him all the way down, but his enormous dick was proving a worthy adversary.

Ten minutes earlier, they'd been happily debating their breakfast options when the urge to suck Carter's cock overwhelmed her. He was just standing there, running his hand over his hair, in that absent way of his, telling a story about how his mother used to make fried peanut butter and jelly sandwiches, when it occurred to her that if she wanted to reach out and squeeze his biceps, then run her hands up and down the ink decorating his arm, she could. In fact, he wanted her to. He'd made that clear. And there was no one here to stop her from doing it: no work colleagues, no bosses, no roommates. He was *here*. For *her*. To touch. If she wanted.

An unfamiliar primal urge to stake out a claim on

him crept over her. Until the only thing she could think about was pulling the heft out of his pants and running her tongue up and down the shaft until it glistened like a lollipop. *Phew.* Her mouth watered.

She worried her lower lip between the cage of her teeth and tongue, until he stopped midsentence, the corners of his mouth twitched up. "What? What's got you so distracted?"

His smile faltered a bit when, with lead for legs, she stepped close to him so they were mere inches apart, her hips tilted into his. Her hand tingled as she let it slide up his naked chest, then she pulled at the nape of his neck, bringing his mouth to hers in a slow kiss, her tongue sliding over his in a wet flick.

When she broke away he leaned in towards her to recapture her mouth, but she craned her head out of reach.

They froze in that position. A smile played on his lips. "What was that for?"

"I—" The heat in her cheeks rose, and her eyebrows knitted together as if she were coming to terms with the idea. "I want to give you a blowjob."

He straightened and choked back a cough, running his hand down his mouth. "Is that right?"

She dropped to her knees in front of him, and his stomach muscles contracted. Her index finger hooked into the elastic at his waistband, pulling on the material enough to expose the bottom of his happy trail. She raised her gaze for permission. "Yes?"

His eyes went wide, almost as if he were in disbelief. "Like I would ever turn down an offer like that, Bad Girl."

At first, when Perdie brought the crown to her lips, daubing it with her tongue, Carter was hesitant, tangling his hand in her hair, but touching her as if she were as delicate as a glass ornament.

But Perdie didn't want gentle, and she certainly wasn't delicate. After licking up and down the shaft, wetting it until it was slippery all over, she'd begun to stroke him aggressively, twisting both hands at the root of his erection while her mouth closed around him, her head working up and down the head and shaft.

Within minutes, Carter's hips were thrusting brutally into her mouth, her throat humming, her jaw sore but still trying to take down more, eventually using her hands as leverage against his body to take in more of his length.

"God, who knew you could suck a cock like that…" he gritted through clenched teeth.

That possessive feeling overwhelmed her again. *Mine.* Her hand came to cup his balls, rolling them in her palm, and his head dropped back a hiss of air escaping him. "Not gonna last very long…" He groaned with a thrust. "Oh fuck, are you touching yourself?"

"Uh-huh." She nodded, mouth full, as she worked one hand beneath the elastic of her silky modal boy shorts.

"Ah, that's so hot…yes…yes…" He was panting now, thrusts becoming more erratic by the second.

Her eyes closed and her moan vibrated around his dick as his fingers reached down to cup one of her breasts, letting his thumb flick the sensitized nipple. Her cheeks hollowed as she bobbed up and down, everything wet and hot and slippery.

"You want it? You want to swallow it down?"

"Mmm-hmm…" She hummed, eyes wide as she nodded up at him. Her fingers worked in a furious circle against her own clit. She was on the edge.

And she did want to swallow him up whole. Take every last drop.

Carter's stomach muscles contracted and he let out sharp puffs of air. Without thinking, she grasped the base of his cock again with her free hand, holding it steady so she could continue to work him as his culmination neared.

"I'm coming…oh god…" The veins in his neck bulged, his words were disjointed.

Perdie held on for dear life as his hips jolted and then the hot jet of semen pumped out of him and down her throat. It was frantic, messy, and hot. She moaned as she swallowed, lurching on her knees as her own orgasm jerked and twitched through her body like little electric pulses.

When it was over, she let him fall from her mouth, her whole body slumping over on the floor, then falling flat like a starfish. Totally spent, washed up to shore.

He yanked up his pants, tucking his wet cock beneath the elastic with a wince and then slid down the wall until he was sitting, knees drawn. "What the…what the fuck was…" He panted.

She let out a strangled laugh. "That was my holiday spirit, I think."

With some effort, she dragged herself to her elbows and crawled over to sit next to him, rubbing her mouth with the bottom of her shirt. His head flopped, eyes still glassy. A lock of hair fell to his eyebrow, which Perdie toyed with between her index finger and thumb before smoothing it over with the rest of his hair. His lids drooped from the simple caress.

"You're a multi-talented woman…" he murmured.

"Hey, Carter."

"Yeah?" His voice was hoarse.

She was searching that little quarter of blue in his eye now, that little cerulean patch that stood out from the rest of the hazelly green. *Damn.* He seemed vulnerable after what she'd done to him. Another surge of possessiveness shot through her. She cleared her throat. "What's your favorite color?"

Warmth crossed his features as a slow smile spread over his face. "I like them all."

"But if you had to pick one."

"If I had to pick one…" His finger flicked up the hem of her shirt, pinning it at her sternum, and he ducked down, drawing the tip of her breast in for a quick suck. "I'd pick the pink color of your nipples."

"Hey. I'm serious." She pushed his head away, yanking the oversized sweater down to her thighs. "Try again."

His eyes glimmered as he settled back against the wall. "You want my *second*-favorite color then? Maybe a different shade of pink somewhere else on your body. Fine, fine. Blue. Like the blue in my eyes that you love staring at so much."

"It's hypnotizing. I can't look away."

He laced his fingers with hers, squeezing her hand. "My birth mother has hazel eyes. But my other mother, the judge, she's the one with the blue. And that little spot is all her even though we don't share genetics. I like to think she argued her way into my biological makeup anyway. Wanting to make her proverbial and literal mark."

She elbowed him gently. "You're a momma's boy."

"Twice over." With her hand in his grasp, he pulled her in against his chest, their stretched-out legs now intertwined. She scraped her big toe over the arch of his foot, fascinated by all of the close-up details of his body she was privy to.

"Ask more," he said, smashing his face against her hair, the heat of his breath sweeping a prickle down the curve of her neck.

"Okay, Pretty Boy. How'd you get to be so successful?"

"Oh, come on. That's a boring one." He shrugged, pulling away so she could rest her head on his shoulder. "Luck. Environment. Genetics. Privilege of all kinds."

"Well, the pretty privilege is certainly a factor. Everyone likes you. And everyone likes to look at you. How many questions do I get? One more?"

"For you? A hundred. A hundred thousand."

"Hmm. A mere hundred thousand. I better be deliberate, then. You know, when we first met I thought you were some kind of fuckboy."

He turned his head towards her, eyebrows raised. "So I gathered. But no longer?"

"The way you're open with your feelings…it feels like a ploy. It's freakish. But now I've come around on the idea that it's—*gasp*—authentic."

"It's freakish to say how you feel?"

She nodded. "Radical even. Didn't you ever learn how to hide your feelings to fit in? Didn't anyone ever…like… make fun of you growing up for being too vulnerable?"

He scratched his head. "Not really."

"Not even an awkward phase?"

Carter laughed. "You'll roll your eyes at this, but I modeled as a kid. Catalogue stuff, did a few commercials and whatever. But no one ever bullied me for it. By the time I hit my teens, I was more interested in surfing and getting into an Ivy League."

"Oh yeah, you're so lucky no one ever bullied you for modeling. Surfing. And Ivy League dreams." She shook her head. "It's a good thing my mother lost all my childhood pictures in a flood five years ago."

"That's...incredibly sad."

Perdie shrugged. "To you, maybe. I'm not sentimental. Some pictures are best kept locked away in your gray matter."

"But your entire childhood?"

"I was a miserable kid. Teeth all crooked, chubby. Disagreeable...*always* getting in trouble for mouthing off to some kind of authority figure. My mother wasn't the most present person in the world. Well, an understatement. There were rare times when she could be like a best friend or a cool big sister. Ice cream for breakfast, liquor when I was a teen, that kind of shit. Let me run free practically. But a lot of the time she was checked out. Or drunk. Or both. She wasn't really committed to anything, including me. I don't blame her for it, I guess. *Immature parenting*, you might call it. I think I read that in a book once." Perdie smirked. "Therefore...ergo...henceforth... some things are safer left in the vault..."

He pressed a kiss against her temple. "You deserve better."

"I found better. I made my own family."

He gestured in the direction of the living room where the painting hung. "Lucille?"

Memories flitted across Perdie's mind. "We met in high school. Lucille was a weird art kid, and I was a total loner. She was my only friend and her family took care of me when my mother didn't. Or couldn't. A real Daria/Jane combo."

"What's Daria/Jane?"

She let out a laugh. "How could I forget you're younger than me? Still, this is a reference you should know. Required education. We can watch it later."

"Ask me more."

She smiled at his insistence. For a man with A+ dirty talk in bed, there was something so pure about him in this moment. "What's something you've always wanted to do that you've never told anyone?"

"Something I've never told anyone? Not exactly a secret, but I don't usually talk about it."

Perdie gestured expectantly. "Well?"

"Climb Denali."

"The fucking mountain?" She snapped her fingers. "Wait, you mentioned that our first night together. But *why*?"

"Unstoppable force...unmovable object..." He shrugged. "This will come as a surprise to you, but I'm something of a people pleaser."

Perdie clutched at her sternum, in mock surprise.

He chuckled. "I spent so much time trying to please my parents with all my accomplishments, I think I forgot to do anything fun. They would freak out at the idea."

Perdie couldn't fathom her own mother caring that much about Perdie's safety. "Ahhh… I see. But nothing's actually stopping you. You're a grown man, you can do what you want."

"Even if that were true, there's still the eighty-hour work weeks, and the new partnership position I took all the way out on the East Coast…and a certain person who seems to be taking up quite a lot of my mental capacity…"

Perdie fiddled with the ends of her hair. "Well, we don't always get to follow *all* our dreams."

Carter smiled affably. "Suppose not. Dreams are just that, after all."

She peeked up from beneath her lashes. "Ever had your heart broken?"

His thumb brushed at the sensitive skin of her wrist. "Most of my breakups have been amicable. I had a serious girlfriend in college but we ended things when I moved back to San Francisco."

"*Amicable* means you've always done the dumping. How inexperienced."

"What about me says *inexperienced*?"

"I mean when it comes to heartache."

Carter rubbed the scruff on his chin. "Huh, I never really thought about it like that."

"Imagine not ever having to worry you'll get your heart broken. That's what I call a fantasy world. I always assume it's inevitable. Misery lurking around every corner."

"You a heartbreak expert, then?"

Perdie scoffed. "Expert? I'm the *queen*. Queen of the Dumped. First time was when I was nineteen. That's when I got the tattoo." She twisted around, lifting her shirt to show him the purple-and-yellow flower. "It was meant to symbolize freedom and beauty."

He leaned over for the view. "Right, right. Of course."

She yanked the shirt down again and adjusted herself against him. "Next time at twenty-three. Then again at twenty-seven, three times with the same guy if you can believe it. He kept convincing me to come back only to dump me again. He was a pastry chef, so you can understand my dilemma. Hell, Lucille made me sign a notarized contract to prevent a fourth go-around. And the last time at thirty-two. Ever since then, I've kept my heart out of the deal. Or maybe I've lost the key to it. That would be on brand, at least. It gets old after a while, you know? Lucille and I can live together forever without anybody else, and I'm just fine with that. Why risk what you don't want to lose?"

At that, Carter's face was thoughtful. "Hmph. And are any of those terms up for renegotiation?"

The jingle of Bananas's collar grew audible from the hallway. The light clacks of nails neared.

"He's gotta go out," Perdie murmured. She rolled to her feet, Carter's hand squeezing hers before letting go.

Chapter Twenty-Three

Rain boots were the wrong choice to wear out in snow, but Perdie didn't have any other kind of inclement weather gear. So, she made do with the shiny black knee-highs, freezing snow particles leaking over the edge against her bare shins.

Luckily, Bananas, sun worshipper extraordinaire, was ready to haul ass back into the warmth of her condo. Perdie caught him by the backside. "No stairs for you, old guy." She scooped him up and trudged through the foot of snow piled onto the outdoor staircase. Luckily the overhang in front of her front door had limited the snowdrift.

She waffled outside for a minute, shivering. She had to level with herself. She was existing in a dream state, a mystical, snowy dream state. And it wasn't just the weed. Getting snowed in had inoculated her against worries about work and worries about her relationship with Carter. Like they were the only two people in the world. And because of that, she'd let her guard down. A dangerous thing to do.

But addictive.

She pushed the door open, and after setting Bananas gently on the floor, the little dog took off running towards Carter.

Carter knelt to scratch the dog's head, distracted as he held his phone to his ear. "Ma… I'll be fine, I promise. It's *one* holiday. There's no way I'll be getting on a plane tonight. Besides, I have a deposition in San Francisco two weeks from now. You can wait two weeks. And don't save me any fruitcake. I still won't eat it."

He straightened up and inclined his head to Perdie, giving her a wink as she hung Bananas's leash on the hook by the door. *Two weeks.* She was supposed to go on that San Francisco trip as well. A mild panic overtook her, but she clamped it down.

Seeing her frozen at the door, Carter padded over, chatting easily on the phone. He was wearing the sweatshirt now, the one that belonged to Lucille's dad. Of course, it was a Knox Family Christmas sweatshirt, this one with a nineties-style puff-painted Christmas tree. Perdie bit her lip so she didn't laugh.

Carter leaned the phone against his cheek and shoulder, then rubbed up and down the faux fur sleeves of the coat she'd thrown on, then he stripped her of it and hung it up on the coatrack next to the door. He caught her hand, bringing her fingertips to his lips in a silent kiss.

"Uh-huh, yeah, I know. I'll make the gallery showing. That's when? Easter? Plenty of time."

His eyes glimmered as he released her, and then his hand snaked behind her waist, yanking her towards him, their pelvises pressed tightly together. She was so close, she could hear the voice on the other end of the phone, although she still couldn't make out the words.

"All right, Ma. I gotta go. Sorry about Christmas." He winked again at Perdie. Perdie's eyes narrowed.

Carter's mother apparently wasn't ready to give up the

conversation because he gave a rueful smile as he continued to affirm her on the line.

"Yes, yes, yes…" He rolled his eyes good-naturedly. "Tell her I'll be there. Okay."

For a brief moment, he caught Perdie's eye. "I love you too. Talk later."

He hung up the phone, and a moment of silence drifted between them until she spoke, her voice creaking. "You were going back to San Francisco for Christmas?"

"Not much to do about it now. The airport's shut down."

She pulled out of his embrace and stalked over to the kitchen. He followed closely, Bananas trotting behind him. "I bet the snow will melt soon enough. You could probably drive out by tomorrow. It's not like you have to stay here with me or anything."

Opening a cabinet, she rummaged around for her coffee mug, the Will Provide Legal Advice for Tacos one, but all she could find was Lucille's ugly Garfield mug.

"If you want me to leave, you might have to wait a day or two. Or make me sleep out in a snowbank." Carter's voice sounded light but serious at the same time.

She whirled around. "Need coffee."

He gestured towards the pot brewed on the counter. *Oh, that's right.* He had made coffee earlier, hadn't he? She swished by him, grabbed the pot, and poured it in her least favorite mug. She sipped the lukewarm liquid. *Fine. That's totally fine.*

Carter leaned against the counter next to her, one ankle hitched over another. She avoided eye contact, lest his puffy-paint Christmas tree shirt lessen her sudden ire.

"You seem angry." He lifted an eyebrow, curious.

Perdie swigged the coffee, then let it bump down

on the counter before hastily picking it up again. She plopped down at the kitchen table and fiddled with the poinsettia sitting there. "I'm not mad… You were going to spend Christmas with your *family*, like your actual family. And instead you're stuck here with me. A colleague you screwed last night. And you probably want to get the hell out of here, but you're too nice to say anything because you know we're trapped." She stared at her coffee mug.

Carter let out a low whistle, which made her eyes up. "Wow." He pulled out a chair and sat down next to her.

She scrunched her nose when he grabbed the coffee out of her hand and took a sip.

"*Ugh*, that's cold." He set the mug down and took her hands in his. "Perdie. Have you lost your fucking mind?" he asked it so deadpan, that a laugh cracked through her icy exterior.

"What!" She snatched her hands away and crossed her arms like a petulant child. "Don't tell me you're not disappointed about being away from your family for Christmas and instead having to hang out with some hookup for potentially days on end depending on when this snow clears up. This is Charleston, we don't have the technology for *snow*."

He winced a bit and his hand scratched his forehead. "Sometimes I can't tell if you're being obtuse purposely or accidentally."

She glared. "Um, *rude*."

He chuckled. Then he pried her hands from their tuck within her folded arms. Again, he held them across the table. His voice was steady. "I'm a thirty-two-year-old man. I don't need to run to my childhood home for holidays. At any rate, I'd rather be with you, right here, right now, than back in San Francisco. Or back at my place. Or any other possible place. *This* is where I would choose to be either way. I happened to have gotten lucky that you can't kick me out." With a wink, he released her hands and leaned back.

Her jaw dropped but then she closed her eyes for a moment, collecting herself. "I want you here too."

"Good, then we agree. We both want to be here together."

"Even if it's the holidays and it's kind of weird for us to be spending them together after only knowing each other for a relatively short period of time?"

He let out a puff of a laugh. "Sure, even if. *Especially* if."

She fiddled with the handle of her mug. "Do you want to watch TV and eat cereal on the couch?"

"Can we make out later?"

At first, she feigned offense. But as she stood to leave, she glanced over her shoulder. "Obviously."

A handful of leftover Froot Loops soaked in two bowls resting on the end table of the living room as Perdie and Carter lay cocooned together under a blanket, their eyes fixed on the television. Carter's hand had crept underneath the hem of Perdie's sweater, the hot, flat flesh of his palm pressed against the bare skin of her belly. She reveled in that touch, in the casual way he drew her near to him, like he had to be touching her at all times.

They rounded their fourth hour of *Daria* together. Perdie and Lucille had bought the box set back when those were still a thing years ago, and they could both practically recite every episode by heart.

"You know, I don't think you're actually like Daria at all."

"No?"

"You're cynical like her. But she's so flat. And you're so…"

"Careful with your words there, Pretty Boy."

"Spiky." He grinned.

Perdie wriggled out of his grasp and padded into the kitchen to collect snacks.

When she returned, squishing a bag of chips and licorice inside her arm and balancing half a cherry pie in her hand—thank god for Lucille providing junk food—she stopped short at the sight in front of her.

Light streamed through the window behind Carter as he sprawled out sunlit on her overstuffed leather couch. The light tinged his hair with fire and created a halo around his frame. He was shirtless again, one arm splayed across the back of the couch, one leg bent up on the cushion.

Perdie shook her head. "Is this a fucking joke?"

"Hmm?"

"I didn't need to waste one of my one hundred thousand questions finding out that you used to model as it is entirely evident right in front of my face. I mean… Jesus, did you mean to pose like that?"

His lips curved up and he rubbed the back of his neck. "What can I say? I'm a man at his leisure."

Perdie shuffled over to the end table and deposited the food, then put her hands out like she was indicating a stop sign. "Don't move a muscle, okay? Just…don't move…"

Carter's expression was questioning, but amusement danced in his eyes. "Okay…"

Perdie ran off to fetch her phone. When she returned, she halted in front of him, assessing.

He cocked his head. "What are you doing?"

"Taking your picture...sending it to Lucille..." She smiled innocently. "Would you mind? As an artist, she'll appreciate this composition. *And* the subject. You're like a goddamn Greek god."

Carter chuckled but then shrugged. "Do your worst."

Perdie snapped a few shots and then turned the camera over to Carter, who was not as impressed by his own image. She nibbled her bottom lip and sent the picture.

Within a few minutes a text returned.

L: IS THAT WHO I THINK IT IS??? MARRY HIM YOU FOOL

Perdie giggled, warmth spreading over her.

"I take it she liked the picture?"

"And she doesn't even know you yet—" Perdie's words were cut short when Carter leapt from the couch, his arms catching her at the waist and rolling her underneath him on the cushions. She shrieked, breathless as he pinned her wrists above her head.

His mouth caught hers and kissed her recklessly, his hand roaming up and down her body, their legs stretched out and tangled.

As things were reaching a fever pitch, a familiar ding in the distance caught Perdie's attention. Her work email. *Ugh.* She already had a lineup of texts she had to contend with that she'd been ignoring all day, Max Goodridge's being one of them. But work wouldn't slow to a halt because of a party, the holidays, a snow day, or an extremely hot man on her couch.

"Waywaywaywait," she murmured, turning her head to the side, holding her breath.

Sure enough, within seconds, several more dings rang out.

With a big exhale, Carter's head fell to the side of her shoulder. "Work emails?"

Perdie clumsily scooted from beneath Carter, falling the short distance to the ground with an *umph*. She went to find her tablet and glanced over her shoulder. Carter was flopped out on his back, rubbing his eyes.

"Get up, Pretty Boy. We've got work to do."

Chapter Twenty-Four

The snow continued to fall in record-breaking inches, melting in the afternoon to a messy slush and then icing at night into a hazardous roller coaster. Charleston life halted to a slippery stop. Perdie cracked the blinds to survey the gleaming vast whiteness, the glare burning her retinas. It hurt, and yet it felt good.

Her body was enveloped in warmth as two arms encircled her rib cage from behind, rocking her back and forth. "Hey, Merry Christmas."

She twisted around so her face pressed against Carter's chest. "I would've gotten you a present had I known you were going to be my extended Christmas guest. Maybe another Knox Family Christmas sweatshirt?" She tugged at the sleeve of his offending shirt.

They'd been making do with what they had to keep Carter in clean clothes, which meant cycling through oversized T-shirts, sweatshirts, and random items in Perdie and Lucille's closet. There was something especially enticing about seeing Carter in these silly clothes as opposed to his normal uber-refined style. It was almost a test of his beauty: Was there anything she could put on him that would take away from his good looks?

Of course, they'd done plenty of lounging in their

underwear, or at times, in nothing at all. In fact, last night they'd sat together at Perdie's kitchen table, tablets, phones, laptops, notebooks, and pens strewn about, Perdie in nothing but her glasses, undies, and sports bra, Carter in his freshly laundered boxer briefs, pouring over their mutual cases.

Working with Carter in the sanctity of her home, without anyone else around or any workplace distractions, had been exhilarating. Perdie resented their power imbalance at the office, but when it was the two of them, they were a good team. She couldn't deny it. Their differences made their strengths. While Carter worked from instinct, from his gut, Perdie was measured, analytical.

When Carter reached a conclusion based on seemingly nothing more than a hunch, Perdie would grab her whiteboard and colored markers and work out the proof. At times it might take her a bit longer than him, but ultimately they reached the same conclusions together. They just found their way there differently. And to Perdie, this played like harmony. Like partnership.

They both also had the ability to summon large swaths of text by memory, something Perdie claimed as her talent alone, but Carter gave her a run for her money.

"In article 4, section 1a, the case stands for the proposition that all contracts more than five thousand dollars must be in writing or are rendered null and void."

"No, I'm telling you it's article 17, section 4c."

When they flipped through the documents for confirmation, they found that they were *both* right; the clause had been referenced twice.

Perdie tossed the document back to the table, chewing her lip.

"Looks like we both win." Carter smiled.

And, of course, it went without saying that the sex they were having could only be described as *unreasonable*. Perdie could never deny their physical connection, which was off the charts.

L: How many orgasms???

Lucille had texted her late into the night, Perdie locked into little spoon position, Carter sleeping peacefully next to her.

P: An unreasonable number. How're things with Noah and the Knox Fam?

L: Terrible. Everyone keeps asking where you are, and they love Noah more than me. Doesn't anyone realize I'm the star of this show?

P: You're the star of my show, Luce.

L: Don't try to butter me up. It won't work.

L: Just kidding, it will. Oh whatever, go have fun with your pretty, pretty, Prince Charming.

And now Perdie and Carter were together on Christmas morning like two newlyweds in a Folgers commercial, embracing each other in front of a snowy window backdrop. Sure, they weren't newlyweds, and sure, the snow was covering palmetto trees instead of evergreens, but nonetheless, the distinctly homey sensation of the holidays permeated. The sensation one discovers when one spends time with someone they love.

Oh shit.

"I have some calls to make, but I was thinking I could do some real fancy stuff with a few eggs for breakfast. What say you?" Carter loosened his grasp on Perdie, peering down at her. They had been surviving off junk food mainly as neither one of them possessed any cooking skills. Perdie half expected Carter to be one of those "clean eaters" who would only consume egg white omelets with kale and raw millet or whatever, but if he had complaints about the local cuisine of licorice and cherry pie he kept them to himself.

Perdie shook her head. "You're my guest. So allow me. Go make your calls."

A few minutes later, Carter had his tablet propped up on the end table while Perdie tentatively opened the drawer in the fridge with the eggs. Perdie was a little ashamed of the fact that she hadn't cooked for herself in years. She'd grown accustomed to takeout or Lucille's culinary skills, which were vast and impressive.

You are thirty-nine years old, you can make a fucking omelet.

For good measure, she set her phone on the counter next to the stove and googled *easiest omelet recipe of all time.*

Thankfully, Carter was too distracted by his video call to watch her flounder around in the kitchen. However, he sat within her view. Voices trailed in from the living room.

As she cracked six eggs into a bowl, his mothers fussed in the background.

"I sent you another bottle of that peppermint essential oil in the mail. I made it with extra love just for you.

And don't forget to take a probiotic, okay, sweetie?" A floaty voice resonated from the tablet.

A harsher, sharper voice chimed in. "Joanne and Michael are here. They brought the kids and everyone wants to know why their favorite uncle is a no-show. Joanne, get over here. Carter's on the video call."

The sobs of children grew in volume.

"Uncle Carter, Uncle Carter, why don't you love us? If you loved us you would be here for Christmas. Uncle Carter ruined Christmas. Uncle Carter doesn't love usss."

Perdie stopped dead in her tracks at the voices. *Jesus Christ, what?*

Carter remained unperturbed. "Joanne, I asked you to stop making the kids say weird things like that. It's creepy."

Giggles erupted in the background as Perdie whipped up the eggs in her bowl, yolk and egg white splashing her thumb. Another woman's voice chimed in.

"Whatever, my little brother-in-law. You deserve it. They've been asking for you *all* day, I can't believe you're ditching us this year you a-s-s-h-o-l-e. *We needed you.* Michael was able to take off the entire weekend, and he cuts hearts open for a living so I don't see how some mergers and acquisitions are so pressing that you can't get on a plane to come see your family who love you very, very much you j-e-r-k."

"I can't change the weather, Jo. I'm not god, unlike Michael, who thinks he is. I bet I can make up for it though. Is everybody ready for a surprise?"

A child chorus of *yes*es rang out.

"Surprise!" Carter held Bananas in his lap so the pug was standing with his paws up as if in surprise. Bananas let out a signature *whao-whao-whao*.

The kids oohed and aahed. "Look at the doggie."

"Mommy, why can Uncle Carter have a dog, but we can't?"

"Because Uncle Carter is a big boy with a big boy paycheck and a big boy house. But seriously, you find a house yet? Can't believe you're going to live in a house all by yourself."

Perdie rustled around for a frying pan, trying not to eavesdrop, and failing. He wasn't exactly trying to hide his conversations.

"Getting there. Have it narrowed down to a few."

"And since when do you have a dog? It looks old. Where are you anyway? That's not your rental. And *oh ho ho ho. What* is that painting in the background?" Sister-in-law *Joanne* was apparently conducting an interrogation.

Carter caught Perdie's eye, at which point she panicked. He gestured to her tentatively, as if he were asking if she wanted to introduce herself *to his family*. Her eyes went wide and she mimed with her waving hands what she hoped communicated the message *hell no*.

Carter turned back to face the screen. "Ah, I'm at a *friend's* house."

"Oh, I see, there's a woman. There's definitely a woman. Michael, did you know your brother has a new girlfriend? Hey, Cindy, Carter's seeing someone."

The dreamy voice from before called out, "Carter, honey. I'm so happy for you. Can we meet her when you come home? Tell her she's invited to my gallery showing on Easter. When am I going to get grandkids? I'm not going to live forever."

A cold shot of adrenaline coursed through Perdie's veins. She tensed, swallowing thickly as she heated the pan with butter and poured in the eggs, pretending not to hear.

Joanne's voice again. "Seriously, Carter. What's the holdup? You have everything, the money, the looks, you almost have a house, you're great with kids. No reason to wait."

Perdie scraped at the edges of the pan, but the eggs weren't setting. Testily, she increased the heat.

"Jesus Christ, Jo. I'm barely in my thirties. Not everyone wants the same things, and not everyone wants them on the same timeline. All right, who wants to see the dog one more time?" The kids cheered again, and Carter held Bananas up for the screen.

"He's so cute. Mommy, I want a dog."

"I'm allergic, we've been over this. It would have to live outside, and that wouldn't be very nice for a doggy, would it?"

"Why couldn't you live outside instead?" The child's voice was so innocent, Perdie let out a snort, quickly followed by a stifled yelp when her omelet began smoking, aggressive flames erupting from the pan.

"What's the noise going on behind you?" Joanne's voice asked.

"Shit, shit, shit, shit..." She flipped off the burner, then raced to the sink with the pan smoking and sizzling. She could hear Carter's rushed voice in the background.

"Okay, Merry Christmas, talk to you all soon. Bye. Bye. Love you. Gotta go. Bye."

The kitchen sink filled with smoke as Perdie sprayed off the singed eggs and pan. Carter appeared besides her, waving away the cloud in front of them. She dropped the pan in the sink, hunched over.

"Pop-Tarts?" she asked.

* * *

They were both a little drunk. At least Perdie was, and as far as she could tell Carter was too. She'd never seen him so tipsy. It'd been her idea to mix the Bailey's in with the instant hot chocolate. A *festive* concoction. But before long, half the bottle was gone.

They tumbled into her bed together, sitting up on their knees and clumsily stripping off each other's clothes until they were kissing naked skin. Then he laid her out on her side, grasping her around her waist, like he did when they slept together at night, spooning. His index finger circled her clitoris as he rocked into her from behind, in slow, steady strokes. She grabbed onto his wrist that was holding her in place, and let the slow waves of their concurrent movements take her away.

Not a word spoken between them.

When it was over, they stayed in position, until his breath heated the curved hollow between her neck and shoulder.

"So, your family really loves you huh?" She said it so quietly, it was like she almost didn't want him to hear. But he stirred, rubbing his face against her hair.

"Don't let them scare you away."

She breathed in her courage, craning her neck to the dark ceiling "They kinda freak me out, if I'm honest. But I've been thinking…"

"Go on."

"You wanna be with me, don't you? In like some kind of…official capacity. You really do?"

Carter's body stiffened behind her. "That's accurate."

She twisted around to face him, their torsos pressed together. She sighed. "Okay. Then…maybe…maybe you're right. There obviously *is* something between us. I… I take a little bit longer to work out the pieces to the conclusion than you do. You know? So. What the hell? I think we should tell HR. And then Frank. I can't be afraid of my own shadow in that office. I do good work, and I deserve good things. I'm done with the games. If they can't take me openly dating a partner at the firm then they don't deserve me secretly screwing a partner at the firm."

"You're serious?"

"Pretty Boy, I'm so dead serious, right now I'm practically the London Guard."

He pulled her in, kissing her in a new way. Intense but not just lustful like she was used to. It made a nervous energy of emotion swirl around the pit of her belly. *Shivers*.

"I want you to know, I won't let anyone speak a single judgmental word about you, Perdie. If anyone has a problem with us, then they can deal with me."

She giggled. "Okay, save your toxic masculinity for a football game or something."

"What I mean is I'll always have your back."

She nodded, rubbing her face against his chest. She could feel the thump of his heartbeat, heavy in the dark. "Looks like we have ourselves a deal."

Carter squeezed her hard. "And we both win."

In the dark of the night, long after Carter dozed, Perdie crept out of bed, down the stairs, and shuffled over the hardwood in fuzzy panda slippers to the living room couch. Settling in, she cracked open her laptop on the coffee table. She was searching for an email address she hadn't used in years. When she found the name of the recruiter who'd gotten her foot in the door at Joy and Schulz, she typed an email furiously.

Melissa, long time, no talk. Wondering if you know any firms hiring a high-level associate with litigation skills? You know I do good work. Best, Perdita Stone

She shut her laptop, drumming her nails on the case, her eyes glazed over. Always good to have a plan B.

"Whaddya doin' up?" Carter's sleepy voice came from the hallway. She turned her head to see him rubbing his eyes, hair a mess.

He scuffled over, scratching his head. The couch shifted beneath her as he plopped down.

"Couldn't sleep."

He laid his head on her lap, settling in, and she let her fingers glide through the soft waves of his hair. "Me neither," he said. But even as he spoke his voice drifted. She stroked his hair some more, taking him in, before letting her head fall back to the blank ceiling.

Welp. Here goes nothin'.

Chapter Twenty-Five

Because of the winter storms, Lucille and Noah remained in Asheville until after the New Year, leaving Perdie and Carter to their own devices.

P: You and Noah still "just friends" or what?

L: Ha-ha. No comment. But you'll never believe the email I got today.

P: Spill.

L: From HAMPTON. An apology. Apparently, he's in rehab. Also, he said he'd wire me ten grand for any damages he caused.

P: Don't you dare respond to that email, Lucille.

L: I won't, I won't. I promise, cross my heart and swear to Diana.

Carter could have left. He could have trekked downtown to his apartment. The roads had mostly cleared and life was picking back up to its usual post-Christmas rhythm. When he did leave, to grab his clothes and other essentials, he returned right back to Perdie and Bananas. She swore she could feel the ventricles of her own heart folding in on themselves when he leaned down to kiss her in her front doorway. Was this dying?

"Don't binge-watch any shows without me. And I'm ordering salads too."

When he returned, he'd changed. Back in his usual expensive but understated style. His stubble gone, jaw now freshly shaven. Work-appropriate attire.

In Perdie's head the countdown had begun. She only had so many days left of snowed-in bliss until the harsh reality of the New Year, and the judgmental drudge of the workplace returned.

An email popped up on her phone. It was from the recruiter.

Perdita,
Perfect timing. Smith and Macher the firm on Meeting Street needs to fill a position right away with someone of your background. Can you go in for a meeting in the next few days?
Melissa

The morning to return to work had finally arrived. Perdie sent Carter back to his apartment before Lucille came home. She wasn't ready for that introduction quite yet.

And for work today, in honor of her personal liberation, Perdie dressed in the spirit of Gloria Steinem. She wore high-waisted, flared, gray trousers with a thin black sweater and a middle part in her hair and everything. *This is feminism, right?* Lucille would know, but she was sleeping.

Before she got out of her car in the attorney parking lot, her phone dinged with a meeting request from Jennifer and Sophia. Perdie pursed her lips. Their relentless nosiness was an irritant. Jennifer and Sophia had gone radio silent over the holiday break, presumably taking the days off to spend with their families, but they apparently hadn't forgotten the talk they'd had at the holiday party two weeks ago like Perdie hoped they would.

Perdie tapped the screen: DECLINE. First, she had a ton of work to do with Carter to prepare for their upcoming trip to San Francisco to meet with the Fletcher Group members. Not to mention the nebulous and looming threat of his entire family within driving distance. Second, she had a clandestine interview with a firm on Meeting Street for later in the afternoon should things take a murky turn at Joy and Schulz. And third, if Jennifer and Sophia were trying to weaponize her secret relationship with Carter against her, well—*ha!*—joke was on them, because she and Carter were about to come out with it that very morning, come hell or high water.

Her stomach flipped at the idea but it was better to 'fess up and control the narrative than get caught and have the story told for you, right? *Right?*

On cue, Carter pulled up next to her, the bump of his car door, and then a knock on her passenger window. She rolled it down.

"Oh come *on*, man." Perdie shook her head.

"What? I just got here."

Perdie opened the door, unfolding out of her vehicle to stand next to him. "Goddammit. We're matching." Carter's gray pants and black sweater were a different cut than hers, but the likeness was unmistakable. "This is going to be a disaster, and we're wearing matching outfits. Of course, you're not nervous, you're not the one with your career on the line."

"It won't go down like that. And even if it did, Frank's only one person. And he isn't the only person in the firm with power. I can use my skills for good as well, you know. Have a little faith." He smiled. "And I like that we match. Signifies we're a team."

Her lip curled in a begrudging smile. "I don't like it, but your cheesiness might be wearing off on me."

They made their way into the building. The plan was to get the easy disclosure stuff with HR done first. Then head to dreaded Frank's office. Perdie was much more concerned with interacting with Frank than Carter was, but she'd made her decision, and she was going to *do* this thing with Carter, right? *Right?*

"Knock, knock," Carter said.

He and Perdie stood outside Frank's office door. Frank glanced up, quickly clicking off his computer screen—but not before Perdie caught a glimpse of women's lingerie. Something told Perdie it wasn't for *his wife, the burden, ha-ha.*

"Ah, to what do I owe the pleasure from such a dynamic duo?" He rolled his chair to his desk, interlocking his fingers and resting them atop the surface. "The Fletcher Group has big things brewing on the horizon, acquisitions galore, so I hope you're ready to wine, dine and sixty-nine 'em on your trip out to San Fran."

"We're more than prepared," Perdie said, crossing her arms, but Carter cleared his throat.

"Actually, we came here to discuss something of a personal matter."

Frank raised his eyebrows, his gaze on Carter. "Oh? Well then, you have my attention."

"Regarding the matter of a newly developed personal relationship between Ms. Stone and myself. We understand the special nature of a relationship like ours and we want you to know that we will take all precautions to keep a safe and harassment-free work environment for all parties involved."

"We—we already sorted it out with HR and everything, so nothing untoward or sordid to worry about," Perdie stuttered. Heat rose in her cheeks at Frank's blank stare. Oh shit. Not only was this embarrassing, but she honest to god had no clue how he would react. Sometimes, she swore Frank had it in for her to begin with, and the last thing she needed to do was provide a loaded gun with more ammo.

Stop yourself, P. You're spiraling. You have another job interview today anyway.

It took a moment for Frank to respond, as if his brain were an old computer with too many tabs open. Then he unlocked his fingers, spreading them on the desktop. "Hmm…okay."

Perdie nibbled her lip.

"And so…" Carter spoke slowly as if to a toddler "…we are disclosing information to you so that you can rest assured that we have the firm's best interest at heart and that our personal relationship won't interfere in any way with our own or anyone else's professional relationships."

Perdie held her breath, waiting. She was so fucked.

Frank narrowed his eyes for a moment, his gaze darting between the two of them. And then he let out a chuckle. "Ah, you kids. So serious. *Relationship dis-*

closure. Hell, back in my day half the second floor was screwing each other. You couldn't walk down a hallway without hearing some kind of personal squabble about an affair. Sorry to disappoint, but nobody cares if you…do whatever it is you're doing together. We're all adults here. We're all human. Plenty of people in this firm date or… eh, who cares." He gave a dismissive wave of his hand.

Perdie raised her eyebrows, tightening her arms to her chest as Frank's gaze wandered there. "Oh." The sound came out staccato. "Well then. Glad we are all at a reasonable…ah…*understanding.*"

"Keep the Fletcher Group on board and that's all that matters at the end of the day. It's about the *work*, isn't it?" Frank pushed his chair back from his desk. "That's all Charles Joy cares about. We on the same page?"

Carter nodded. "Of course, the Fletcher Group is my client after all."

"And you're the smartest hire we ever made at this firm, Leplan."

The words scraped against Perdie's ego like a cheese grater, but she put her emotions on hold until they could escape Frank's office. She turned to leave. "Great. Thanks." It was only a matter of time until Frank said something cree—

"And hey, while we're on a personal note, if you two ever wanna do some *swinging*…ah…stop by my office sometime after hours, if ya know what I mean."

Perdie dug her nails in her palms as she pivoted slowly back to Frank. "Excuse me?"

"Ah ha-ha. It's called a joke, Perdita. Not sure when everyone got so *PC* about everything anyway…"

Carter cleared his throat. "Maybe we'll save that discussion for another day. Thanks again, Frank." He signaled towards the door for Perdie and they rushed out of the room.

Without a word to one another, they walked in parallel strides towards the elevator, where Carter hit the down arrow. The giddiness of relief flowed out towards Perdie's hands and feet.

Ding.

Swoosh. When the door closed they both began talking at once.

"Can you believe he asked us if we wanted to swing?"

"Wanna make out in the elevator?"

Carter stilled. "Really? Right now?" Then he sighed, as if world weary from her demands, and snatched Perdie by the waist, his large hand pressed against the side of her rib cage, thumb brushing at the underside of her breast. "Better make this fast."

At five thirty a.m. Perdie and Carter sat together in the first-class cabin, sipping dull coffee in tiny paper cups, preparing for their five-plus-hour flight to San Francisco. Carter's long legs stretched out, while she crossed hers, her black patent leather heel bouncing against his pant leg.

She breathed in deep, eyes closing. He smelled so, so, *so* very good.

Good enough to ruin your career over? The thought snapped like a reflex. *Perdita Stone, it is time to get over yourself. You are nothing but paranoid. Nobody gives a good goddamn if you're screwing Carter. Hell, not even Frank.*

All that paranoia had been for nothing. Nothing. They could've been screwing the whole time and not a damned person would care. Well, maybe Jennifer. But that didn't matter now.

Plus, she had two big things working in her favor: her work with the Fletcher Group and her burgeoning case with Noah. As long as she kept her nose to the grindstone, and her ass out of petty drama re: Jennifer and Sophia, no one could take that from her.

And if, in the meantime, she privately wanted to feel Carter up on a first-class flight at five thirty in the morning, well, then, who was stopping her exactly?

Only herself. The problem was that there hadn't been a problem the whole time. It was all in her head. She could almost laugh.

The pressure shifted in her ears and belly as the plane ascended. She let her gaze drift out the window when the creak of the armrest drew her attention. Carter had lifted it, removing the barrier between their two bodies. Instinctively, she moved to scoot closer when she almost stopped in realization.

That's what he did. He removed barriers. Barriers she had put up for what she thought were good reasons. But maybe it was okay to let her guard down for a while. Try it out…test the waters…

"We'll have fun on this trip." Carter rested his head against the back of the plane seat. "And we can use all the hours you billed here for a good leveraging chip for your partnership nomination."

"We?"

"Of course *we*. I'm infiltrating the executive committee. Use my powers for good."

"Okay, Spider-Man. But I should warn you that I'm not much of a Mary Jane type."

"No, you're not. You're your very own type. One of

a kind. No red hair either." His mouth was curved in a smile. That beautiful fucking smile.

A rush of warmth filled Perdie like that feeling she got when she first stepped foot into a warm bubble bath.

Carter's head tilted, his eyes regarding her with amusement. "Why are you looking at me like that?"

"Like what?"

"Like I'm some birthday candles you're about to blow out."

Perdie narrowed her eyes.

Motherfucker, she had gone and fallen in love with him.

Perdie rolled over on her back, the white down comforter tangled and hot around her torso and legs. She was hungover. *Again.* But she'd done her job for the evening, with Carter. The Fletcher Group outing had been mild, relatively speaking, compared to some of the Joy and Schulz client schmoozing of old. For one, there'd been no strip club or lines of coke off a bathroom sink. Instead, Perdie and Carter had taken the four Fletcher Group representatives out to a nice steakhouse, ushering in expensive bottles of cab and chardonnay one by one by one.

There had been laughing and small talk and the usual drunken test of keeping things personal-professional. Personal enough to keep the client seeing them as human, *like friends*, and professional enough not to cross any boundaries that might cause outcries. Perdie was already a pro at toeing that line anyway. And she was aware of how Carter's presence legitimized her to those around them.

She patted the spot next to her, but no Carter. She propped up on her elbows, head pounding, and gazed down to see that she was wearing one of Carter's off-kilter button-downs.

Last night, as they'd stumbled into his hotel room, she'd stripped out of her fuchsia sheath, kicked her heels across the room, and pulled on one of his shirts. It was supposed to be *sexy*. Maybe not so sexy when it was all crooked—why was she so bad at buttons anyway?—but it hadn't bothered Carter as his hands wandered beneath the material, pulling her to the luxe hotel mattress and whispering filthy things into her ears.

She let her fingers slide up and down the buttons. They had done good work both in and out of the bed last night.

The lock whirred and the door opened. Carter emerged, two cups of coffee in his hands.

"I see Sleeping Beauty has arisen." He sat down on the bed, handing her one of the cups.

She squinted, opening the lid to blow the liquid cool. "How are you up so early? And why do you look like that?"

Carter was in workout gear, pants and a zip-up sweatshirt with a pair of fancy but unidentifiable-to-Perdie running shoes. His hair was windblown but otherwise he appeared fresh as a daisy. "Best cure for a hangover is a run."

"Get outta here. How come I keep forgetting you're a masochist?"

He leaned over to trail his hand up her thigh and under her shirt. "Because we do so much stuff that feels so good together…" His breath against her made her eyes shutter as he kissed her lightly on the vulnerable shell of her ear.

"Ah, speaking of."

Perdie jolted from her daze when Carter pulled away to show her his phone.

"Email from Frank and Charles Joy already. Looks like the Fletcher Group is very, *very* happy with us. They want to debrief first thing tomorrow morning."

Perdie sipped her coffee tentatively. "Ugh, is this a nightmarish monkey's paw type scenario where I wished for success and all success turned out to be was a bunch of meetings with old men who say inappropriate shit to me?"

"Don't be such a pessimist. Someday fairly soon they'll die."

Perdie snorted in her coffee. "We have a while until our flight, don't we? I'm gonna need a bit to kick this hangover. Unless you want to make the trek to a dispensary and procure me some hangover weed. It's what Spider-Man would do for Mary Jane."

Carter unzipped his hoodie, tossed it to the bed, and reached behind his neck to pull off the shirt underneath.

Perdie leaned back against the headboard to ogle him. *Nope, never gets old.* "You ever gonna tell me what those tattoos are all about?"

He shook his head. "I don't think we've been on our *third* date yet. But I'll tell you what, I know where to get you the best hangover weed on the planet. There's just one caveat."

"And that is?"

"Don't freak out."

"Commencing freak-out. *What.*"

Carter scratched his ear. "It's my mothers' house…"

"Freak-out intensifying."

"I understand, but I told them I'd stop by before the end of the trip. Also, if you come with, I'll tell you—no, I'll *show* you—all about my tattoo. Even before the third date. Scout's honor."

Perdie winced as if the very act of thinking was painful. And in all honesty, it was. Every muscle in her body screamed *absolutely the fuck not*. She didn't need to meet Carter's family, what a *committed* thing to do.

But she fought the impulse. Fought the fear. She'd created enough negativity in her life by finding problems where problems didn't exist. It was time to push her own boundaries a little. Emphasis on *little*.

Deep breath in. "I know I'll regret this but..." her lids squeezed together "...*fine*."

Carter clapped his hands. "I'm impressed with you, Bad Girl." And he leaned to kiss her before heading towards the bathroom. "Meet me in the shower and I'll show you my gratitude."

Chapter Twenty-Six

Bernal Heights was a quick fifteen-minute drive from the financial district near their hotel. They packed up their suitcases and went on their way.

"This is absurd, right? Me meeting your family? Like it's totally absurd. How about instead I walk straight into the Pacific Ocean?" Perdie was hastily braiding her damp hair as they pulled up to the driveway of a midcentury two-story. While in Charleston, it would have been a modest house at best, Perdie couldn't begin to imagine the price tag on this kind of place in San Francisco. More than her mom could afford working the lunch shift at Shooters that's for sure.

Carter parked the car in the driveway, the hum of the engine falling silent. His soft expression made her stop fiddling with the ends of her braid.

"I'm going to ask you for something, okay?"

She chewed her lip, eyeing him suspiciously. "Okay…"

His hand snaked over her lap, enveloped her own and gave it a squeeze. "I'm asking for you to be brave."

It was a plea, a plea for her to rise to the occasion. Meet the family of the man she probably…very likely… most definitely…*loved*? *Oh shit, oh shit, oh shit.*

She swallowed hard. "I can be brave."

He lifted her hand to his mouth, kissing the outside. "Never doubted you. All right. Let's go."

They headed to the front door but before Carter's knuckles even made contact with the painted wood, it swung open.

"Ah. Carter, darling, right on time as usual. Come in, come in." A curvy, ethereal woman in a long, flowy taupe gown ushered Perdie and Carter into the living room of the beautiful open-concept home. Perdie recognized Cindy from her dreamy voice.

Perdie's eyes went wide. The walls were adorned with paintings with colorful, bold graphic lines. *Awfully familiar, that style of art.*

"And you, *you*…" Cindy held Perdie by the upper arms, examining her face-to-face. "You must be Perdita. Perdita Stone, I believe. Is that right? Will you look at these colors on you…" The woman inspected Perdie with such intense scrutiny that Perdie didn't even protest. Just withstood the inspection. "Perdita. *Per-di-ta*. Latin for *lost*. Unless my Latin is rusty."

"Um…it's my mother's name. And her mother's name."

"Carter, will you go to the back garden and fetch your mother please? And let's see. *Stone*. Like a cave. Ah. Wait. But that's not right. *Like a mountain*. Hmm…it makes one wonder."

"W-wonder what?" Perdie asked.

Carter touched Cindy's elbow. "Ma, take it down a notch, please. Let her sit before you start with the spiritual analysis. I'll be right back."

Cindy smiled and gestured for Perdie to sit on a long L-shaped cream sofa. "Of course, where are my manners? Perdita, darling, my name is Cindy, I'm Carter's mother, and Jesse, his other mother, will be here momentarily. May I offer you a joint? Carter says you woke up feeling ill."

"I'm not going to lie, Cindy. I feel a little awkward about this."

"Nonsense, nonsense. In fact, I'll have some with you, then we'll all go to the kitchen and enjoy a nice cheese and fruit platter together. Cashew cheese, I hope you like that."

"I like anything I don't have to make myself." Perdie smiled.

Cindy patted Perdie's knee and stood to retrieve the hangover remedy.

"Mom, this is Perdie." Carter entered the room with another woman, this one lean and tall, in jeans and a T-shirt, her dark hair cut close at the sides, almost in a Mohawk. "Perdie, this is my mother Jesse."

Jesse offered her hand to Perdie, prompting her to stand and shake. "Sounds like you and Carter are quite an effective team," Jesse said, her voice sharp, especially compared to Cindy's. "And I hear you do good work for that firm of yours. I know you scored a great big settlement out of that oil guy…what was his name, Brown or some nonsense. Actually, who cares, fuck 'em."

"Thanks, Mom, I was on the losing end of that case," said Carter, but there was amusement on his face.

Cindy returned, lighting a tightly rolled joint as she walked to the center of the room. She took a drag and then handed it off to Perdie. "This is our own special blend. We grow it in the yard. A little bit goes a long way, so I might advise you to go slow."

Perdie nodded, taking a tentative drag, then offered it to Carter and Jesse, who both waved her off. Instantly,

Perdie's dull hangover headache began to ease. She took a big, relaxed breath and handed it back over to Cindy. "I think I'm ready for some cashew cheese."

Only once before had Perdie met the parents of a man she was seeing, and that meeting had been tense, awkward, and stiflingly unfunny. Perdie never once acted as herself, avoiding making the jokes she would normally make, or using the kind of language she liked to use.

But it wasn't so with Carter's mothers. They were warm and open and *cool*. Like, she could say anything she wanted and they would run with it, laughing and improving along the whole way.

And *wow* did they dote on Carter. Lucille's parents were bad, but they didn't hold a candle to Jesse and Cindy. Carter was clearly the light of their world. Or at least one of them, as they had another son, Michael.

"Cindy, your artwork is beautiful. My friend Lucille would go bonkers over it too. Are all the pieces in the house your work?"

"They are. We are often changing the artwork around here though. Swapping it out as my style changes."

"Except for the artwork on me. That never changes." Carter smirked.

"What does that mean?" asked Perdie. The other three were exchanging glances around the table.

"I thought that wasn't something you talked about with your…" Cindy glanced at Perdie. "With your friends."

Carter shrugged. "You can tell her."

Cindy raised her brow but then leaned in like she was about to spill a secret. "I designed Carter's tattoo. It took me forever to get it right, and we searched high and low for the best tattoo artist in the city to execute it, but well,

I think it turned out rather amazing, don't you? Carter is, after all, my greatest creation."

"Ma, this is half the reason why I don't want people to know. Don't call me your greatest creation, it's *objectifying*. I'm an entire person separate from you."

Cindy straightened up. "Oh, you're quite right. I'm sorry. But we can all agree that it looks quite phenomenal on you."

"Besides, Cindy, Michael is our greatest creation." Jesse chuckled. She leaned back in her seat to sip her chamomile. "Carter was always an emotionally intelligent kid. So popular. Homecoming King *and* Prom King. Imagine the two of us with a kid like that."

Perdie smiled and laughed with the conversation as she ate cashew cheese on sea salt and cracked pepper nut crackers. *Being brave pays off.* This wasn't hard at all. A strange and new sensation of joy surged through her soul.

"We have to head out soon," Carter said, as he helped Cindy move dishware to the sink. "I made good on my promise to visit. But the airport awaits us."

"Oh, but Carter darling…" Cindy's hand touched her son's cheek. "Can't you stay for a while longer?"

"Afraid not. We've got a plane to catch. And I'll be back soon enough for your gallery opening."

"Fine, it's fine, Cindy," Jesse cut in. "He's busy. He's important. But, Perdie, before you go, why don't you come out to the garden with me? We can pick a few oranges from my new orange tree."

Perdie glanced at Carter, who lifted his brows. Would she dare?

She jumped to her feet. "Sure, sounds great."

Jesse led Perdie through the living room and out a

large glass panoramic door to a sun-drenched back garden and patio.

"Perdie, I actually wanted to talk to you about something important." Jesse stopped in front of the orange tree and twisted off a piece of fruit. "Woman to woman. Lawyer to lawyer."

"Oh?" Perdie accepted the orange Jesse plopped into her hand.

"My son is in love with you."

Perdie almost dropped the orange. "*Shit.* I mean…oh, I wouldn't say— I mean—we haven't talked about anything like that be—"

"I know my son. And he is. And you're in love with him too. Uh-uh-uh, don't even try to deny it. I know that of which I speak. May I be blunt?"

"Could've sworn you were already doing that."

"I don't mean to overstep my bounds. But I don't waste time anymore, and you shouldn't either. *Don't* waste time."

Perdie tilted her head. "Don't waste time?"

"If you love him, don't waste any time. Cindy and I wasted so much time, and regretted it."

"I'm afraid I don't understand…"

"Look, the age gap. It's no big deal, I'm hip to it. Except you're pushing forty, huh? Never married? Don't answer, I looked up your court records."

"You did what?"

"And people are marrying later nowadays and using IVF and all sorts of stuff, but let's do the math. You take a year to get married, another year to settle down? That puts you at what? Forty, forty-one? Risky. Cindy and I…we waited too long to have Carter…we struggled for him. I wouldn't wish it on anyone. Take my advice and do it now."

For a full thirty seconds, speech evaded Perdie. Her heart pounded in her chest. "Okay, thank you for the advice."

Jesse's face softened. "I've freaked you out, haven't I? We just met, we're practically strangers. But I wouldn't say any of this if I didn't absolutely with all my heart believe that you and my son belong together. Call it a hunch, and my hunches have never been wrong. *Just* like my judgments. So, take it from me, *capisce*?"

Perdie nodded slowly. "Sure. Yeah, I…uh… I got it."

Jesse handed Perdie another orange and then wiped her hands off on her pants. "Now that that's settled." She opened her arms. "Come on in for a hug."

On the way to the airport, Perdie clammed up, her brain oversoaked like a sponge. She had been *too* brave today perhaps. Eventually she managed to banter with Carter as usual. But she couldn't ignore the pit in her stomach.

She tossed the oranges in the trash at the airport terminal when Carter wasn't looking. Their flight had been canceled, but there was another one heading out the same time, and he'd gone over to the ticket agent to book new seats.

"I've got good and bad news." Carter strode over to her. "So, the good news is we got tickets on the next flight out of here. The bad news is we got downgraded to coach."

"I'll take it." Plane seats were the least of her worries.

Once boarded, the atmosphere irked her. Different than when they'd flown to California. The seating was cramped, and Perdie and Carter were squished together

like a panini. Their shared armrest was jammed halfway up, forcing her to cross her arms over her chest in
a makeshift hug.

Perdie longed to zone out.

A lot had happened in the last few hours. So much.
More than she was ready to handle. She needed to de-
compress. She needed to get home and talk to Lucille.
For now, she could only concentrate on the things right
in front of her. Like this grimy table tray. *Keep the mood
light, P.*

"You want some of my ginger ale?" She held up the
clear plastic cup. "Tradesies for that bag of pretzels."

"Perdie."

"Huh?"

"I love you."

Perdie choked on her drink. When she regained her
breath, she squeezed her eyes closed.

Carter's voice was soft. "Did you hear me? I love you."

"Carter, I…" She gulped. Suddenly, the world was
fuzzy. So much for keeping things light. "I don't want
kids."

Chapter Twenty-Seven

A record-scratch moment. The air chilled between them.

Carter's brows knitted together. "Kids? Who said anything about kids?"

"Well, you want them, right? Soccer practice, chicken nuggets, white fences, the whole nine?"

His lips parted to say something, then he shook his head. "Is this because I asked you to meet my parents? I know I pushed your limits, but don't you think this conversation is a little early?"

"Early for whom? I'm seven years older than you. I'm too old to wait around for you to be ready for these kinds of conversations."

Carter let out a big exhale. "Okay…" His eyes closed. "I guess I really never thought that hard about it before. Starting a family is—"

"You mean a family *with kids*. Just because I don't want to have my own kids doesn't mean I don't have a family."

"You interrupted me." He stabbed his hand through his hair. "I'd be happy without kids."

"I don't believe you."

"You don't—" Carter paused, then spoke in a measured tone. "What's this really about?"

"It's about kids. I just told you what it's about, don't look at me like that. I don't want them, and you do."

"Stop. I don't give a fuck about having kids."

"I should've seen it before, but I ignored the red flags of our relationship. I pushed forward with us anyway, but I knew better."

"Better than what? What's going on with you?" But from the cast of his face, she could tell he already had an inkling.

"Better than to hope this could work. You and me. We don't belong together, it's like pairing a moose with a field mouse. You're the wholesome hero home for the holidays, and I'm the drunk spinster in the weird glasses crashing the party. I'm not the droid you're looking for. Orange trees, parents, commitment, living together... *marriage*... Do I look like someone interested in that? I'll *never* be ready. We had a fun time playing house, but to quote your own sentiment: commitment isn't in my DNA. Just ask my mother. Better yet ask yours."

Carter's spoke softly. "If you're afraid to admit you're in love with me, you can just say that."

She scoffed. "Don't pretend like you don't understand exactly what I'm saying."

"This hot-and-cold game has an expiration date. You were just fine meeting my parents. In fact, the whole meeting went great."

"That's what you think."

Carter blanched. "Then enlighten me. What's changed?"

But she dug deeper into her defiance. "That's the problem, *nothing*'s changed. I told you I'd disappoint you, and now I'm sticking to my word. You should've listened when you were warned."

"Bullshit. Answer the question."

And tell him what? That the conversation she'd had with Jesse had put things into laser focus: she couldn't commit to him. She would never be enough in the end. Not enough for a perfectly kind, perfectly beloved man like Carter. The disparity was too great and the risk of losing her heart too high. In comparison to him, she felt like orphan Annie. Like somebody's discarded lunch. They could never be equals. Better to end things now before she got in even deeper. Before she drowned. She lifted her chin to stop her lip from quivering. "Your good looks are like hypnosis. I fell for it. But we don't have anything beyond the physical."

Carter's nostrils flared. A stretch of silence passed before he spoke again. "That's a really fucking shitty thing to say."

She'd been willing to take risks for this man, but now she was at a tipping point. No, *passed* her tipping point. He'd pushed her too far, and now she'd fallen off the ride. She shrugged. "Hmm. I guess it is."

Carter's voice was hoarse. "Don't do this. Don't fucking do this. Not now."

She'd believed the lie that work kept them apart. She'd blamed Jennifer and Sophia and Frank and the law firm and rules and propriety. But that'd been a farce. A red herring. Too easily resolved. Too simple. Her problems were deeply rooted within her, and they wouldn't be fixed by a lunch with the parents. What choice did she have? She elbow-dropped the halfway-stuck armrest, locking it firmly between them.

"I'm sorry, it's over."

He wanted eggs, and all she had were Pop-Tarts.

Perdie leaned against the door once inside her house, toeing off her shoes, dropping her jacket and luggage to the ground. Bananas didn't greet her, which meant he was asleep with Lucille.

She climbed the stairs, legs like boulders, heart like a rock. She knocked softly on Lucille's door and then cracked it a little. "Hey, Luce."

Lucille rubbed her eyes, voice thick with sleep. "P? That you? What's wrong?"

"Can I sleep in here with you and Bananas tonight?"

"Yeah. Yeah, of course."

Perdie crawled in next to Lucille, pulling Bananas to her chest. He didn't stir when she moved him, just settled in against her. So frail. She was frail too.

"You wanna talk?"

Perdie pulled the blanket over her shoulder. "What difference would it make?"

Perdie took a deep breath and made her way to the seventh floor for her meeting with Charles Joy, Frank, and Carter. She looked like shit, and it didn't matter.

She'd awoken late. Lucille had already left for an early shipment from the wholesalers, but she propped a little card covered with watercolor bluebirds on the nightstand.

Sweet Pea, Whatever it is. We'll get through it. Call you later <3—L

In some kind of blissful cosmic reprieve, Perdie didn't feel sadness. Nor did she feel hurt or despair. Instead, mercifully, she felt nothing at all. An empty, all-encompassing nothingness.

She rounded the corner to the sole office on the floor, where an assistant at a desk notified Charles Joy that Perdie had arrived and then motioned for her to head in.

When she entered, the wall-to-wall window overlooking the harbor practically blinded her with sun. Frank and

Carter were already seated in front of the large oak desk with Charles Joy reclined behind it, like she had walked in on a meeting already in progress.

"Perdita. Thank you for joining us. Have a seat." Charles indicated the empty chair next to Carter's.

It brought her no joy to see that he looked like hell. Dark stubble framed the stiff line of his jaw. His eyes were droopy, his hair an uncharacteristic mess. He stared ahead, one leg stretched out with his hands folded in his lap.

"So, we'll make this a quick one." Charles leaned back in his large, leather chair. "Right, now that we're all present, first off I want to thank you both for your excellent work. The Fletcher Group had a great time, and that means *we* had a great time, if you know what I mean. Well done there."

"That's what I'm talking about, Charles," said Frank. "I knew I trusted the right lawyers with this client."

Perdie bit her tongue.

Charles Joy's eyes cut over to Frank, shutting him up in a heartbeat. He cleared his throat "Now onto the bad news. And by bad, I don't mean bad *bad*, I simply mean we'll have to do some adjusting, that's all. As you know, Fletcher Group has been acquiring a great many companies lately as part of their growth structure. And it has been brought to our attention that one of their recent acquirements is none other than Zelen Corp, the pharmaceutical company."

Perdie's senses tingled. Zelen Corp, the company she was preparing to sue for patent infringement with Noah. *Oh no*.

"I don't need to explain to you that this has become a conflict of interest in your patent case, Perdita."

Oh no, no, no.

"As such we've decided to go ahead and pull out of the patent case against Zelen."

Carter sat up. "You can't be serious?"

"But the Fletcher Group can waive the conflict." Perdie frowned.

"They refused the waiver. They don't want any muddled interests between us and them, and we, of course, defer to their wishes."

"But we can create in-office firewalls. Prevent the cases from leaking information within the firm. Firms do this kind of thing all the time." Perdie's heart was racing.

"Let me talk to the Fletcher Group." Carter's eyes darted to Perdie only for a moment. "I brought them on. They'll consider what I say."

Charles Joy shifted in his chair. "Carter, as always, I appreciate your willingness to show such admirable leadership qualities, but it wouldn't be prudent for you or this firm to jeopardize our relationship with the Fletcher Group."

"But the Fletcher Group is Carter's client. If he's willing to talk to them, why can't we at least try?" Perdie's foot was bouncing, her blood pressure rising.

Frank shrugged. "Sorry, kiddo. I told you that case was a bomb."

"Don't call me kiddo, you asshole. I'm thirty-nine years old." The words came out before she could think straight.

Frank bristled. "Well, no need for name calling. How unbecoming of a professional female. I guess, Charles, *some* associates can't handle the pressure. They're too *emotional*, if you know what I mean."

"Frank, I'm right *here*. I can hear you talking about me."

"Watch your attitude, or you'll buy yourself a one-way ticket to a bad end of the year review," said Frank.

Now she was pissed. "You propositioned Carter and me for a three-way not two days ago. *You're* too emotional. *You're* unbecoming. You're…you're disgusting, you…you…fucking *fossil*."

"Excuse me?" sputtered Frank.

Carter scoffed. "Frank, do you hear yourself? Even if you weren't being entirely sexist, which *you* are, don't you have even a shred of empathy? This was Perdie's big case, the first case she brought in on her own, and you've pulled it out from under her and acted like a condescending ass."

Perdie was grateful for the support but too furious to process. "And you won't even listen to reason."

Charles Joy's voice was deadly calm. "Perdita, I'd advise you to calm *down*. This is not appropriate behavior."

"Appropriate behavior? It's not appropriate behavior to hire Carter as a partner after I *smoked* him in a deposition."

Frank huffed. "First you're insulting me, and now Carter. Carter, who's done nothing but stand up for you? Did you know he came and talked to me about putting you up for partnership, did you know that? Said he believed in your talent. Really says a lot about your character, doesn't it, that you'd stab him in the back. Maybe you should consider how your own behavior has prevented a promotion instead of blaming those around you."

Perdie's mouth gaped. She almost fell speechless.

"No, she's right, Frank." Everyone's head turned to Carter. "Everything she's saying is true. She handed me my ass in the depo, and look at our respective positions now. Does it even make sense that I would *have* to go to bat for her? Maybe we all need to examine our actions a little more closely. Think about how we've been culpable in creating an unfair environment. Make some changes around here. The firm would be stronger, not weaker, for it."

"Do I look like a camp counselor to you, boy?" Charles said. "This is a *law* firm not a *feelings* firm."

But then Frank and Charles exchanged a look, a knowing look. A *possible sexual harassment lawsuit* look. They might attempt to get rid of her first. Claim poor performance.

"You know what? Fine. I'm *feeling* magnanimous this morning. I'll cut you a deal, Perdita," Charles said. "You go back to your office, get back to work as usual, and we'll all pretend like this little outburst never happened. Your bonus will remain intact provided you behave."

Carter shook his head. "This isn't right."

Perdie dug her nails into her palms, the bite of pain an odd relief. Hypocrites. *Inappropriate behavior.* They were only in the positions they had today because *everyone* had always let them get away with all kinds of inappropriate behavior. These old men partying on yachts, snorting cocaine, bringing clients to strip clubs, and judging *her*. Why did they get to make all the decisions about everyone else anyway? Where was the justice in that?

Whatever sadness she couldn't feel before manifested itself in rage. "No." The word came out harsh. "I won't go back to my office. And I won't go back to business as usual. No." She sprung to her feet. "I quit! Fuck you. Fuck all of you."

"Good lord in Heaven! You're proving my point!" Frank yelled.

"Oh hell," Charles grumbled.

"Jesus *Christ*, Perdie." That last voice, Carter's.

But she'd already run out to the lobby of Charles's office. Familiar footsteps chased after her. She halted, spun around, her eyes clenched. "Don't follow me. Don't talk to me. Don't say we can work things out because we can't. Don't say you want to help because you shouldn't. Delete my number. Pretend we never met. As far as you're concerned, I'm a ghost."

Carter's voice was deadly calm. "So, you're giving up. On us. On your job. I'm not fighting if you say there's nothing to fight for. I won't keep chasing you."

For one stinging moment, Perdie's desire to wrap herself around his body like a boa constrictor, cleaving him forever to her heart, almost won out over fleeing the scene of the crime. Almost. Instead, she wiped the threatening tear from her lower lid before it could drop. "No. You won't. Goodbye, Carter."

She pivoted on her heel and escaped to the elevator, and punched the buttons until the cheerful ding of its arrival. Carter didn't follow. Fifty percent relieved. Fifty percent devastated. One hundred percent not looking back.

When she reached the third floor, she ran to her office, ripping through her drawers, throwing her belongings in her briefcase. No more tears. No more sadness. She was *done*.

She hurried down the hallway.

"Hey, Perdie, back from your trip?" Jennifer's voice.

"Not now, Jennifer. I'm leaving."

Jennifer called after her. "Leaving? But I have to talk to—"

Perdie's back was already turned, her hand waved in the air as a dismissal. Her heart raced a mile a minute, walking briskly until she reached the parking lot. Then her phone began vibrating.

Lucille Knox.

Oh thank god, Lucille. Yes, she needed Lucille. *Lucille would help.* Lucille would have the right words. She brought the phone to her ear.

"Luce, you won't believe what happ—"

"P, shut up, shut up, shut up." Lucille's frantic voice stopped Perdie dead in her tracks. Muffled cries staticked on the other end. "You gotta get home, right now. Oh my god, it's bad. It's so bad. I don't know what to do!"

Perdie's heart raced like a wild horse, adrenaline coursing within her. She rushed into her car and turned on the engine. "I can't understand anything you're saying. Talk slow. What is it?"

Two, loud sobs came through the receiver. "It's Bananas. I came home for lunch…and *oh my god*…he's not okay. I don't think he's gonna… I don't think he's gonna make it."

Chapter Twenty-Eight

The vet said he'd lived a good life.

She said that in the end, he suffered little. That they had done the right thing. That they had done right by him.

Lucille and Perdie sat on the floor next to the window overlooking the water, where Bananas used to snore under the warm sun on cold winter days. Between them sparkled a bright yellow-and-gold vase Lucille had filled with Bananas's ashes.

"I don't think I'll ever find love again, P."

Perdie wiped at the corner of her eye, raw and burning, before grasping Lucille's hand.

"Maybe, someday…" She sniffed. "Maybe someday, you'll find a distant second. Maybe we both will."

Lucille's head dropped. "How're we gonna tell Pudding she's a widow?"

Perdie hiccupped. "We'll have to spread his ashes in the ocean, to commemorate their love."

Lucille smiled a bit. "Yeah. I think he'd like that. I wanted to keep him forever, you know? I guess I was in denial. But in the end, everyone needs to be free." She stared out the window. "Will you put on some music? I can't stand how quiet the house is without him."

"You want something so we can be more happy or something so we can be more sad?"

"Neither."

Perdie tapped through her phone until she found the song: Bleachers' "Stop Making This Hurt."

As the upbeat poppy tune pulsated through their condo, they both fell back, hand in hand, their heads resting on Bananas's old bed.

And together, they wept.

Perdie accepted the offer from the Meeting Street firm. It was something of a bum deal—not only was it a less prestigious firm, but she'd start at associate level, take less pay, work on lower-scale and local cases—but at least she didn't have to care. And as the named partner had a personal vendetta against Charles Joy (Charles had slept with his wife), they didn't give a good goddamn if Perdie had told Charles Joy to fuck off.

The only condition from Perdie was that she requested two weeks before her start date.

Because holy shit did she ever need a fucking break.

At first she and Lucille were wallowing hunks of dough, puffy and moist on the couch together. Either one might burst into tears at any given moment, depending on who was feeling what at the time.

"We're really going *Grey Gardens* up in this bitch, aren't we?" Lucille pulled an errant sock from Perdie's makeshift bun. "How'd this even get in there?"

Noah complicated the situation further when he turned up on their doorstep, sending Lucille scampering out of the house. Perdie called him on her new phone, having mailed the firm its phone after a full swipe of her personal data. She had to explain to Noah that Charles and

Frank had forced her to drop the case and her new firm had no interest in taking him on as a client either.

But when he arrived and leaned down to envelop Perdie in a bear hug, she sniffled.

"Don't be freaked out." She wiped her raw eyes with a tissue. "This has been happening all week. I'm very dehydrated. It's not you, it's me. I promise. Although I'm sorry to have let you down. You trusted me, and I failed you."

Noah shook his head. "I value our friendship a great deal more than I ever could a settlement check."

Noah's kind words made Perdie burst into tears, prompting Noah to reach into his wallet and hand her a card.

"What's this?"

He gave an understanding smile. "The number to a therapist. Might not hurt to have another person to talk to."

"Therapy is for people who are capable of change. Not only am I not capable, I'm not interested."

"Maybe you aren't. But maybe a therapist is capable of listening. And we all deserve to be heard, just as we are."

Hmm. His argument was concise, which Perdie respected. She'd never considered if she'd ever been *heard* before. What might that even feel like? "Fine. I'll consider it."

Noah nodded. "A wise idea."

Naturally Noah wanted to know what was going on with Lucille, not having heard from her in several weeks, but Perdie didn't have any good answers.

"She's had a lot of events lately. Baby showers. Weddings. I'm sure she'll call soon."

The furrow of Noah's brows told Perdie he knew she wouldn't.

Lucille was busy with the flower shop anyway. And Perdie, well, she couldn't lie to herself. Every night she dreamt about Carter showing up at her doorstep, asking her to come back. Saying they could work things out.

But in her dreams, it wasn't Carter who was different, it was Perdie. She was optimistic. Determined to follow through. Ready to work things out, like the kind of person who had faith in their abilities to love another. Hopeful. Relieved.

"We can live together, happily ever after," she said to a dream Carter at the end of a hotel bed. Sometimes they ate dream cookies together. In the darkness, she could believe anything.

In the cold stark light of day, not so much.

Real life wasn't a fairy tale. Carter wasn't a Disney prince. They were two grown-ass adults who didn't live in the same realities.

She sat up with a start, sweat staining her sheets, her face crusty and sore. Crying in her sleep? Honestly, a new low. She reached over to her nightstand and slid the therapist's card from the surface. "You win this round, Noah Crain."

Chapter Twenty-Nine

"Whatever happens in this room today, I'm not gonna be one of those people who blames everything on my mother. In fact, I'm not talking about my mother at all."

"Okay." Therapist Jacqueline Mei, a thoughtful woman in her fifties, regarded Perdie with the calmness of an elementary school teacher waiting for her class to stop talking. "What would you like to talk about?"

Perdie shrugged. The therapist's office was cozy with a plush beige couch and a plethora of mismatched throw pillows. She hugged one to her chest. "I don't know, isn't that what I pay you for?"

Jacqueline said nothing, sitting in silence with Perdie for an entire minute. As an attorney, Perdie was familiar with this tactic. Silence compelled people to talk. It wouldn't work on her. She was only here to make Noah happy and to help fill the hours of her day so she wouldn't have to spend any of them thinking about Carter.

Carter.

Her new job was a boring, unfulfilling dead end. And that was good because Perdie didn't want to care anymore. Aspirations hurt. And success was a trap. The people at the top, in her experience, were predatory dickheads. And it simply wasn't worth it. She shouldn't have tried to play their game in the first place.

She'd been through a lot in one year.

Her voice was creaky. "I'm here because I want to be heard."

Jacqueline nodded. "Then I'm relieved this isn't a Home Depot. They're bad listeners."

Perdie let out a laugh. Then she sobered. "I don't think my mother loved me, and as a result I don't think I know how to love me. Or other people...sometimes."

Jacqueline scribbled a note on a pad. "Do you want to talk about it?"

Perdie sighed. "I guess I should since I'm not here to buy hurricane shutters."

Jacqueline suspected Perdie was depressed. (*"Uh, doi,"* Perdie said. "I wore my pants backwards yesterday and didn't even feel it. You ever put dress pants on backwards?") She scheduled Perdie three times a week. Overkill in Perdie's mind, but then, surprising herself, she agreed anyway.

The more she focused on other projects, the more she could banish Carter from her mind: like how she and Lucille were buying a new house. She couldn't believe it, but it was a welcome endeavor.

Lucille brought up the topic one evening at dinner. It was out of the blue, but that was Lucille. "So, I've been thinking. Maybe we could use a little more space."

Perdie pushed her mac and cheese back and forth on her plate. All food tasted like trash. "Oh?"

"What do you think about this? Lucille Knox Handcrafted Cards. Sell them at the shop and online. Charge an arm and a leg, like I do my arrangements. But we would need extra room for a studio. I know we love this place, but…we've outgrown it. Space-wise that is."

Perdie had several of Lucille's watercolor cards, all adorned with beautiful wispy bluebirds and little hand-written notes. Perdie would always gamble on Lucille's talent.

"I'm in. I'll find the Realtor." Good thing she knew one.

"So, Lucille is taking on this new chapter of her life, and of course, I'll be right there with her. But…why do I feel so stagnated? Empty?" Because she missed the hell out of Carter, and she couldn't even feel a thing about it.

Dr. Mei nodded sagely. "Sometimes in order to feel that we're moving forward, we have to put ourselves in uncomfortable positions. Growth comes when we exert stress on ourselves. Take risks."

Perdie blew her hair out of her face. "But I do take risks. I risk sleeping with opposing counsel. I risk an il-licit affair at work. I risk getting wasted at holiday par-ties."

"It sounds like you only take risks that you're certain won't pay off. But do you ever take risks when it really counts?"

"What do you mean?"

"Risks where you might get hurt. Risks that really pay off. Do you take those risks or do you cut and run?"

Lucille's words echoed from all those months ago, the first time they'd met Noah. *Sometimes things are meant to be, and you have to stick with them to find out. You can't cut and run because things aren't perfect.*

She hugged the beige pillow from the couch. "My mother wasn't interested in anything I did. We never had money, but it was more than that. She didn't have emotional currency either. Good behavior or bad behavior, I couldn't get her attention. I think I began to think of myself as inherently disappointing. I reinforce those feelings at work and in romantic relationships. I think I'll disappoint everyone in the end."

Jacqueline nodded. "And so what if you do? Disappointment never killed anyone. Are you meant to be a perfect person? What if...you take the risk, and you *don't* disappoint simply by being yourself?"

"Wow. Somehow I never considered that possibility. I guess this is why I pay you."

Jacqueline chuckled. "May I offer you a challenge?"

"You may."

"Next time you feel yourself running away, running out of fear of letting down others, decide that disappointment is a risk they'll have to live with if they want to live with you. Just like with anyone else. Make a choice and believe that you're worth it."

Perdie crossed her arms. "Hmm. I'm skeptical but..."

Perdie was wiping out the inside of her kitchen cabinets in preparation for future condo showings when a knock came at the door.

Life had calmed to a dull point after an initial wave of grief. She was empty and complacent at her new job. To a certain degree, she welcomed the numbness. Her career ambitions were effectively on life support. Her love life a distant and hazy memory. She was almost like a ghost, and while the therapy was helping, she wasn't back to breathing yet. Maybe she was closer to a half-resuscitated zombie. Maybe she needed a good zap like Frankenstein's monster.

And maybe she had one final idea to do just that.

Knock knock knock.

"We having company?" Lucille bounded down the stairs in Perdie's *Spring Breakers* T-shirt and a pair of holey leggings. Perdie's heart sank a little. Bananas wasn't trotting behind her.

"Not quite." Perdie had changed her outfit for this meeting, wearing her black cigarette pants with a white button-up. *Professional-ish.* Not a sock in the hair to be found.

She cracked her knuckles as she walked to the door and swung it open. "Hello, Jennifer."

Before responding, Jennifer ducked her head to the side to peer behind Perdie. "Oh my goodness, Lucy?" she squealed.

"Oh my god, Jenny!" Lucille squealed back.

"Lucy?" Perdie murmured as Jennifer breezed in past her.

"Where's Bananas? I thought you had a lovely little dog."

Lucille shook her head, a frown on her face. "He didn't make it."

Jennifer pulled Lucille in for a hug. "Tragic news."

"Sorry, but are you two *friends*?" Perdie asked.

Jennifer released Lucille. "Lucy did the flowers for the baby shower. I know I told you, but you *never* listen." She straightened her periwinkle silk blouse. "Anyway, I'm here at your request, Perdita. After storming out of the office like a tornado…people are still talking about the stir you caused."

Perdie stiffened. "Well, that's comforting."

"*Awwwkward.* On that note I'm outta here," Lucille called as she disappeared up the stairs.

Perdie gestured towards the kitchen table. "Welcome to my home, Jennifer. I've missed you. Have a seat."

Jennifer sat, primly crossing her legs. "Well?"

Perdie took a big breath. "I want to start a firm. With you and Sophia as partners."

Jennifer blinked. "Excuse me? But you don't even like us. We couldn't even pin you down for a simple meeting at Joy and Schulz."

"I know, I was avoiding you. I—I thought you wanted to scold me about dating a partner. But look, I get it now, I deserved it anyway."

Jennifer gave an incredulous look. "Who? Leplan? Who cares?"

Perdie scrunched her face. "But you made comments… and you jumped in on that patent case as soon as he agreed to take it on with me."

Jennifer pinched the bridge of her nose, shaking her head. "Yes, I did. I wanted to have your back in case the firm tried to give Carter credit for all your hard work. We were trying to work *with* you."

"Oh. I didn't realize."

"Yeah, *oh*. I think there are many things you don't realize. Do you think you're the only overlooked person at that office? Do you think the rest of us sail on through to partnership? Sophia and I have been at that firm nearly as long as you, and we haven't made partner yet either. I went to Duke. Heck, Sophia brought on a client last year. Not to mention she's one of only *five* Black lawyers in the entire firm. Out of two hundred and fifty! Did you ever think about that? Especially now that she's pregnant. They'll roll right past her once she's on maternity leave."

"Sophia's pregnant?"

Jennifer's eyebrows shot up. "Who do you think the

baby shower was for? Oh my god, Perdita, you really are the most selfish bitch."

Perdie's eyes went wide, but then she bit back a laugh because Jennifer was right. She really was. She'd misjudged them by a league. "Can't argue facts. And speaking of facts, I have a case with no home. I'm sure you're aware they dropped my case at Joy and Schulz."

"Of course I know! I was one of the lawyers helping you." Jennifer paused before she spoke again, her words measured. "Look, I'm going to level with you. Sophia is staying with me and Owen. She's divorcing that awful husband of hers right now, and after that she'll be on maternity leave. It's a stressful time, she's going through some nasty stuff, and as her best friend, I'm trying to get through it with her. This isn't a great time for huge changes."

Jennifer and Sophia were best friends. Like Perdie and Lucille. She and Lucille had been going through a lot…but wow. Still, all the more reason to push forward with her argument.

"You said so yourself, nobody's getting promoted over at Joy and Schulz, they pass people like us up until we're shriveled and old. *Now's* the chance for all of us to work together. You wanted a meeting with me, and you got it. I'm ready to talk to Sophia too." Perdie pulled a business card from her pocket and plopped it in front of Jennifer. "Here. I had these made. Look pretty good together, don't they?"

Jennifer picked up the card in the middle of the table with the partner names *Stone, Stein, and Steele*. She glanced up at Perdie. "It's not the worst thing I've ever seen."

"Aw, don't flatter me. Now c'mon, Jenny. What do you say? Partners?"

* * *

Jacqueline applauded Perdie at her next therapy session.

"Keep your momentum. It's hard work to challenge deeply ingrained beliefs about yourself, but you can do it."

Perdie nodded. "Aye, aye, captain."

Chapter Thirty

"As you know from the links I sent, this is the only available duplex option, and I think it's perfect for two modern gals like y'all," Aubrey chirped. "Kitchens and bathrooms are newly renovated, and appliances are all up-to-date. And would you check out these beautiful marble countertops." She slicked a hand over the smooth surface. "To die for. Hard to tell with this rainy weather, but the skylights in the foyer offer great natural lighting. Of course, if you really want an upgrade, I've got a four-thousand-square-foot colonial with a marsh view that's new on the market."

"Sounds a little out of our price range, Aubrey," Perdie mused as she strolled around the kitchen island.

Aubrey adjusted the pendant on her delicate gold necklace. She wore a bright red cardigan. The correct shade. "You know the owner. Carter Leplan?"

Perdie's hand froze over a shining chrome faucet handle. "He's selling his house? But he must've just bought it?" The words tumbled out a little too fast.

"Mmm-hmm, such a shame he's leaving tomorrow. Back to San Francisco. He's a looker, that one. Sweet though."

Shit. Shit. Shit.

The news sent a bolt of panic down Perdie's spine. She had questions. Although things were already over, Carter moving away meant it was *really* the end. It meant he wasn't secretly pining for her like he had been in her dreams. He wasn't trying to bump into her by accident at the grocery store. He was moving. Moving *on*.

Lucille wandered in from the dining room in a Pussy Riot shirt and a sucker hanging from her mouth. She popped it out. "We'll take it. You think we could convert this room into a studio?" She glanced at Perdie. "The hell's wrong with you?"

"Nothing, nothing at all," Perdie snapped, but her internal systems short-circuited.

Later that night, while the sky rained and thundered, Perdie did the one thing she swore she'd never do again, not since the day they'd first met: she googled Carter Leplan.

"Whatcha doing, P?" asked Lucille, who was strolling through the house inspecting every nook and cranny for a potential future move-out day.

Perdie jumped in her chair, her body involuntarily tense. "Torturing myself."

"Don't torture too late. You have an important meeting tomorrow."

She did. Perdie, Jennifer, and Sophia had been working hard on Noah's case. "No promises."

A rumbling of thunder had her jumping again. A nervous energy permeated. What was she searching for? A sign? A Google search sign? For what though? Perdie scrolled through the lawyerly results, pictures of Carter wearing expensive suits and professional smiles, links to the Joy and Schulz website and Carter's old firm.

Then something caught her eye. Exhibition: SF

Museum of Modern Art, Cindy Leplan *The Paths We Choose.*

Don't you click that fucking link, Perdita.

She clicked the fucking link. Carter's mother's exhibition from Easter.

Her heart dropped. In the cover shot of an embedded video was Carter, almost hidden in the background near an enormous painting of a multicolored fluorescent and gold-brushed mountain.

Against good self-preserving sense, she played the video. Cindy Leplan, in a gold-and-blush gown/muumuu hybrid spoke to the camera interview-style, her voice floaty and calm. "It's about 'The Road Not Taken.' The Robert Frost poem. People often misinterpret it, but I've endeavored to capture its imagery here. No matter what road we choose in life, we might always ask ourselves what could have been. The colors of life are multitudinous. Both the regret and the joy of choice is one of life's inevitable tortures."

But Perdie's eyes fixated on the action behind Cindy. "Yeah, yeah, yeah…now what's going on over here?" She zoomed in on the corner with Carter.

He was chatting with someone out of frame, smiling, doing that thing where he rubbed his hair back and forth, and then…then *she* came into view. The person he was talking to. They were both dressed in all black, the woman with thick, dark hair much like Perdie's, curvy. Pretty, definitely pretty even from a low-res video. The woman clasped both Carter's hands, leaned in towards his ear, and they shared a laugh. The actions portrayed a special sense of intimacy Perdie had once herself been familiar with, there was no denying it.

A wealth of energized fire welled up inside her, inactive for months. Her anger, her spark, her passion had lain dormant until this very moment.

He was fucking dating? That *motherfucker.*

At the very least, he was hand-clasping. He and the woman appeared to like each other very, very much.

And he was *moving* back home. Like a light in a dark room, the video illuminated a terrifying truth.

Carter was moving to San Francisco for this new woman. Of course he would. It sounded unreasonable, but with Carter it made perfect sense. He'd moved to be with Perdie once too. He went after what he wanted. An unbridled optimist who was always dealt a lucky hand.

They would do all the things Perdie swore she could never do: move in together, share a closet, go to the grocery store. Juice those fucking oranges. The family Carter and his mothers wanted. A woman who wouldn't disappoint.

Against her better judgment, she replayed the video, but this time instead of the dull pain eating her insides, furious anger enflamed her heart. Who was this woman? A knockoff Perdie Stone. *Agh.*

She scrunched her hair in her hands, ready to scream. And then it dawned on her. She needed to see him. Right now. Right *fucking* now.

Jacqueline's voice twittered like a little bird in her ear: *Take the risk. What's the worst that can happen?*

Thunder snapped hard outside.

Fuck it. She googled his address. How had she never even been to his house before? She really was selfish.

Her arms were numb as she shoved them through her wool coat to cover her mini sleep shorts and camisole-clad body. Her knees shook when she pushed her feet into Lucille's fuzzy rabbit slippers. And before she left, she grabbed the extra key off the credenza and shoved it in her pocket.

The soft slipper material soaked instantly when Perdie's feet hit the pavement of the parking lot.

Complete madness. Her actions would likely end in humiliating disaster.

But some risks were worth getting hurt for.

The four-thousand-square-foot colonial with a marsh view had an expansive driveway, and her windshield wipers fought overtime against the downpour as she neared. The vehicle slid on a diagonal when in haste she threw it into a lurching stop. She tumbled out, then sprinted.

Bang. Bang. Bang.

She pounded the door with a wild intensity she had never used against a piece of wood before. Rain pelted her sideways, hair already plastered to her face and neck.

No answer.

She stepped back to view the windows. *Fuck it.*

"Carter!" she yelled. "Carter! *Open the door!* Open the *fucking* door!"

Rain drowned her out, and her skin slicked from the heavy, sopping coat. An internal countdown. *One Carolina two Carolina three Caro—*

A light illuminated a window. Then a few seconds and the door opened.

Perdie froze. The woman from the video stood before her.

The woman tightened the knot on her bright floral silk robe. Her raven hair was mussed but still better than Perdie's on a good day. She really was pretty. Maybe Perdie was the knockoff?

But adrenaline compelled momentum. She'd made it

this far, time to bust the yellow tape. "Ahem. Can I talk to Carter?"

"Who're you?"

"A ghost come to life."

"That's a weird thing to say."

Perdie's voice caught in her throat as Carter appeared behind the woman. He was shirtless, somehow more muscular than she'd remembered, and god help her, in her heightened state even now he sent an extra thrill to her toes. But also terror. *Shirtless with this other woman*.

"Perdie?" He rubbed his eyes. "What are you doing here? It's two in the morning."

She winced, futilely wiped at the slick skin on her cheek, then squeezed her eyes shut and let the words spew. "I only need forty-five seconds. Sixty tops. And if you won't talk to me, then—then..." she sputtered. "I don't even know what I'll do. Have to go to therapy every single day? I'm already there three times a week." Her eyes snapped back open, desperate.

Carter and the woman exchanged a concerned glance, but then he nodded. "Go to bed. I'll take care of this."

The woman's features wrinkled, but then she shrugged and turned back into the house. "Say the word, and I'll get the Taser."

As soon as the door shut, Perdie blurted out, "Are you with that woman?"

Carter stepped beneath the protective overhang in front of the doorframe. Sprinkles of water decorated his eyelashes while Perdie stood drenched, uncovered.

"Give me your phone," he ordered.

"Excuse me?"

"A timer. You're lucky I'm giving you sixty seconds." He held out his hand.

Perdie wasn't used to this Carter. Stern Carter. Her jaw dropped at his audacity but in reality *she* was the audacious one turning up like a wet rat on his doorstep in the middle of the night, in the middle of a storm, in the middle of what might be a complete nervous break-down. She dug into her sports bra and handed him the unlocked device.

"Lucille says you're out of tampons."

"Huh?" Was he making a joke?

But his stern expression remained, challenging. He tapped the screen a few times and held up the countdown display. "Well?"

She should've come prepared. A PowerPoint, maybe. Few index cards. But in the absence of a full TEDx speech, she'd have to speak from the heart. *Shit.* She stared blankly at that perfect face and those beautiful hazel eyes. They were smudged with dark shadows be-neath. "Goddamn, you are so handsome."

He shook his head. "Try again."

She pointed her index finger with slow deliberation as truer words came to her. "But it's not your looks that matter, looks fade, and… I…uhhh…okay, I fucked up. I'm a USDA grade A asshole. I freaked out and ran at the first sign of something real and it's inexcusable because you're amazing inside and out. There're a million reasons why I want to be with you including but not limited to the fact that you're handsome and amazing in bed." She paused to redirect herself. "You're also kind and funny and smart and were good with Bananas and I think Lu-cille would quite frankly love to put you in an oil paint-ing. And you make me feel…you make me feel *happy*. Like a person deserving of a real relationship. The kind of relationship where you don't cut and run at the first sign of conflict. The kind of relationship worth fighting for. Which, if we're being honest, I don't really know a good goddamn about. Fighting for something, that is. Pretty scary for a coward like me."

When his Adam's apple bobbed, she paused again, hoping he'd jump in and save her. *Nope, keep going.*

"I've been seeing a therapist, and she's really got me on a self-reflection train...and..." She stuttered, the turbocharged energy with which she'd arrived dissipating.

The timer ticked on. "And?" he prompted.

"First stop: Apology Station..." She squeezed her palms until her nails dug into the flesh. "I'm sorry. I'm so sorry. I've missed you. So much. I was wrong, about everything really."

Carter pursed his lips, finally, closing his eyes for a moment. "I've missed you too."

"I want you, Carter. Back to the way we were. You and me. I won't be a fuckup this time, I swear."

Carter hung his head. "Do you think that's what I want...to return to how things were? Keep playing the same old games?"

"Carter—" A loud boom exploded in the sky, and Perdie jerked, giving a little yelp. But before she could recover she was interrupted.

Beep beep beep. Beep beep beep.

Both their gazes traveled to the screen and the zeroed-out timer.

"Time's up." He handed her the phone. "I think you should go."

The inside of Perdie's chest crumpled. Had she thought it would be so easy? No, Carter wanted more from her, he'd made that clear from the start. And that's what she'd come with: more. And she was going to offer it up if it killed her, goddammit.

"You didn't let me finish! Closing statements. Five more seconds. P-please."

Carter crossed his arms, eyebrows lifted, as if to say *well?*

She dug inside her soaking coat pockets for a metal object and gestured for him to take it.

He held out his hand. "What's this?"

"A key." She placed it in his palm and clasped it to hers. Then she pressed his hand against her soaking chest, against her wildly thumping heart. Suddenly, she understood all those times when he'd done this to her. She understood what he meant. "Move in with me."

She squeezed his hand. "I don't want things to go back to the way things were. I want to move forward. With you. I want to wake up and see you every morning. I want to make up for the absolute mess I've made of the two of us." This time, soreness tightened in her throat. Oh, fuck, she really loved him.

"Perdie…"

"Good risks, you know?"

Gently, he lowered their hands, near their waists between them. "Perdie. I can't."

Her brain searched for the right thing to say. "I'll beg if I have to."

She went to drop to her knees, but Carter caught her fast by the elbow, drawing her up. "Please don't do that. I can't stand to see you do that."

Perdie sniffled, blankly staring up at him, her vision cleared. His hand fell away from her elbow. The loud rainstorm reduced to a quiet, misty drizzle.

Her head hung low. "Because I'm too late? Because you're with someone else now?"

"Because I'm leaving tomorrow."

"Back home, I know," she mumbled, defeated. "Where you belong."

"Well…" He shook his head. "It's complicated."

"Oh god, I've really fucked up, haven't I?"

"You're not exactly batting a thousand."

Her lip quivered a bit. "I don't know what that means. I don't watch sports."

Then he reached out and curled his finger under her chin. "Hey, look at me." His eyes had softened, not steeled as they had been before. "I quit the firm. Right after you, actually, the whole place went up in arms. Never thought I'd see Frank so scandalized. Considered moving back to San Francisco…lick my wounds somewhere comfortable…but then something strange happened."

"You dreamt about me?"

"I ran into Aisha Wakely."

"Not where I thought you were going with that. Aisha from Lowcountry Pro Bono Access? Tom's wife?"

He nodded. "She offered me a job. Associate position. Terrible pay, tough work, lotta prostrating in front of donors…but a chance to contribute to the community. Use my skills for good."

"Yeah, but what kind of person takes a downgrade like—"

"I accepted her offer."

"You…you did?" *Oh.* Oh! "You're staying here?"

"Well, almost. I told her there's one thing I have to do first before I start work again."

"Which is…"

"Climb Denali."

Perdie shook her head, a bit amazed. "Wow, you're actually going to climb that fucking mountain."

"Been training for months. Had energy to burn without you around. Look, I figure now is as good as time as any. Instead of following the yellow brick road, I do what I actually want to do. For no one but myself." That explained the extra muscles.

"But—but…what if you *die*? What if you don't come back?"

"I won't."

"You won't come back?"

"I won't die."

"How could you possibly know that?"

"I have something important to return to."

Perdie gazed up from beneath her lashes. "Your new job?"

Carter shoved his hands into the pockets of his sweatpants and shrugged. "Well, there happens to be this woman who walked out on me and ruined my life not so long ago. She gave me the runaround and broke my heart and then showed up at the worst possible time on my doorstep soaking wet… I thought I'd give her another chance to ruin my life."

Perdie's throat tightened when his words registered. She couldn't believe it. That her risk could pay off. That she was someone worth taking a risk on too.

A smile curled on her lips. "You're a masochist. She sounds like a real bitch."

"Understatement." He pulled Perdie in beneath the overhang and smoothed the wet hair from her forehead. Her sagging wet coat clung to her shoulders. "But that's what I love about her."

"I love you too." The words escaped quietly.

He nodded. "Yeah, I know."

"So, you'll do it? Move in with me?"

His fingertips grazed her exposed upper back. "We'll talk when I return, and we can discuss all the ways you'll make things up to me. When we've both had time to think on it. No offense but you're a little bit—" he tilted his head to regard her "—desperate right now."

She whapped his chest. "Hey!"

He caught her hand and smiled. "To be honest with you, I can't afford this huge house any longer. It's going up for sale. Maybe the Porsche too."

She gave him a sideways look. "Seems that the universe is telling us something." Then she nestled her head against his chest, breathing in deep the familiar scent. "I'll wait. Whatever it takes. But, Carter...*who* is that woman? She's not your girlfriend?"

Carter squinted, confused. "Joanne? My sister-in-law. Joanne, Michael, and their kids are staying in the house while I'm away."

Perdie's hand slapped her forehead. "Of course it's your sister-in-law! It's always a sister of some kind... You'd think I'd learned a thing or two by now."

"Carter?" As if on cue, Joanne's voice came from behind the door. Had she been eavesdropping the whole time? "Do we finally get to meet your girlfriend or is she another one of your stalkers?"

The door opened and Michael stood with Joanne. They looked an awful lot like Carter and Perdie but...better.

OMG Carter and Perdie were the knockoff Michael and Joanne.

"Jesus, let her come inside, get her dried off. Mom

would kill you if she knew you let her stand outside in the rain."

Perdie pushed away from Carter, sadly attempting to straighten herself. "No, I can't... I have to be somewhere first thing tomorrow. And besides, I'm completely mortified."

Carter gave them a pointed look. "Sorry, guys, private matter."

Michael went to protest but Joanne grabbed him by the biceps. "Michael, leave them alone. They want privacy."

"Fine, fine, but at least I didn't tell her she was running out of time like Mom," Michael grumbled.

"Sorry for showing up in the middle of the night!" Perdie called after them as the door shut again.

Then it was just her and Carter and the silence that fell after the storm.

His hand sneaked inside her coat and he hooked a finger into the waistband of her shorts, drawing her close. "I'm going to kiss you now."

"Okay, yep, I'm ready..." But she wasn't, she would never be ready for big love like the kind Carter had to give. But being ready didn't matter a damn bit. Because she wanted it anyway. All of it.

Carter's lips met hers in a gentle caress, making her eyes flutter like butterflies.

He squeezed her wet, puffy, sopping body against his dry one.

"If you die on that mountain, I'll kill you."

He smiled, and kissed her again. "Fair enough."

Chapter Thirty-One

"We are crackin' bottles tonight, baby!" *Pop!* The cork sailed through the air. Perdie rushed the overflow to the sink, then doled out glasses. "This is the good stuff, y'all. The twelve ninety-nine shit, not that three ninety-nine swill."

They originally planned to hit the town for the evening, but Sophia, Jennifer, Perdie, and Noah were all too tired and too deeply into their thirties to muster up the will. Instead they decided on getting drunk and ordering pizza.

With their powers combined and a little bit (a lot) of good fortune, the three women had settled Noah's patent case against Zelen Corp. Normally these cases would go on for years, wringing so much money out of a small firm that they'd simply give up, but the pharma company was in a tenuous place after the acquisition by the Fletcher Group so they wanted to wash their hands of the case. The millions they settled for was peanuts to the corporation, but a hell of a lot for Perdie, Sophia, Jennifer, and Noah.

So, after all that, the acquisition that had lost her the case at Joy and Schulz had ultimately won her the case

with Stone, Stein, and Steele. She should send Joy and
Schulz a fruit basket.

Perdie couldn't wait to tell Carter, who was returning tomorrow. She was also sick to her stomach with
nerves. They hadn't been able to speak while he was on
the mountain, and for all she knew, he might've totally
changed his mind while gone. Summits could do strange
things to a person. Offer clarity where there was none.
Perdie could only hope the kind of clarity that came to
Carter meant he'd missed her as much as she missed
him. In the meantime, she'd take her wins where she
could get them.

As a settlement, the win was symbolic only. Well, and
monetary. But they were still going to party like it was
1999. Perdie had, indeed, turned Noah into a rich man.
"A person of her word," Noah called her.

"To many more wins." Sophia lifted her flute. The
light reflected the gold wrapped into her long balayage
locs. After leaving Joy and Schulz, Sophia had changed
her hair for easier upkeep with her baby, Winter (Lucille
had generously offered up the name). Sophia, Jennifer,
and Perdie were the bosses now so they could dictate the
terms of employment. Fuck the boys' club. The glasses
tinked as they cheers-ed.

"Don't drink too much, you're a lightweight now."
Jennifer fussed over Sophia. "You have to ease back into
these things."

"This is my first full night off without the baby in
months. Momma is going to town…" She took a big gulp
from her glass. "Metaphorically at least."

The front door burst open and Lucille rushed in, a boat
bouquet of flowers in her arms, a suspicious glint in her
eye. She placed the flowers on the counter. "Hey, P. Hi,

Soph, Jenny, uh, Noah. No time to chat. P, you're gonna
wanna change into something real nice." She paused
at Perdie. "Here, fix this and that…and that berry lip
stain too. Wait, no, I take it back, you don't need the lip
stain, it'll make a mess. Okay, *mwuah*. Love you. Be
right back."

Perdie gave the others a nod. "One sec…" she said,
following Lucille up the stairs. She stopped Lucille in
front of her bedroom. "Why are you acting suspicious?"

Lucille bit her lip. "I don't know anything, I am but a
humble shopgirl selling her wares in the village."

Perdie eyed her, but this was typical Lucille behavior.
"Mmm-kay. You're 'fessing up at some point."

"That's what you think." Lucille's door shut.

Perdie shuffled to her own room and inspected her
clothes in the mirror. Changing into something more
presentable wasn't a half-bad idea. They were celebrat-
ing, after all.

With a sigh, she pulled off her T-shirt and fraying
denim shorts, deciding a fitted cotton ribbed tank dress
would be enough of an upgrade. She'd need to change
her bra though. She flung open her dresser drawer and
found the red silk bra, the one she wore the evening
Carter went down on her on a conference table. *Oh boy.
Talk about memories*.

Once dressed, she stepped out into the hallway.

"Ah, you listened. Amazing. You look good." Lucille
gripped Perdie by her shoulders. "Don't worry, when the
time comes, I'll get everyone out of here."

Perdie crinkled her nose. "Huh?" But Lucille was already gone.

She was making her way down the stairs when the
doorbell rang. *Pizza's here*.

"Coming! I got the tab," Perdie called before opening the door. "It's you. The man of my dreams."

"Uh…" The pizza deliveryman blushed at the greeting, handing over the stack of boxes. "Sign here please, ma'am."

Perdie scribbled a signature, then handed it back. "A real American hero," she said as the guy walked away. She was one second from closing the door when a shadow rounded the corner.

She almost didn't recognize the bearded man with shaggy hair and a familiar gait who neared. "Carter?" *Lucille.* Somehow she'd known he'd return early. Perdie almost dropped the pizza.

She'd missed him.

When he made his way to the door, he gripped her by the waist, his quiet voice sending prickles all long her neck. "I've missed you, Bad Girl. You've got ten seconds to get upstairs or I'm fucking you right here."

Perdie froze, but then slowly set the pizza boxes on the floor.

Wordlessly he grabbed her hand and as if entranced she followed him through the group in the kitchen.

"Carter?" Sophia's head turned as they passed by. "Wow, you look…just, wow."

But he remained singularly focused on Perdie. "Hey, Sophia, talk soon okay?"

"Should we, uh, offer him a drink?" Jennifer asked.

"Nah." Lucille's voice came from behind. "I don't think we'll be seeing them for a little while."

Carter clomped up the stairs with Perdie close behind. Her heart pounded. He opened the door to Perdie's room and gently guided her to the bed before sitting himself.

The man in front of her was worn. He'd grown a beard

and his hair had gone shaggy. Older looking even though it'd only been a month.

And did she need an eye exam or had she spotted a gray hair or two sprigging out near his temple? Her instinct was to touch it, trace the silver with her fingertips.

Endorphins ran high from the physical chase and this new look on Carter... She licked her lips. Well, life really wasn't predictable, was it? He was usually so urbane. But now he looked...rough.

"Kissing you with a beard is gonna be weird," she whispered.

"I can assure you it's the only appropriate course of action." His voice was equally soft.

Succumbing to temptation, she gently caressed the hairs at his temple, his eyes drooping from the touch.

Then like a flash, they were on one another, mouths and tongues desperately seeking, her hands frantically finding the buttons of his shirt as his hands trailed up her thigh beneath her dress, kneading the flesh roughly.

His fingers found the waistband of her underwear and yanked hard to uncover her. She lifted her hips to assist, then kicked the scrap of fabric to the floor, abandoning the pursuit of shirt buttons for the more important one at his pants.

"You...owe me...new panties," she gasped against his mouth. He wasted no time, greedily locating her clit with the pads of his fingertips, circling the hot bud with unbridled, messy enthusiasm. Her eyes rolled back in her head, moaning, but her hands managed to free the bulging erection from his boxer briefs.

He growled when she stroked his dick, pulling her to his lap, groping her breasts, her waist, her thighs.

His voice reverberated into her ear. "If you don't jump

on my cock and ride me like I'm the last rodeo right now, I'm gonna have to turn you around and rail you against the wall, and believe me when I say I won't be fucking gentle."

They both froze in realization after the words. Then a flustered rearrangement of bodies. Before she could blink, Perdie was on her knees, hands white-knuckling the headboard, her ass rocking back and forth on the tip of Carter's cock. When Carter slammed inside her from behind, she gasped, the entire bed lurching with thrusting momentum.

"Fuck," she groaned. "You're still good at this."

"It's been too long since my cock's been inside you." He panted.

"Practically a lifetime. *Goddamn.*"

"You left me, Bad Girl. You left me, and you better never do it again." He gave her a hard slap against her ass.

A sharp cry escaped her. *Surprising.*

"Now I'm going to punish you for it."

"I'll never do it again," she pleaded, hoping for another smack.

He delivered, his palm hitting with enough force to burn brightly, hurtling her towards an orgasm. "Say it like you mean it."

"I love you, don't stop."

He didn't.

Perdie's reality shifted as Carter flipped her over again, now on her back, his lips and tongue covering her nipples, then a hot tongue trailing up along her neck, finding its way to her mouth. He cupped her breast, pinching her nipples, lacking all the usual finesse, as he shoved harshly into her again. And Perdie, could do nothing but hang on for dear life. Quickly, she reached her limit, her muscles clamping around him, threatening to convulse.

"Oh no, Carter, I'm…coming already." Her body tightened like a cord.

He bucked against her, burying his head in her neck, hot breath heating her from the inside out. "Good. Me too."

When she began to come, he muffled her cries with the palm of his hand against her mouth. Blinking hard, tears streamed down her cheeks, she held on, nearly blacking out, as the orgasm exploded and then subsided in dying bursts inside her. He pushed his weight heavy against her, finally toppling, body broken. A sated slackness overtook her every sense.

He ducked his head to kiss her lightly on the collarbone and then rolled away, spent like a mannequin with his legs stretched out.

"It feels different this time," she whispered.

He squeezed her hand tightly in his.

She squeezed back. "We didn't do much talking."

"And yet, we said it all."

Awkwardly Perdie rounded the corner down the stairs. Although she and Carter had made efforts to keep quiet, she was well aware that the whole gang would know what they'd been up to.

Soft music played in the room, no voices. They'd left.

In the middle of the coffee table was the boat vase filled with the flowers, champagne in an ice bucket, two flutes, and pizza plated on the nice white plates Lucille and Perdie almost never used. Also, a few candles fluttered in a glowy light.

Perdie grabbed the bottle of champagne, sat down on

the couch, patting the seat next to her. She popped the cork slowly so she didn't spill, and champagne smoke whirled from the top. Carter sat, his arm reaching out behind her, pulling her in close by the shoulder. She swigged from the bottle, then passed it over to him.

"Here's to the first day of our lives together."

He accepted the bottle, pulling big. Then he smiled. "First of many."

Epilogue

"Well, I just can't get over how you and Lucille have lived together for *so* long. It's like a marriage, isn't it?" Aubrey ran an immaculately manicured fingertip over the marble countertops of Perdie's newly purchased duplex. After the closing, Aubrey had stopped by to drop off a housewarming gift for Perdie and Carter: a wedding topper of the two of them designed by a local sculptor.

Perdie liked the gift but she and Carter weren't quite *there* yet. Or at least, Perdie wasn't. Still, things had progressed quite a bit by Perdie's standards. After all, it was the first time Perdie had ever lived with a man.

"Yep, longest relationship I've ever had. How are things going with Max by the way?"

Aubrey gave a coy smile. "I can't thank you enough for giving me his number. Long distance is a challenge, but we're in that exciting, fun new phase."

"Yes, I know it well." Perdie stretched on the tips of her toes to place her Will Provide Legal Advice for Tacos mug back into the kitchen cabinet.

Within a few moments, the front door opened and a plethora of sound overtook the house. Carter appeared in the hallway.

Perdie's heart fluttered just a bit at the sight of him.

After a few weeks of role-playing some very campy Mountain Man sex, Carter was back to looking like himself again. He was dressed in expensive denim and a T-shirt. The new job working for Aisha was a lot more casual than Joy and Schulz, which actually suited Carter's personality quite well.

"I come bearing gifts." Carter pocketed his phone and set a box of donuts on the counter. Peanut Butter scurried over to greet his dad.

Perdie leaned over and kissed Carter on the lips, then leaned down to kiss Peanut Butter on the head.

"Hey, Aubrey." Carter waved.

Aubrey smiled. "Hey, sweetheart. I owe you big for this double commission."

"Always good to help a friend."

"Ferris says the office isn't the same without you."

Carter shrugged, laughing. "Somehow I'm sure they'll make do."

"He's doing that nervous thing again," Perdie said as Peanut Butter paced along the hardwood floor. While returning from the mountain, Carter had encountered a sickly dog. The vet suspected it was some kind of wolf-dog hybrid abandoned out in the park. Carter had called in every legal favor he had to get Peanut Butter over to South Carolina.

Carter knelt to the dog's level, scratching his ears as Peanut Butter looked to him expectantly. "It's not me he wants."

He whistled over his shoulder and walked to the far end of the kitchen, where he lifted the extra-large, custom-installed doggy door cover that led to Lucille's side of the duplex. Peanut Butter's ears pricked up and he ran to the opening, jumping to the other side in search of Lucille. "What can I say? He prefers his aunt Lucille."

"She does have a special way about her," Perdie agreed.

The day after Carter and Perdie had reunited, Lucille and Perdie had a recapping session together sitting at the kitchen table with mugs of chai.

"I'm proud of you, P. Shit was pretty touch and go for a minute there, wasn't it?"

Perdie had brought the mug to her lips. "I think I might be *happy*." She whispered the word, superstitious of its cosmic weight. "But I won't stop seeing Dr. Mei. I've still got tons of work to do." She contemplated for a moment. "Although I miss Bananas. It's so empty without him around. He was a part of our family. The three of us."

Lucille nodded. "How can you replace perfection? The only way I could even think about getting another dog right now is if it knocked on the front door and walked right in. It would have to be fate. It really would. At least that's what my psychic said."

Perdie cocked her head. "Since when do you have a psychic?"

"She also said I need to stop falling in love for at least a year."

Perdie's jaw dropped. "Seriously, how did I not know this?"

"You're a bad listener."

Just then, there was a knock on the door. Perdie and Lucille exchanged a look.

Lucille tiptoed over, opening the door slowly to find Carter and Peanut Butter standing right in front of her. Lucille gasped as the enormous animal nosed her hand for pets.

"Hey, I forgot my— What?" Carter had asked. "Are you okay?"

"Is this your dog, Carter? Because I'm sorry, this is my dog."

Carter had taken it all in good humor. He didn't mind sharing joint custody of Peanut Butter.

And just like that, a new family unit had emerged.

Lucille fell into the habit of bringing Peanut Butter to the flower shop with her. Peanut Butter would return home with daisy chain crowns adorning his head. Quite the sight.

Perdie checked her phone. "All right, well, I've got a deposition to get to."

Carter tapped the side of his cheek with his finger and Perdie pushed up to kiss him. "I know you're busy with your new job, but don't forget to give your orchid ice cubes today before you get out there doing good."

Lucille had been teaching Carter the way of the flower lately, their bonding activity. Perdie relished the blossoming friendship between the two.

"I would never neglect my orchids." She walked by and squeezed Aubrey's shoulder. "Aubrey, you did right by us with the house. I can't thank you enough. And tell Max I say hi."

Unexpectedly, Aubrey pulled Perdie into a hug, talking directly into Perdie's ear. "I'll let him know. This has been the most exciting year of my life."

"Um, okay." Perdie extracted herself from the overly exuberant embrace, double-checked the buttons on her shirt, and adjusted the underwire digging into her flesh. *Some things would never change.*

"Ah, you're finally here." Jennifer handed Perdie a stack of documents, and then with a disapproving frown began to smooth the hairs of Perdie's ponytail. "Your hair is everywhere."

Sophia tapped idly at her phone and glanced up at Perdie. "You ready for this? This is gonna feel real good."

Perdie nodded, hand on the door to the deposition room. "Born ready. Let's get 'em."

The three women filed into the room and took their seats.

Perdie set her vintage Louis Vuitton briefcase in front of her, snapped it open, and regarded the men across the table with a smile. "Why hello, Charles. Hello, Frank."

* * * * *

Acknowledgments

There are so many people to thank for the completion of this book.

First, to everyone at the writing critique site that shall never be named—Ann, Sierra, Shruti, Bigga—your critiques, advice, friendship, and encouragement were invaluable. I'm so grateful you took interest in my chaotic first draft.

To Mary Ann Marlowe, thank you, thank you for the kindness and generosity you showed me during a mega freak-out period of my life and the amazing help you provided with my query letter.

To my Tall, Dark & Fictional podcast cohost and fellow romance writer, Beatrix Strand, your why-the-fuck-not attitude, patience, humor, and brainstorming capabilities have gotten me through so many hard writing times (and there have been many). 10/10 would recommend friendship again.

To fellow romance writer Elaine Reed, for giving me feedback that soothed my prickly soul during a period of great tumult. Thank you for your considerate, smart words and willingness to invest your time in my manuscript even though I'd done nothing to deserve it.

To Instagram stranger turned real friend and all-around cool person with a monkey-dog like mine, Bailey (and Roscoe), your exuberant willingness to read a near stranger's unpublished romance novel was both exciting and touching. And thank you for your smart story suggestions as well, which I implemented. And thanks for all the memes too.

To Lottie Lucille. Another Instagram stranger and fellow romance writer who agreed to read my manuscript and then went above and beyond with smart, thoughtful, thorough, on-the-money feedback. What amazing luck. Can't wait to return the favor.

To Beth. You were the first person to ever read this story. I would have quite literally quit on chapter one if it weren't for your quiet encouragement. Your kind, non-judgmental presence gave me the will to continue on to the next page and then the next. Forever grateful.

To my partner. You were the first person to ever call me a writer even though I'd proven myself exactly zero times. You are never surprised when I succeed. Your incredibly thoughtful and exacting insight make me feel seen. Thanks, boo.

To K-pop. For obvious reasons.

To Deborah Nemeth for walking me through every step of the process and being such a skilled, patient, calm, and talented editor. Thank you so much.

And lastly, to my dogs Ozzie and Griff. The real MVPs. You can't read, but you are/were always, always there for me, and that's way more important. And to Ozzie, my Ozzie Bear, the little dog of my heart and soul, thank you for unselfishly staying with me until the very end. Had I known you'd have to go when I finished, I would've never finished. I'd give anything to have you back, but you were and are too good and pure for this whole bad world. I love you so much. Thank you.

About the Author

Cat Wynn lives in a cozy house in Charleston, South Carolina, with her longtime partner and geriatric rescue dog. You can find her website at www.catwynnauthor.com and her Instagram and Twitter @catwynnauthor.

*A meet-cute gone wrong is the start
of a surprising courtship in this fresh,
modern take on the workplace romance.*

Keep reading for an excerpt from Hot Copy
by debut author Ruby Barrett.

Chapter 1: Wesley

This elevator is sweltering. Or maybe it's just the combination of my nerves and this suit that's making me feel like the air is thick enough to choke on. I tug at my tie. After two years of wearing nothing but jeans and T-shirts, the silk feels like a noose. The only piece of clothing I am comfortable in are my socks.

I stand shoulder to shoulder with a guy almost my height, in a similar suit and tie. Though his looks much more expensive and he seems more at home in it. His blond hair and Rolex glare under the fluorescents. The volume on his phone is turned up so loud I can hear his horrible taste in music clearly through the earbuds.

"Hold the elevator!" a woman calls as the doors start to roll closed.

I step forward, pressing my hand to one side of the sliding doors as she darts in. Her head is down, her thumb scrolling quickly across her phone's screen.

"What floor?" I ask, but she doesn't respond, instead tapping the toe of her high-heeled shoe in a metallic rhythm. She sighs audibly, shaking her head at the screen. I shrug and step back again.

"You part of the Hill City internship?" Bad Music Guy

pulls an earbud out. The tinny sound of his music fills the small space. What I wouldn't give for the dulcet tones of the Beastie Boys' mid-'90s discography so I could avoid conversation with him. I was such a nervous wreck this morning I forgot my earphones on my bedside table.

I nod and hold out my hand. "Wesley Chambers."

"Mark." He smiles wide, showing all his teeth. Like a chimpanzee. "Who's your mentor?"

My father's friend Richard Skyler is the CEO of Hill City Marketing & PR, one of Boston's premier agencies. Dad considered his paternal duties fulfilled when he got me a spot in this program two years ago. After that, it was back to sporadic emails and missed birthdays. I'm not mad at him, though. My father is just a dick. He can't be fixed.

Luckily, his buddy Richard isn't an incurable phallus.

"Uhhh." I scratch the back of my neck, stalling for time. "I actually interviewed for this internship two years ago and I was going to be working with Richard? The CEO? But…" I clear my throat. Sneak a peek at Mark. The sharp edge of his smile assures me that I will not explain the past two years of my life to *this* guy.

"But I had to defer it," I say. "So, now I have to work with Corrine Blunt." I can't keep the dismay from my voice.

I'd met Richard Skyler when I was a kid and he'd remained friends with my parents until their divorce. When I interviewed for the program, Richard and I got along like old buds. And when I had to decline his offer of mentorship to take care of my mom, Richard promised me a spot when I was ready. And he kept in touch: emails, even the occasional phone call.

"Honestly, I'd assumed Richard would be my mentor again. But…it didn't work out."

I rock back on my heels, surprised by how disappointed I feel in this moment. The woman is a powerhouse, after all: graduated with an MBA from Boston College at twenty-four. At thirty years old, she's one of the youngest executives at Hill City Marketing & PR and the only woman in the executive suites. She's won countless awards for her marketing campaigns and was Richard's protégé in the first Hill City mentorship program years ago.

Plus, I know I'm not supposed to think about my boss this way, but it's not the worst thing that she's pretty. In her picture on the website she sported a bouncy, dark bob and a bright smile. She seemed happy and welcoming and young, like whatever they mean when they say "bright-eyed and bushy-tailed." I'd felt an affinity with her immediately. I shouldn't complain about having to spend a whole year working with her. In truth, I'm excited, if not mildly intimidated.

I open my mouth to admit that but bite my tongue when Mark says, too loud in this small space, "*Dude*, your mentor is Corrine Blunt?"

I rub my hand over my closed mouth and wince through a nod.

"The lady boss?" Mark laughs, and the cruel sound sends a shiver up the back of my neck. I've been the subject of a laugh like that before.

"You know what they call her, right?"

I stifle a cough and avoid his gaze, staring at my fuzzy reflection in the chrome elevator doors, at the digital numbers counting our ascent. I look anywhere but at this asshole. My eyes finally come to rest on the back of the woman standing in front of me. She stares up at the numbers as well. Her neck is long and elegant. The red temples of her glasses hooked around her ears are the only pop of color on her otherwise crisp black outfit. The scent of coconut wafts from her long, dark hair, pulled up into an intricate, tight bun, not a single strand out of place. It looks painful, to be honest.

She's wearing a black blazer and the type of skirt that makes a woman's ass look spectacular. And the blazer has that ruffle thing around the waist. *"Peplum, Wes,"* Amy's voice echoes in my head, tinged with frustration at the number of times she's had to repeat an irrelevant fashion-related fact to me.

"Wes, my man, you're in for quite a year," Mark says, as if I haven't ignored him for the past thirty seconds. The elevator dings our arrival on the Hill City floor and the woman walks down the hall, her head lowered over her phone again.

"My frat brother Sean got an internship here and worked with her. He coined her nickname: Blunt the Cu—"

I make a spluttering sound. A combination of *no* and *what* and *stop* that comes out sounding like, *"Nuhwst."* I don't need him to finish his sentence to know what he was about to say.

"Look, buddy," I say, and a shocked, stilted laugh tumbles out of my mouth before I can close it. Relief that she didn't hear him washes over me. "Can you *not* say that word?" I hiss into the empty hallway.

Mark throws his head back and laughs, the sound booming down the halls, solidifying exactly how much

I don't like him. He grabs my shoulder, shaking me roughly. "Oh my god, Chambers. You're precious."

All the interns gather for a breakfast meet and greet in one of the conference rooms. I lean against a wall with a plate of fruit and a mini chocolate chip muffin, chasing a piece of melon around with my plastic fork. Everyone here seems to know everyone else. They're fresh from the same graduating class and it shows in their excitement, the overlapping convocation stories. After two years, my own graduation is a distant, hazy memory. I've launched a few smiles at some fellow interns, but mostly I eat my complimentary breakfast alone, watching people avoid eye contact with me.

While I've grown into my legs, feet, and hands and gotten better at shooting the shit with the guys, I still feel like the sore thumb in any crowd. Amy calls it Ugly Duckling Syndrome. I call it being lucky a twin is a built-in best friend.

The piece of melon slips off my plate and bounces off my shoe. I hike up my pants to stoop down to get it and when I rise, Mark stands in front of me.

"Come on, bro. Let's mingle."

By mingle, Mark means hit heavily on the only women of color in the room, two interns from Finance. Marisol, a Northeastern grad from Pennsylvania, ignores us for her phone. But the one Mark lays it on thick for is clearly uncomfortable with the attention. With every one of his jokes, Abila's smiles morph into cringes. Her shoulders inch toward her ears when his hand brushes her arm. He stares at her chest and she pulls her cardigan together. I open my mouth. Close it again. If Amy were here, she'd let fly with some asshole-puckering swear words. If my best friend, Jeremy Chen, were here, he'd find a calm way to explain to Mark why his behavior was inappropriate.

I'm just afraid that if I open my mouth to do either, another nervous laugh will end up escaping, especially if Abila has it in hand. I catch her eye, lifting a brow. She rolls her eyes, shaking her head.

"I'm...going to get another coffee," she announces, earning a glare from Mark for interrupting his story of "epic drunken debauchery." "Please don't follow me," she says, her voice laced with quiet disdain.

"Christ, uptight much?" he mutters.

Or maybe she didn't feel like being sexually harassed on her first day, Mark.

Mark's elbow digs into my ribs, spilling my, luckily, lukewarm coffee. I pat at my hand with a napkin, putting the cup on the conference table behind me.

"Wesley! I see you've met my intern, Mark."

Richard pats my back hard enough that I buckle a little under the pressure and I'm so glad I'm not still holding my coffee because I would have spilled over more than my hand. Mark and I greet Richard, Mark smiling that chimpanzee smile again.

"If you'll excuse us, Mark. I need to borrow Wes for a moment."

Something shifts in Mark's smile as we walk away, his eyes snagging on Richard's hand on my shoulder. He suddenly seems a little less primate-like and a little more sharklike.

"I'm so sorry I couldn't be there for Laura's funeral," Richard says, once we've found a private space in the corner of the conference room away from Mark's dead shark eyes.

At the mention of Mom, my stomach drops.

I really don't want to talk about this today.

"Did you get the flowers I sent?" he asks.

I nod, swallow past my dry throat and dread, and try to get the words to come out. I'm at that point where I think it's okay. I think I'm okay with my mom being gone. But then someone asks about her or how we're doing and my stomach clenches, my tongue ties. I realize I'm not okay. I'm small again, a skinny, scared kid who really, really misses his mom.

"Yes, we got the flowers. Thank you," I manage.

Richard smiles and not for the first time, I wonder how this kind man could ever be a friend to my father. Richard speaks fondly of Mom, repeating stories he's already told me about the three of them—my mom, my dad, and Richard—in college. The longer he talks about her the less my lungs feel like they're being crushed in someone's fist.

"I'm sorry." He smiles ruefully. "I'm sure I've told you all of these before."

He has, and each story hurts like a knife to the gut, but I'm starving for them nonetheless. Memories of Mom where she was the happy, healthy version of herself. Our last few months together, when she was sick and so tired of being sick, are imprinted on my brain. It's a relief to be reminded that she wasn't always that way.

Richard walks me through a maze of hallways, pointing out departments. We pass a large, open concept area he calls the Pit where teams already work together, walking until we reach a sandblasted glass door, the words Marketing Director etched across it. He claps his hand on my shoulder and squeezes, smiling warmly.

"This is Corrine's office. I know the two of you will

get along well." He points to me and winks as he walks away. "Pay close attention. You'll learn a lot from her."

I take a moment alone on this side of the door. I check my tie, catch a glimpse of any stains on my suit in the reflection of the glass. But all I see is a blob of brown on top of my head and dark shapes where my glasses sit. Fuzzy and undefined. That feels depressingly on brand.

I adjust the pant leg I'm in an ongoing battle with, but it creeps up my leg again, displaying my lucky socks. Taking a deep breath, I knock.

"Come in," a voice calls from the other side of the door.

I step into an all-white office. It's so bright I squint. So clean, so sterile I want to take off my shoes to not to leave footprints. A small white couch, an armchair with no arms, and a glass coffee table sit in the open space in front of a white desk. Two pocket doors bracket the crisp white wall behind the desk.

And standing across the room, one dark eyebrow arched, her red lips tightly pursed, casting a stark black silhouette in this crisp white space, is the woman from the elevator.

My brain stutters, stalling on the image of her there and now here. Her hair shining under the elevator lights still lingers on the backs of my eyelids. The smell of co-conuts doesn't belong here. That scent belongs back in that elevator. But after two good sniffs, here it is still.

I close my eyes tight, like if I turn my brain off and on again it will work better. But when I open them, it's still her, with that severe bun and the peplum top and red glasses. The Corrine Blunt I found on the company's website looked nothing like this woman, who glares at me like she eats bright-eyed and bushy-tailed things for breakfast. Whatever similarities I thought we had have been surgically removed. Every possible reason for why this woman is in Corrine Blunt's office runs through my head. But it keeps returning to the only horrifying explanation:

Corrine Blunt *is* the woman from the elevator.

Don't miss Hot Copy *by Ruby Barrett,*
out from Carina Press.
www.CarinaPress.com